"Halloween is trick or treat, Des....

"It's ghost parades and horror movies. It's when the leaves change and black cats come out and you sneak into the woods and tell spooky stories around a bonfire." She hesitated. "I don't know, maybe it's all in my mind. I'm not used to curses, or a housekeeper who looks like the living dead or a mansion built by an architect on the verge of insanity—"

"It's all right, Rowen." His soothing tone tried to calm her. "It'll be all right." He caught her chin before she could look away and, lowering his head, set his mouth on hers.

She'd wanted him to kiss her. But the shock of his action sent her mind into a spin. It was only a kiss, but it was doing the strangest thing to her, making her hot and shaky and hungry for more of him.

Sexy. She hadn't consciously thought of that word for him; it flitted into her mind. He was neither rough nor gentle with her. His hands on her body were far from chaste, but it was only what she wanted.

In fact, it wasn't enough....

Dear Reader,

What better time to snuggle tightly with the one you love than on All Hallows' Eve—when things truly go bump in the night!

Harlequin Intrigue is ringing your doorbell this month with "Trick or Treat," our Halloween quartet—filled with ghastly ghouls and midnight trysts!

For Jenna Ryan, a trip to Madame Tussaud's Museum of Waxworks provided the inspiration for *Midnight Masque*. "What would Halloween be," Jenna asks, "without fog and graveyards and a good ghost story?"

Let's not forget the strong man to share it with!

Be sure not to miss any of the TRICK OR TREAT quartet this month.

Regards,

Debra Matteucci
Senior Editor & Editorial Coordinator

Midnight Masque

Jenna Ryan

Harlequin Books

TORONTO • NEW YORK • LONDON
AMSTERDAM • PARIS • SYDNEY • HAMBURG
STOCKHOLM • ATHENS • TOKYO • MILAN
MADRID • WARSAW • BUDAPEST • AUCKLAND

To my uncle, Thomas Francis Goff, who will never really be gone. He made so many lives happy just by being himself. We will remember him always with love.

To my aunt, Kris Goff, one of the strongest, most genuine people I know. To my cousins, Brent, Terry, Shelly, Cam and Laurie. We love you all and share your loss.

ISBN 0-373-22251-3

MIDNIGHT MASQUE

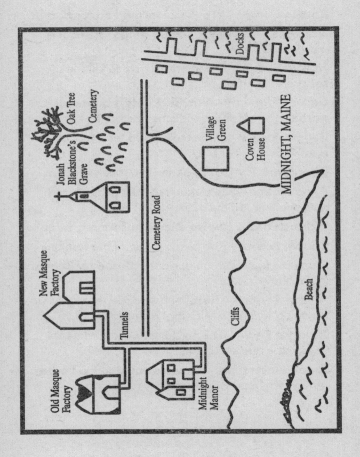

MIDNIGHT, MAINE

Docks

Oak Tree

Cemetery

Jonah
Blackstone's
Grave

Village
Green

Coven
House

Cemetery Road

New Masque
Factory

Tunnels

Cliffs

Beach

Old Masque
Factory

Midnight
Manor

CAST OF CHARACTERS

Rowen Hunter—Why was she marked for death?

Des Jones—He set himself up as the target of a murderous curse.

Harold Forbes—Did the family curse kill the reclusive tycoon?

Lester Ridgeway—Would Harold's business partner ''kill'' for the Masque Factory?

Reggie Forbes—His secrets could lead to Des's death.

Darcy Forbes—He hid beneath a meek facade.

Anna Forbes—She'd married the Forbes name; now she wanted the money.

Richard Forbes Lewis—Did he harbor a grudge?

Cooper Forbes—The black sheep of the family.

Franz Becker—Did an accident caused by Reggie leave him crippled?

Almira Adams—The loyal housekeeper would do anything to inherit Midnight Manor.

Terrance Poole—The mysterious groundkeeper with many hidden talents.

Jonah Blackstone—His curse haunted the Forbes family two hundred years after his death.

Prologue

He may as well have been a ghost.

Harold Forbes walked along the docks past closed shops and creaking boats that bobbed at anchor on the ocean. It was nighttime, the middle of October, and to anyone who passed he was simply an eighty-year-old wraith in patched jeans, wearing a navy pea jacket and a pair of floppy rubber boots.

His scruffy white beard hung down to midchest, his wispy hair almost grazed his shoulders. But Harold Forbes was no wraith, and he was no salty dog. He was a retired business tycoon with holdings that stretched from Maine to Hong Kong.

"Van Winkle," someone on the dock remarked in his wake.

For once he didn't smile. His mind was absorbed in other matters.

The Midnight Masque Factory, the foundation upon which the Forbes family fortune had been built, was about to be reopened. It had taken him almost two years to get the place in working order, but he'd done it, and all without disturbing the old ruin that had been the factory's original home.

He hadn't dared touch the ruin. It had burned down seventy-odd years ago after more than one hundred and thirty years of putting out masks—first death masks, then as that trend faded, more traditional Halloween masks and costumes. To restore the ruin would have been sacrilege. Tam-

per with that and you tampered with Blackstone's legend.
Even a Forbes wasn't permitted to do that.

"This is an October town, Mr. Forbes," Harold's partner Lester had said in his usual somber way. "People make pilgrimages to Midnight just for Halloween. After all, we've even got witches.

Witches, fishermen and one reclusive tycoon whose face few people in the world, let alone in the coastal village of Midnight, Maine, would recognize.

Harold gave a dry chuckle as he left the docks and started for the heavily treed Cemetery Road.

He wanted to contemplate the Masque Factory and a sordid history he didn't buy for a minute. He wanted to picture Jonah Blackstone in all his dark, forbidding glory, composing the letter that would haunt the Forbes family forever. He wanted to light a cigar, find a bottle of whiskey, fire his incompetent grounds keeper and send his spooky housekeeper off for a complete make-over, so she'd look something less like Dracula's widow and more like a human female.

Oh, yes, there were lots of things he wanted to do, but the best he could manage, as he tromped toward the misty town cemetery, was a host of thoughts about his grandson Reggie and all his other unpromising grandchildren.

God help him, there wasn't one among his late children's offspring whom Harold could think about without shuddering. "Weak-willed wimps" was how Reggie disdainfully summed up his cousins on the Forbes side. Not that Reggie was in a position to be throwing stones, but he did have one redeeming quality: he was a genius in business. He kept a low profile at Harold's insistence, and yet he ran the corporation as easily as if it were a corner grocery store.

The cemetery came into sight briefly, then faded back into the night mist. Harold had intended to stop at Blackstone's grave, but that dubious pleasure could wait. The wrought-iron gates of Midnight Manor stood in foggy view. Directly across from them, between manor and ruin, sat the new Midnight Masque Factory.

Actually, it wasn't new at all. It was a combination of the old family mill and the stone barn, refitted, refurbished and ready to open. They would hold a costume party there on Halloween night, then on November first, All Saints' Day, the factory would be back in operation, producing carnival and Mardi Gras masks, costumes and accessories as it had so profitably done in the late nineteenth century.

Harold's eyes twinkled. "Sorry, Blackstone," he said without a scrap of remorse. "But those gruesome death masks you and my ancestors cranked out are a thing of the past, as are you and the skull mask you employed to convey your curse."

The night was damp and cold. Harold could see his breath in the pale light from the manor. He bypassed the distant house and walked on to the factory, a brooding mass of peaks and brick walls backed by a broad stand of oak and maple trees.

Unlocking the large front door of what had once been the mill, he entered, letting the night-lights guide him through the display area.

Harold loved the witchy New England atmosphere of the place. Nothing fake about it. They said that Jonah Blackstone had been heavily into the occult. Judging from his portrait, which still hung in the manor, Harold could believe it. Who but a disciple of the black arts would curse an entire family by means of a skull mask and a letter written prior to his death?

Harold shook his head. Blackstone must have known that his partners were plotting to kill him, and yet he hadn't once tried to stop them, at least not according to the story.

"Must have had a death wish," the old man declared. "Either that or he really was crazy."

He started through a thick plank doorway, pleased that the worn brick-and-wood partitions hadn't been touched. The death mask of some long-deceased witch stood on a shelf inside the door. Next to it was the plaster head of a woman who'd gone crazy Halloween night and, in the manner of Lizzie Borden, chopped her husband and brother to pieces.

Infamy, thought Harold. Maybe this *was* a Halloween town at that.

He halted suddenly, his gaze falling on a third mask. This one hadn't been here this afternoon, he was sure of that. If it had, there'd have been hell to pay. Harold disliked practical jokes.

Reaching out his thin hands, he snatched the mask from its peg. He would have smashed it on the floor if his sharp eyes hadn't glimpsed the yellowed piece of rubber beneath it.

An angry threat formed on his lips. "Lester, if you've taken to black humor, you'll be back riding bulldozers by morning."

The rubber mask leered at him, all teeth and bones, menacing in its implications. By long-standing tradition, the skull mask was taboo in Midnight. This was a very sick joke indeed.

Behind him, Harold heard a soft swish followed by the heavy tread of feet. Blackstone had limped, he recalled, but Blackstone was long dead. This was a prank, nothing more.

Turning, Harold located the specter in the shadows. He couldn't quite fight the feeling of mild shock that started deep in his belly. The person before him looked wrong somehow, and had no business being here in any case.

"What do you want?" he demanded, flinging the mask away. "Why the cape and black boots? And what's that thing you're carrying?"

There was no answer, only an eerie chuckle as a pair of gloved hands withdrew the hidden object from the cape's voluminous folds.

Harold frowned. "Blackstone's original skull mask! Where on earth . . ."

He broke off sharply as the figure lunged at him. He smelled chloroform on the handkerchief that was clamped hard over his mouth and nose. His head slammed against the brick wall. His mind spun.

"Call me Death, old man," he heard his attacker whisper softly. "I've come to fulfill Blackstone's curse."

Chapter One

"This city's obscene," Reggie Forbes complained as he made his way down a gritty alley in the center of Marrakech. "It's hot and dirty and it stinks."

Dark-haired Rowen Hunter glanced back at him. "And British alleys are cold, and damp, and they smell just as bad," she teased.

He scowled at her. "People *live* in these alleys, Rowen. If you can call this living," he added in a sour undertone.

Rowen could have made a comment, but she found it better to ignore Reggie when he got disagreeable.

Young women in batik prints pushed past a group of old men gathered in one of the low doorways. The men smoked American cigarettes, and only about half of them wore the traditional North African clothing. The rest were dressed in pants and T-shirts. Ah well, nothing was forever, Rowen supposed.

Behind her, Reggie swatted flies and grunted noisily. He could be a total wuss sometimes. Today was one of those times.

Turning down a hotter, smokier alley, she remarked, "I think this is the place."

"It better be," Reggie muttered. "Honest to God, only Des could live in a Moroccan hellhole and enjoy it." He stopped dead, staring in disbelief past Rowen's bare shoulder. "Good Lord, tell me that isn't what I think it is."

Delighted, Rowen moved closer. "It's a snake charmer," she exclaimed. "I didn't know there were such things anymore."

Reggie gave her a disgusted push. "Filthy, depraved city," he snorted.

Rowen laughed, ignoring him. Reggie was brilliant in business, but as a companion he tended to be a bit of a bore. Not that it mattered. She wasn't in love with him and he knew it. She enjoyed his money and his position; he enjoyed her nerve and her inventiveness. It was an equitable enough trade. For now.

Giving the snake charmer a final admiring look, Rowen zeroed in on a young man wearing an "I Love New York" T-shirt.

"Do you speak English?" she asked hopefully. After a moment's hesitation, he responded to her smile.

"A little."

"Good. Do you know a man named Desmond Jones? He's supposed to live around here. I believe he's an artist."

"I might know him," the man said. The crowd around them had thinned slightly. The flies hadn't. Neither had the man's mistrustful expression. "Are you sent by Mr. Kalish?"

"Who?"

"He runs..." The man stopped suddenly and peered at Reggie. "Wait a minute, you look like Des. Who are you?"

"I'm Reggie bloody Forbes, Des's cousin from London," Reggie growled. "I have no idea who Mr. Kalish is, although knowing Des, I can imagine the type. Now kindly tell us where the hell my cousin is so we can get out of this disgusting city and back to civilization."

Wrong approach, Rowen thought, covering a smile. The man wouldn't tell them anything now. Before dismissing Reggie with a rude gesture, however, he did glance down the alley at one of the rounded doorways.

"Come on," Rowen said while Reggie glowered at the departing man.

When he didn't move, she left him and started toward the door. The air was thick with the odors of cigarette smoke and spices, scarcely the worst things she'd ever smelled. Reggie was being predictably difficult. He might also be upset over his grandfather Harold's recent murder, but

Rowen doubted it. Emotional closeness was not a Forbes family trait.

Unhappily, it wasn't a Hunter family trait, either, but you couldn't have everything. At least her parents and brother were still alive.

Shaking those thoughts away, Rowen approached the half-open wooden door. She gave a quick knock, then pushed her way inside with a bold, "Hello, is anyone here?"

There was, and he was sprawled in a rattan chair facing the entrance. A shadow from the partly curtained window hid most of his face, but his body looked tall and thin. Deceptively so, she suspected, because his bone structure was anything but small. She caught a glimpse of long brown curls and a scruffy brown beard. His feet were bare, his khaki pants loose-fitting, his white cotton shirt untucked.

She could feel his gaze on her when he responded with a dispassionate, "Who are you?"

The British accent and deep voice—he sounded like Reggie all right. Yet this man's tone held a trace of amusement. Reggie's never did.

"My name is Rowen Hunter," she said. "I came with your cousin, Reggie. He's out in the alley, complaining about the heat."

The man dropped his feet to the floor. "Sounds like Reggie. How did he track me down?"

Rowen decided she wanted a better look at this person and headed for the window. "He didn't—*I* did—assuming you're Desmond Jones, that is. Do you mind?"

She set her hand on the muslin curtain. At his shrug, she pushed it back.

From his pocket the man produced a pack of cigarettes, lit one and studied her through a veil of smoke. "Pretty," he said. "And bright. I'm surprised. I thought Reggie favored airheads."

Rowen smiled, unperturbed. "Reggie hasn't noticed my brain yet. If I'm lucky, he never will."

"Still likes to be superior, does he?" His eyes glinted with humor. "Naturally, you let him pretend."

"It suits my purpose." Rowen surveyed Reggie's cousin. They probably did look alike, if you could get past the beard and long hair.

While neither man could be called handsome, she had to admit this one possessed some very nice features. His mouth for one thing. It was long and sensual and well shaped. He had an engaging smile, and eyes that were nothing short of hypnotic. Changeable as well, she realized. They might range in color from pale green to hazel, depending on the light. His nose was very strong and had almost certainly been broken at some time; still, it fit the rest of his face. And no one, not even Reggie, could fail to notice Des's beautiful patrician cheekbones.

At best, he was an odd jumble of similar features, but no ringer for his cousin. Rowen didn't really see Reggie's plan working for any length of time.

When Des stood, he did so with the grace of a cat. She shook her head. There were just too many dissimilarities.

Taking another drag from his cigarette, he stared back at her. "Do I pass?" he asked with a faint arch of his eyebrow.

"Not as far as I'm concerned," Rowen replied, although he couldn't possibly know what Reggie meant to propose. "I bet you drink, too, don't you?"

His smile startled her a little. Or was the word *captivated?*

"Frequently," he said. "Are you sure you're with Reggie?"

"He probably saw a black cat in the alley and is afraid to move until it leaves."

"Still superstitious?"

"Highly, but it doesn't matter. I can tell you what he wants. It's Des, isn't it?"

His nod was slow, assessing and mildly amused.

"Well, Des," she said, coming to stand in front of him. As she'd expected, he was extremely tall, six foot three at least. "The plain truth is that Harold Forbes, Reggie's grandfather, has been murdered. Reggie believes that the killer is one of Harold's lesser heirs. According to the terms of Harold's will, Reggie is to inherit the bulk of his grandfather's estate. However, if anything should happen to him—Reggie, that is—before the will can be read and probated, the so-called lesser heirs will stand to inherit a much larger share of the pie. That makes Reggie a target, or so he believes."

Des removed a bottle of whiskey from a cabinet on the stone wall. There were easels everywhere and a number of partially painted canvases, but nothing complete that Rowen could see.

Blowing the dust from two glasses, he poured some of the whiskey into them and handed her one. "When did the old man die?" he asked. It was not the question she'd been anticipating.

"Two days ago." She tasted the whiskey. Not bad. "They say it was horrible."

"Who says?"

"Whoever Reggie spoke to in Midnight. That's the town where Harold lived."

"Did you know him?"

"Harold? Not really. I think I might have met him once, I'm not sure. He was a recluse."

Des downed his drink and reached for another cigarette. "An eccentric recluse. What makes Reggie think the killer's one of old Harold's heirs?"

Rowen had no idea what to make of this man, so she simply responded to his questions. "He didn't say, although it seems a logical assumption. Reggie did mention something about a family curse, but he said it was nothing but a lot of mumbo jumbo."

"As opposed to avoiding black cats and throwing salt over his shoulder." Des's grin was infectious. Rowen found herself wanting to smile back. "Have you heard about Blackstone's curse?" he asked.

She leaned against the wall, sipping her drink. Her eyes took in Des's Spartan living quarters. "I was born in Alamogordo, New Mexico, not Midnight, Maine. Alamogordo's in the desert. My family worried about snakes and scorpions, not dead men's curses. I do know that the victims of Blackstone's curse are supposed to die under brutal circumstances. I also know that Harold Forbes's body was discovered hanging from an oak tree above Jonah Blackstone's grave. But I don't believe it was any curse that put him there, if that's what you're implying.''

Crossing to the window, Des glanced out. ''I wasn't implying anything, actually. What does Reggie want with me?''

''I want to borrow your body, cousin.''

Rowen turned to discover Reggie in the doorway, his linen suit immaculate despite the heat. His smile was slick. ''I want you to take my place for the next few weeks in Midnight, Des.''

DES WAS TOO CURIOUS to dismiss his cousin offhand. He listened patiently to Reggie's plan, smoked three cigarettes and watched with humor as Rowen explored his studio like a child on a treasure hunt.

''Look, Des,'' Reggie said, taking a seat on the sagging cot. ''I know the idea sounds crazy on the surface, but you could pull it off. You're a born actor.''

Resting his head on the chairback, Des blew a stream of smoke at Reggie's face, not so much to be belligerent as to avoid looking at his cousin's clean-shaven features. They were too like his own for comfort.

''I'm an artist these days, Reggie,'' he said, fighting a smile as Rowen went down on her knees to examine a stack of his aborted paintings. ''I'm not sure I want to set myself up as a target for murder.''

''Why not? You've done it before.''

Rowen laughed. ''Really?''

''Other times, other places,'' Des remarked obscurely.

''You've also worked with Scotland Yard,'' Reggie persisted. ''Something to do with a misunderstanding between you, a deck of cards and a duke with clout, wasn't it? The police offered you a deal. The duke would be dealt with in return for your cooperation. I heard you spent three months on the London docks helping them catch those smugglers. Don't tell me you weren't a target then.''

Rowen continued to laugh while she went through the rest of the paintings.

Des slid her a curious sideways look. She wasn't Reggie's type at all. For one thing, she was sharp. Tracking him down in Marrakech couldn't have been easy. For another, she was completely oblivious to dust, dirt and heat.

Maybe she liked money. Reggie had plenty of that. She was certainly pretty, with long black-brown hair, a gorgeous Latin nose, a generous mouth and a proud tilt to her head that even an arrogant creature like Reggie couldn't misinterpret.

"Well?" Reggie demanded. "What's it going to be? I'll pay you, of course. You'd have to leave right away, change your clothes and a few of your more antisocial habits, but it could work. I assume you have the same face I remember under that beard."

Des sat back. "How much?" he asked, but his eyes were no longer on his cousin. He pinched the burning tip from his cigarette as the shadows in the alley deepened.

"One hundred thousand."

"Pounds?"

"Dollars, you idiot. I'm not made of money."

Des kept his gaze fixed on the shifting shadows beyond the door. Shoes crunched on the gritty stones outside. "Pounds or no deal," he said.

"Bloody crook," Reggie muttered.

"You can always go to Midnight yourself," Des told him. As soon as the crunching faded, he relit his cigarette. "After all, how many antagonistic cousins do you have on the Forbes side? Five?"

"Three. Four if you count that witch, Anna."

"Who's Anna?"

"Darcy Forbes's wife," Rowen answered. She was going through his sketchbooks now, unconcerned that her Indian cotton skirt was trailing on the floor. "Apparently, Darcy's the family wimp."

"I haven't seen any of them for twenty years or more," Reggie added. "I only know about Anna from what Harold told me."

"So I'd be dealing with four potential murderers in Midnight."

"Well, there might be a few others."

"With motives for killing Harold?"

"How the hell should I know?" Reggie snapped. "Look, someone hanged the old man over Blackstone's grave. And there was a skull mask stuck on his face, which implies that whoever murdered him is using Blackstone's curse as a cover for his crime. Now you and I both know the story, Des. Any Forbes whose name appears on the Midnight Masque Factory's ownership papers is fated to die on or shortly before Halloween. In case you've lost track of time in this Moroccan sewer, it's October eighteenth."

Des's eyes were again drawn to the alley. Men's voices outside sounded grim and purposeful.

"A hundred thousand pounds, Reggie," he maintained, putting out his cigarette for the second time.

"Crush it," Reggie said, indicating the ashtray.

Des frowned. "What?"

"Never light the same cigarette three times," Rowen remarked from behind his chair. "First law of superstition." Eyes sparkling, she leaned over and whispered, "I think one of those men in the alley just mentioned the name Kalish."

Des was on his feet before Reggie could demand to know what was happening.

"Is it a deal?" Rowen asked as he slipped the blackened cigarette and a pack of matches into his shirt pocket.

"Talk him into the money and I'll let you know."

Her smile was confident. "We're at the Hilton."

"Of course you are." Des headed for the window.

"Wait a minute, where are you going?" Reggie snapped. "We're not finished."

Rowen intercepted him neatly. "Des has to run, I think. We can finish this later."

Reggie's blustering response was drowned out by the noise of the city. Des hoisted himself through the window and up onto the roof just in time to see five men enter his studio through the alley door.

A crack in the shingles allowed him to look in. He chuckled to himself when two of the men grabbed Reggie's arms.

"Come along, Mr. Jones," the small one said. "Mr. Kalish would like a few words with you."

Reggie's face mottled. "I'm not Desmond, you idiots. My name is Reggie Forbes. I'm Des's cousin. Tell them, Rowen."

"He's Des's cousin," she said, not sounding particularly hopeful.

"Of course he is." The man snapped his fingers. "Bring them both."

"This is ridiculous," Reggie snarled. "I'm an American. You have no right to force us..."

Pushing the mop of brown curls from his eyes, Des sat back. Kalish would realize his mistake soon enough. He wouldn't hurt them. The man was a bookie not a murderer.

Lifting his eyes, he surveyed the polluted Marrakech sky. Mid-October already. He wondered what it would be like in Maine at this time of year. It might not be a bad idea to find out. Kalish wasn't the only man to whom he owed money.

Resting his arm on one upraised knee, Des removed the half-smoked cigarette from his pocket, smiled down at the alley—and lit the blackened tip for the third time.

IN THE SOLITUDE of a candlelit room, the first letter was composed. It seemed a fitting device. Jonah Blackstone had written a letter prior to his death two centuries ago, and while the person in the room didn't claim to be a ghost, the word *vengeance* might be applied to both human and spirit. A gloved hand began to write.

Dear Dr. Sayers,

It's me, the patient you treated a short time ago, the one you said needed to find a purpose in life. Well, I've given the matter a great deal of thought, and I've found one. It's called revenge.

Harold Forbes has fallen victim to my purpose. I killed him two nights ago. I knocked him out and hanged him over Jonah Blackstone's grave. Now Jonah Blackstone is dead, but he left behind a curse and a wonderful skull mask that I was fortunate enough to unearth after my purpose had been established.

I'm looking at the skull mask, Dr. Sayers. It's very old and eerily detailed. They say Jonah Blackstone made it before he died. I hope that's true. I know Harold was frightened when he saw me that night in the Masque Factory. I can only hope Reggie will be frightened, too.

Because I've learned something, Doctor. I liked Harold's fear, the way a vampire likes blood and a child likes trick or treat.

My purpose takes a new direction now. I'm going to be in Midnight with Reggie. I'm going to kill him the way I killed his grandfather. I'm going to make Jonah Blackstone's curse come true.

Please rest assured,
A former patient

Chapter Two

"At least you don't have a tan," Reggie said irritably. "But you might have cut your hair a bit. And stop looking so damned amused. You knew those men would mistake me for you. Rowen and I spent an hour getting that toad, Kalish, to believe that you and I are not one and the same. And I don't mind telling you it cost me more than bus fare to make him listen. I'll deduct it from your blood money."

Des listened in tolerant silence while Rowen straightened his tie and collar. "Stand still," she ordered. Then she stood back and smiled proudly. "There. All done. What do you think, Reggie?"

"I've never looked so Bohemian."

"I'll take that as a compliment," Des said, lighting a cigarette.

Reggie scowled. "You would. And I don't smoke."

Des inhaled deeply, letting his eyes roam the platform of the darkened Portland, Maine, train station. "I'll remember that when we get to Midnight."

"We" being he and Rowen, which was a situation he hadn't bargained on, but one he didn't object to in the slightest.

"I'll be at my Boston apartment." His cousin sighed. "Rowen has the number. Are you sure you have everything straight?"

Des couldn't resist grinning. "Don't you worry, Reggie. I'm a born actor, remember?"

"Oh, knock it off. And get rid of that stupid hat. I don't wear hats."

"You do now," Des said around his cigarette.

"Do something," Reggie growled at Rowen.

"I will," she promised and gave the lapel of Des's gray-green raincoat a final tug. "Come on. Our train's ready to leave." She glanced at Reggie. "We should be in Midnight by ten o'clock tonight. I'll let you know how it goes."

Des didn't object when she took his hand. "One hundred thousand pounds, Reggie," he said over his shoulder. "In my bank account tomorrow morning, or the deal's off."

"Minus what Kalish..."

Des silenced him with a look. "Minus nothing. Tomorrow, cousin. Eleven a.m. I'll check with the bank."

Reggie grumbled but didn't argue. Rowen chuckled and pulled Des along behind her.

"No goodbye kiss?" he asked, tugging his hat down over his eyes.

"Nope, Reggie doesn't like kissing."

"Should be an interesting marriage," Des murmured.

She glanced back at him, not the least bit upset. "I told you on the flight over, we're not officially engaged. I'm not sure I want to marry a magnate. I'm not sure I want to marry at all." She motioned to her left. "We're here. Put your cigarette out and try to look pompous."

Des took a final drag from his cigarette, then dropped it.

"Reggie doesn't usually back down from people," she remarked in a curious tone. "What did you do, beat him up or something when you were young?"

"No."

"But you wanted to, huh?"

Banking his amusement, Des followed her onto the train. "You don't have a very high opinion of your unofficial fiancé, do you?"

"I'm not blind, I know what he's like. I also know you're not going to be overly popular in Midnight. I don't think Reggie the child was very nice to his cousins, and I'm not sure how kind old Harold was to his employees. Compassion and consideration aren't Forbes's traits. From what I've heard, Harold just up and decided one day to leave London and go live in Maine. The housekeeper and her husband had been running the estate there for close to two decades—although I think he's dead now.''

''The housekeeper's husband?''

Rowen nodded. ''These are our seats. Her name's Almira Adams, and unless Reggie's exaggerating, she's appropriately ghoulish and disgustingly capable, a sort of spooky Mrs. Danvers. She knows every inch of the manor, and it's supposed to be huge.''

Des dropped into the seat next to hers, propping his feet up on the cushion opposite and watching her from under his hat. She wore a black raincoat and a tan silk dress. Her dark hair, layered at the front and sides, had begun to curl, probably from the dampness in the Portland air.

It had been pouring ever since they'd landed in Boston yesterday. No thunder or lightning, only buckets of rain and a coastal chill that reminded Des strongly of Cornwall in the fall.

Rowen's eyes moved about the car. The curiosity in their depths had his lips curving in faint amusement. Her eyes were deep blue, large and exquisitely shaped, but then she probably knew that and used it to her advantage. Reggie might be slick, but no one had ever accused him of having bad taste.

Except, Reggie didn't seem to want to kiss her, and that couldn't be considered normal. Any man with a halfway active sex drive would want to kiss Rowen Hunter straight into the nearest bed.

''Boring bunch of passengers,'' she said at last, subsiding. ''Oh well, do you want to go over any details? How old are you by the way? Reggie never did say.''

''Thirty-eight.'' Des eased the tie away from his throat, sighed over his missing beard and pulled his hat down farther over his eyes. ''Reggie's thirty-five going on fifty, and you—I don't know.''

''Twenty-eight,'' she said as the train started forward.

''And you work for one of the Forbes family companies?''

''No.''

He pushed his hat up slightly. ''No?''

"A friend of mine works for one of the Forbes family companies, in the antiques division to be precise. She introduced us. That was three years ago. I lived in Los Angeles then, which I'm told is where Reggie was born, although it's hard to believe that listening to him now. He sounds as British as you do."

"He's been in London for twenty-three years. Did you meet him at a party?"

"At an inquest. There was a fire in the building where my friend worked. The officials thought it might be arson. I was called as a witness."

"Sounds like a dull first meeting. What do you do for a living?"

"Probably not what you think."

He gave his head a vaguely humorous shake. "I never jump to conclusions about people, Rowen."

She laughed. It was a wonderful sound in the humid confines of the train, rich and somewhat husky. "Reggie does," she said. "He thought I was either an actress or a private detective."

"And are you?"

"No. I illustrate children's books."

His smile widened into delight. "Really? Witches with curled toes and things like that?"

"All kinds of things like that, but shouldn't we be talking about Midnight and Blackstone's curse and Reggie's creepy relatives? After all, someone murdered Harold. Reggie could be right. The killer might decide to come after him next—or you as the case may be. Blackstone's curse would be a good smoke screen, especially if the murderer is one of Reggie's cousins."

"Murder for money." Eyes half-closed under the brim of his hat, Des watched a little girl eat Halloween Hershey bars from a plastic bag. She had a Catwoman mask on her lap and chocolate all over her face. "An obvious motive," he agreed. "But obvious isn't always correct. Who else will be at the manor?"

"A man in a wheelchair whose name I don't know, the household staff—I think there are two of them—and Harold's partner from the Masque Factory. I understand Harold formed a recent partnership with someone in Midnight, a local man, I think. Reggie's never met him and he didn't really have time to get any information on him, but I gather he's a loner, and a brooder. Very dark.''

"Like Jonah Blackstone?''

"If Blackstone was dark and brooding, yes.''

"Oh, Jonah Blackstone was dark all right,'' a new voice interjected. "He was a wizard.''

Tipping his hat back, Des surveyed the man who'd paused to lean on the back of his seat.

This could be trouble. He was in his mid-thirties, tall and fair with silky blond hair, narrow features and a scarf tucked like an ascot into his shirt. His accent said Wales, but there was a hint of South Africa mixed in there as well.

Des decided to let Rowen handle the awkward moment, which she did with ease. "You know of Jonah Blackstone?'' she inquired while Des dropped his feet to the floor.

The man's smile had a wicked edge. "It's family history. I'm family. Richard Forbes Lewis.''

She held out her hand. "Rowen Hunter.''

"My fiancée,'' Des said, sliding an arm around her shoulders. "It's been a long time, Richard.''

"Twenty-one years,'' Richard said, taking the seat where Des's feet had been. "Not counting that night in Birmingham, of course.''

Des didn't flinch. "I've never been to Birmingham.''

"No?'' Richard sat back, his forehead knit. "Must've been Cooper. Neither of you had any sense of fun. You're about as adventuresome as dormice.''

"Off of which Cooper used to pull the whiskers,'' Des returned blandly. Despite Reggie's lack of faith in him, he'd done his homework, as much as he could at any rate in the short time available to him.

He glanced at Rowen, expecting anger over the fiancée remark or the arm resting on her shoulders. Instead, her eyes were focused on a woman in the aisle.

"That's your cousin Darcy's wife, isn't it?'' she said. "I've seen her picture.''

Richard didn't bother to look. "Thin woman, straight red-brown hair with bangs, drab dress, husband in tow?''

Rowen nodded.

"That's Anna," he confirmed. "Harold used to call her the Wisconsin witch."

"Harold?" The woman paused in passing. Her colorless eyes took in Des's face and long curly brown hair. "Cousin Reggie, I presume?"

Des smiled his response.

She took the only available seat across from Rowen. "Say hello to your soon-to-be-rich cousin, Darcy," she instructed her husband, an equally thin man with light brown hair and pale, nondescript features.

"Nice to see you again, Reggie," Darcy said. "I see you brought a friend."

"Fiancée," Richard corrected while Des began to wonder how much longer it would take them to reach Midnight.

With the rain and the night and the trees lining the tracks, he had no idea where they were. He only knew that this seemingly coincidental meeting was no coincidence. Any one of these people might be a murderer, and for money he'd just agreed to become the next target. If the trio before him was any indication of things to come, he'd have been better off in Marrakech.

Of course there was no Rowen in Marrakech...

"It was grisly, I tell you," Anna was confiding. "The housekeeper found him. She almost bumped into his swinging legs in the fog."

"How do you know there was fog?" Rowen asked.

"There's always fog in Midnight at this time of year," Darcy said quickly.

Anna's features tightened. "Mr. Pettiston, Harold's lawyer, told us all about the discovery of the body. I gather the young man's been having a hard time since his father died. Apparently the elder Mr. Pettiston was not an organized person, and he carried quite a caseload. Naturally, that's now fallen on his son's shoulders. I gather he has been having some trouble locating Harold's will."

"Not that it matters," Richard noted, crossing his long legs. "The will can't be probated until the police have completed their investigation of the murder. Maybe not even then.''

Des offered them a cheerful, ''Interesting, isn't it, that we're all rushing up to Midnight under the circumstances?''

Anna's eyes narrowed. ''Some of us want to pay our last respects to Harold.''

''Harold was cremated,'' Rowen reminded her. ''His ashes were interred in the family's London tomb yesterday.''

''You sent a telegram of sympathy,'' Des added with deliberate mischief. ''Remember?''

Anna's lips compressed. ''I wasn't aware you had a sense of humor, Reggie.''

Des shrugged. ''People change.''

''Harold didn't,'' Richard commented. ''He was always a strange old duck, reclusive to the point of obsession. He wanted you to be the same way, didn't he Reg? Low-profile and all that?''

''Oh, Reggie likes to keep a low profile.'' Rowen sent him a teasing smile. ''Don't you, Reggie?''

''It suits my purpose,'' Des agreed straight-faced.

He noticed Anna staring at him. Her expression was contemplative. Des decided to direct the conversation back to Harold's death.

''We heard the murderer put a skull mask over the old man's head before he hanged him. It wasn't Blackstone's original mask, was it?''

''Good Lord, no,'' Richard exclaimed. ''That old thing was locked up in a safe room more than seventy years ago, before the old Masque Factory burned.''

''What do you mean 'safe room'?'' Rowen inquired. ''Was the skull mask considered dangerous?''

''It was believed to contain the essence of Blackstone's curse,'' Darcy revealed. ''You could say it was the instrument through which he worked his black magic. It was locked up but removed any number of times over the centuries.''

''What exactly is a safe room?'' she pressed.

Richard leaned forward. "A man they called a diviner created the room not long after Blackstone died. No one really knows much about it, except that the room is supposed to neutralize the evil in the mask. As long as the mask remains in that room, all will be well. It is only if someone removes it that the curse becomes active again."

Rowen exchanged a doubtful look with Des. "In other words, for Harold's death to have been caused by Blackstone's curse, someone would have to have found the original mask and taken it out of its sanctuary. Sounds a bit farfetched if you ask me."

"It would to you," Richard said, "but not to the people of Midnight. According to my mother, who went there a few years before she died, there are a lot of superstitious people living in that town."

"There are a lot of superstitious people everywhere," Des said. He caught Rowen's warning look and added with a dismissing shrug, "Me, for instance. But even I know the difference between fact and fiction. No ghost hanged Harold in that cemetery."

"Perhaps not," Anna said, folding her hands primly in her lap, "but one has to wonder why a being of flesh and blood would want the old man dead."

"Oh, money." Rowen's smile was pleasant. "That's a strong motive, don't you think? With Harold moving back to Midnight and opening the new Masque Factory, together with an old curse and Halloween only a few weeks away, the situation would have been perfect for anyone wanting to commit a murder. The method would confuse things nicely."

"Yes, but surely Harold had enemies," Darcy said. "The motive doesn't have to be money."

Des closed his eyes. He wanted a cigarette quite badly. An hour of sleep wouldn't hurt, either. It had been a long flight from Marrakech to London, then there had been that marathon session with Reggie in his Mayfair flat, and of course Harold's cremation. The problem was, how did he ditch his newfound relatives?

He endured another ten minutes of morbid conjecture, then shoving his hat back, leaned over and brushed teasing lips across Rowen's cheek. She looked vaguely surprised but covered it well. "I'm going between cars for a smoke," he whispered. "If I don't come back, tell them I fell off the train."

Her lips twitched but she managed not to smile.

Offering no explanation, Des stood and started toward the rear of the train, passing the chocolate-smeared child who was engrossed in a book about animated jack-o'-lanterns. He wondered briefly if Rowen had given those pumpkins life, but all fanciful thoughts dissolved when he glanced out the window.

The train was approaching a coastal fishing town. A swinging sign took shape through the rain. To his tired mind it seemed almost human, a corpse wearing a skull mask. But was it Harold's face he pictured on that sign? Or was it his own?

"MY NAME IS Almira Adams. I'm the housekeeper."

It was close to eleven p.m. and the woman standing at the door of Midnight Manor was a perfect horror. In her early fifties, she wore a black ankle-length dress, black stockings and enormous flat black shoes. Her hair, also black, hung in rats' tails over her shoulders. Black liner gave her eyes a frightful look. She could have been Dracula's daughter or the star of a 1950s horror movie. She was tall and deceptively frail-looking, although Rowen suspected her sinewy frame probably hid sufficient strength to knock Darcy back onto the porch.

"Take their bags upstairs, Poole," she instructed the sopping, sandy-haired man who'd met them at the station.

"I'll help you," Richard volunteered since the man was quite obviously incapacitated. Walking seemed an effort for him—an accident on a fishing boat, he'd explained curtly—but at least he didn't limp.

Jonah Blackstone had limped. Rowen discovered that tidbit on the interminable journey from Portland to Midnight. No one knew why, but it was Richard's grisly conjecture that in order to obtain dark powers, Blackstone had been forced to sacrifice a portion of his leg—flesh in exchange for favors. After being reattached, his left leg had purportedly come up a full inch shorter than his right.

It was a creepy thought for a rainy night, especially in a town where Rowen had already spotted a group of people in black robes entering a stark-looking Early American house. It hadn't helped when Terrance Poole unceremoniously informed her that these people belonged to a group of witches who gathered each year in Midnight. It was a Halloween tradition, he said, like Blackstone's curse.

"Come this way," Almira said without expression. "Your cousin, Cooper Forbes, has gone to his room for the night." She glanced coldly at Des. "So has Mr. Becker."

"Who's Mr. Becker?" Rowen immediately asked, surveying the shadows of the entry hall.

From what she could see, the manor was an even greater horror than the woman who looked after it. An odd combination of a Gothic castle overlaid with the macabre elements of an Edgar Allan Poe story, it was dark, gloomy and freakishly decorated. And there were no railings on the carpeted staircases or on the upper landings.

"Mr. Franz Becker," Almira informed them, "arrived yesterday afternoon. He came with his canes and wheelchair. I gather he isn't expecting a warm welcome from you, Mr. Reggie."

"Just Reggie will do," Des said, looking around in distraction. "Why is that, Almira?"

Rowen held her breath, but the housekeeper merely lifted her head. "He mentioned something about an accident."

"Did he?" Des's smile gave nothing away. "Well."

It was Almira's cue to continue walking, which she did. She led them through a double stone archway to an area of the house that looked like a cross between a great hall and a living room.

A wood fire burned low in the carved grate. The table in front of it was mahogany. The marble floor was covered with a threadbare Moroccan rug. The walls were adorned with dark portraits. Black velvet curtains hung at the pointed windows. Electric sconces, simulating candlelight, cast a dull orange glow, creating more shadows than they dispersed in an already ghastly room.

Rowen sidestepped Des who'd stopped to study the portraits and headed for the fire, murmuring a sarcastic, "Harold must have had some sense of humor."

Des gave a short laugh and glanced at the empty tabletop. "No dinner, Almira?"

"Dinner is served at seven, Reggie."

"How nice. But we weren't here at seven."

"Really," Darcy protested weakly, "I'm not very hungry."

"I am," Rowen said. Actually, she wasn't, she just wanted to see how Almira would react.

Almira didn't utter a word. She didn't need to. Her hostile expression said it all.

"We'll go up, I think." Darcy looked meaningfully at his wife. "We can unpack and read a little before we go to bed."

Almira gave an approving nod. "This way." She glided toward the door. "I'll see about a cold supper for you and Miss Hunter," she remarked to Des over her shoulder.

"Thank you."

In the archway, she turned to face him, her black-rimmed eyes a mask. "Don't expect too much, Reggie. My husband, Gilbert, was the cook in the family. He had a fatal heart attack last year. As you might be aware, that attack occurred shortly after your very demanding grandfather came to live in Midnight."

Chapter Three

Rowen waited until they were gone before poking Des in the ribs. "I don't think Almira likes you very much, Reggie."

Des removed a cigarette from his coat pocket and tapped it absently on his wrist. "It doesn't sound as if she liked Harold much, either." He squinted up at the portrait of a narrow-featured man with long black hair, a heavy black beard and eyes that shone like polished silver. "That must be Jonah Blackstone. He looks like a wizard."

Rowen ran her hand lightly over the fireplace stones. "He looks like a wild-eyed maniac if you ask me." She glanced backward in an unruffled warning. "Don't light that. Reggie's a fanatic about cigarette smoke. It's one of the few things that everyone knows about him."

Des chuckled dryly. "What does he do, send out notices?"

"Let's just say he makes his opinions known." Picking up a brass figure from the mantel, Rowen turned it over. Made in Taiwan. She smiled and put it back. "What's this cousin Cooper like? You mentioned something about him pulling the whiskers off dormice earlier."

"I gather that pretty much sums Cooper up."

"Sounds like a sadistic creep. I wonder why he'd be in Harold's will."

Des walked over to one of the portraits, hands stuffed in his pants' pockets. "Why would any of us, if you'll pardon the expression, be there? We're not the nicest collection of people."

"Well, you are all Harold had. It's not unusual to leave your worldly possessions to your descendants, whether you love them or not." She spied a blue crystal bowl on a shelf and headed toward it.

With a sly grin, Des tapped the canvas in front of him. "This is very good."

"Shouldn't it be?" Rowen asked absently.

"It's a fake."

She studied the bowl in her hands. "Well, this isn't. Look." She brought it over. "It's Lalique, probably worth a fortune."

"Fake Daumiers and genuine Lalique." Des pursed his lips. "Interesting."

"Extremely. Oh, hello, Mr. Poole."

"Just Poole," their former chauffeur corrected, making his way through a darkened archway at the far end of the room. "I've brought you some food."

He'd changed, Rowen noticed, into an ill-fitting black suit and white gloves. "You double as a butler, I take it," she said when he'd deposited his tray on the table.

He nodded, avoiding her eyes. That would make him either shy, evasive or antisocial, she decided.

Clumsily, yet without spilling a drop, he unloaded the heavy tray. He wasn't as slight as Rowen had first thought. Nor was he as old. Forty at best. It was the deep grooves around his eyes and mouth that suggested more. He was a tall man, but still shorter than Des by a good three inches. His hair was a thick sandy blond, his features hawklike, his movements labored but steady.

"I used to be a fisherman," he said quietly.

His remark told Rowen that she'd been staring. She blushed slightly. "I didn't mean to be rude," she apologized, slipping into one of the carved chairs. "Your accident must have happened quite some time ago. You get around very well."

He kept his eyes on the tray. "I'm better off than Mr. Becker and grateful for that."

Des glanced at Rowen who offered a smooth, "Yes, I hear Mr. Becker needs a wheelchair and canes to get around. What happened to him?"

Poole darted a quick look across at Des. "That's not for me to say."

"I see." Shaking out her napkin, Rowen smiled. "Thank you, Poole, we can serve ourselves. Oh, and thank Almira too if you see her. Such a gracious woman."

A tiny smile touched Poole's mouth, then swiftly vanished. With an awkward bow, he disappeared through the archway.

"Jellied ham, stale bread and a suspicious-looking sausage." Des eyed the food with amusement. "The old bat outdid herself."

Rowen wrinkled her nose. "Are you sure Reggie never mentioned anyone named Becker?"

"I'm sure. Ham or sausage?"

"Bread, thanks." She broke off a piece. "I wonder who he is."

"And what Reggie did to him."

"Oh, well, never mind. I'll find out tomorrow." She set her elbows on the table. "I think everyone's buying you as Reggie, so they can't have known him very well as children. Either that or they think he's changed." Reaching for the dusty wine decanter, she poured two glasses and pushed one at Des. "Were you a nice little boy?"

He tasted the wine, then frowned into the glass. "Not especially. This tastes like vinegar."

Rowen returned her untouched glass to the tray. "Was Reggie a nice child?"

"Reggie was then as he is now. He wanted the best toys, the best clothes, the most freedom."

"In other words, he was a brat."

Des's eyes, gray-green in the light from the fire, gleamed. "Does that surprise you?"

"No. But let me get this straight. He knew his cousins on Harold's side and he knew you, but you never knew them?"

"I'm not related to 'them.' Do you know all your married-in relatives?"

Standing, Rowen began to pace the room. "Not at all. I don't even know my own first cousins." She paused, aware that he was watching her. Her skin warmed, but there was something beneath the purely physical sensation, some dark cloud forming in her mind. "Does something here feel wrong to you?" she asked. "Beyond the obvious, I mean?"

His eyes, which could be unnervingly intense at times, followed her past the fireplace. "It feels like fall," he said. "And Halloween."

She glanced at him, marveling briefly at how distinctive his features were despite his resemblance to Reggie. His was not a face you'd forget, and while handsome might not be the word to describe him, intriguing most definitely fit. She half wished he would smile at her, then she recalled the topic of their conversation and shivered.

"Halloween is trick or treat, Des. It's ghost parades and horror movies. It's when the leaves change and black cats come out and you and your friends sneak into the woods and tell spooky stories around a big bonfire." She hesitated. "I don't know, maybe it's all in my mind. I'm not used to curses, or a housekeeper who looks like she comes from *Night of the Living Dead,* or a mansion that must have been designed by an architect on the verge of insanity."

Des didn't seem the least bit perturbed by her remarks. In fact, he looked vaguely amused by the whole thing.

"I'm talking to a brick wall, aren't I?" Rowen finished, sighing.

In one swift motion he sat forward, transferring the hat he still wore from his head to hers. "Yes. And now that you've gotten that off your lovely chest, let's explore a little, shall we? Maybe we'll get lucky and run into Jonah Blackstone's ghost."

"POST-REVOLUTION ROCOCO," Des concluded thirty minutes later. "With a few Gothic flourishes thrown in for good measure." He glanced down at Rowen on her knees on the floor. "What's that?"

"A ghastly jack-o'-lantern." She peered at the flame inside. "It won't last till Halloween. It's already drying out. Look, there's a whole line of these things along this hall. One at every window, and all lit."

"Maybe Almira puts them here to keep Blackstone's ghost away." Grinning, Des nudged her shoulder with his knee. "Come on, let's see what's at the end of this horror trail."

Rowen stood, started to dust off, then stopped as something creaked ahead of them. "What was that?"

Des squinted into the shadows. "A door maybe? Come on, I think there's a fork down there."

"I think there's a fork in your brain," she retorted. "If anyone sees us, they'll know right away you're not Reggie. He doesn't like to explore."

"Tell me something, Rowen," Des said with a glance at the slanting rain. "Does Reggie like anything that doesn't involve the making of money?"

She gave his jacket a teasing tug as they started forward. "He likes shopping for clothes. Silk, linen, velvet, Harris tweed. He only buys the best. Wait!" Setting a hand on his arm, she halted. "There's that creak again. It's like floorboards."

"Or door hinges." Des searched the shadows. "Someone spying on us maybe?"

"Oh, there's a comforting thought."

He nudged her forward. "If it's all the same to you, I'd rather find this killer before he or she finds me."

"So would I. I just happen to think that sneaking around dark hallways in the middle of the night is a rather stupid thing to do when you know there are a bunch of spooky people in the vicinity, most of whom would be ecstatic if you walked into a butcher's knife."

"Shh." Pressing a hand to her mouth and his cheek to the side of her hair, Des nodded toward a patch of black near the rear wall. "It came from over there." His eyes strayed to her neck. "You're wearing Ombre Rose, aren't you?"

She smacked his hand from her mouth. "Don't be so pedantic. And let go of me."

He kept his lips deliberately close to her ear. "Why? Doesn't Reggie like to touch you?"

She twisted on his wrist until it hurt. "That," she said defiantly, "is none of your business."

He was contemplating kissing her neck just to see what she would do, when the creak came again.

Rowen pushed his hat and her hair from her eyes. "Maybe it's a window shutter," she speculated, her fingers still curled around his wrist.

"Maybe we should go and look, hmm?"

She made some remark he couldn't hear above the splashing rain, and he started for the darkest section of the hall. There were five doors at the end.

"Locked," Rowen affirmed, rattling one of them. She sniffed. "It smells musty here, doesn't it?"

"We're probably over the cellar," Des said. "This is the north end of the house."

"What does that mean?"

He nodded at the appropriate wall. "The cliffs are over there."

"I need a bit more than that, I'm afraid."

"Cliffs," he repeated. "Ocean, boats, smugglers. At least it works that way in England."

"Yes, well not in America." Leaning her shoulder against the third door, Rowen pushed. "This one's jammed. Anyway, Reggie never said anything about smugglers, only a curse and greedy relatives."

"I wouldn't depend on Reggie for accurate information." As he spoke, Des twisted another handle. The latch gave, and he stepped across the threshold. "This one's..."

The final word lodged in his throat as the floor suddenly opened up beneath him. He landed hard and began to slide. Toward what, his startled mind couldn't imagine, but he was going down and there was nothing but smooth wood for his hands to grab.

A huge black pit loomed before him. He remembered shouting at Rowen to keep back. Then as abruptly as it had begun, the slide ended.

Unfortunately, his momentum drove him forward into something that felt like a stone wall. His forehead slammed into it, then his chest. The next thing he knew, he was on his knees, dazed and wondering whether he was conscious or not.

His muscles were numb from the impact. A sudden glare of lights overhead blinded him. He squeezed his eyes shut against their brightness and slowly pushed back from whatever it was he'd hit.

"Des!" Rowen's urgent voice came into his ear. Her hands touched his hair and shoulders. "Are you all right? Are you hurt?" She gave him a gentle shake. "Answer me."

Easing his eyes open, he located her face. "I'm fine, I think. What happened?"

"You tumbled down a ramp."

The light still hurt, so he kept his eyes closed and grimaced. "What kind of an idiot would put a ramp behind a door?"

"I don't know but some idiot obviously did." Brushing back his hair, she ran her fingers over his cheek. "You're going to have a big bruise tomorrow."

"And a headache tonight. What did I hit?"

"A support beam." She slid her hand to his chest. At his hissed breath of reaction, she moved behind him. "Come on, I'll help you up."

Not by pressing her breasts into the back of his head she wouldn't. Des thought about going limp and enjoying the moment, but a saner instinct prevailed. Gritting his teeth, he climbed to his feet.

The room spun, then slowly began to settle. Rowen steadied him by wrapping both hands around his arm.

"You're bigger than you look," she said, brushing the tangle of hair from his eyes. Her fingers lingered on the bruised bone, then returned resolutely to his arm. Despite the pain, Des smiled.

"Don't look so smug," she warned, reading him with unnerving accuracy. "I was checking, not enjoying."

"Shrewd little thing, aren't you?" he noted.

"I like to think so." She eyed the ramp. "Well, we can't climb that thing, which only leaves this other door."

His vision clearing, Des looked around for the first time. The room was clean and empty, barely larger than a storage closet.

"It's an outer door," Rowen told him, peering across the threshold into the rain. "We'll have to go around to the front and hope Almira or Poole answers. Assuming Poole leeps here, that is." She paused, and he heard a closer, "Excuse me, but what are you doing?"

Crouching down, Des examined the iron railings that bordered the ramp.

"Des?"

She tapped his shoulder, and he sat back, a slow smile curving his lips. "It's a pulley system."

"Really?" Leaning over, Rowen tested the strength of the cable beneath the rail. "For something heavy, huh? Furniture maybe?"

Des arched a speculative eyebrow. "Or a wheelchair."

"Ah. As in our mysterious Mr. Becker."

Eyes on her mouth, Des nodded. She had a sensual way of expressing herself, not to mention an incredibly sexy voice. He had the strong feeling that he was going to want her quite badly, quite soon.

"It's rude to stare," she said, her eyes not leaving the pulley.

Amusement shimmered through him. "Don't tell me, Reggie's painfully polite, right?"

"He can be," she agreed, then gave his shoulder a shake. "We have a visitor," she murmured. "Look up."

Even knowing who it had to be didn't diminish the shock of seeing Almira Adams in a bloodred bathrobe and a pair of black men's slippers. She didn't have fangs but they wouldn't have been out of place in her white face.

"What are you doing down there?" she demanded.

Des stood, irritated more by her attitude than by his recent fall. "We're looking around *my* house," he said evenly.

"Well, you shouldn't be."

"Why not?" Rowen asked. "Does it upset you?"

Almira's features remained frozen. "I know this house, Miss Hunter. It has many traps and dangers."

"Deliberate ones, I'm sure." Des offered her a dangerous smile of his own. Like Rowen he had a range of expressions, some of them not particularly pleasant. "Open the front door for us, will you, Almira? And as long as you're up, fix us something to eat."

Her dark eyes radiated hostility, but she said nothing.

"Very good." Des congratulated her self-restraint. "Now go and open the door."

Almira moved away in furious silence. Rowen moved around him, nodding toward the top of the ramp. "It's her, Des," she said softly. "That's where the feeling I had earlier came from." She started for the outer door and the rain beyond it. "There's something very weird about that woman."

THE MAN CONCEALED in the shadows outside the Ancient Mariner Bar had begun to think that Peter Pettiston was never going to leave. But the lawyer finally tottered out at one-thirty a.m., and turned for his lighted, dockside office.

Damn the arrogant lush, he'd taken forever, and it was a cold night. The man wondered belatedly if he should have taken the risk and broken into Pettiston's office, but then breaking and entering wasn't his strong suit, and unless he was mistaken, there would be an elaborate alarm system to deal with.

No, it was better done this way.

Slack-jawed, Pettiston staggered toward the outer staircase. Some lawyer. Bleached-blond hair, artful stubble on his jaw, he looked as if he belonged on a surfboard. Still, he was probably plenty strong. This would have to be handled carefully.

The man waited until Pettiston reached the top of the stairs, then slowly began to creep up. The rain had subsided but his shoes still squelched on the wet wood. Fortunately, the lawyer was too busy trying to find his keys to notice.

He located them at last, stumbled forward, then pitched through the door. The fingers of his left hand depressed a series of buttons on the wall. His charge timed, the man outside threw his weight against the closing door, knocking it and Pettiston aside with a loud crash.

"Hey, wait a minute," the lawyer sputtered. "What's going on here? Who...?"

The room was dark. Only the misty lights from the Ancient Mariner broke the office gloom. Using a short pipe, the man cracked Pettiston on the back of the skull, then watched dispassionately as the lawyer's body dropped to the floor.

He tossed the pipe down next to Pettiston's head. Good. Now maybe he could get what he'd come for. How simple everything would be if he could just find that one little envelope that Harold had almost certainly entrusted to his lawyer...

A full hour later, the man flung the last file from the last drawer to the floor in disgust. He kicked aside a stack of legal papers and looked around at the shambles. Why in this whole damned office did he find everything but the one thing he wanted?

"Oh, to hell with it," he muttered at length. "Murder is easier." A cold smile grazed his lips as he started for the door. He let his eyes stray in the direction of Midnight Manor. "Easier," he repeated, clenching his gloved fists in an obsessive gesture, "and a lot more enjoyable."

Chapter Four

"You. Girl. Help me get to the elevator."

Rowen turned slowly in the second-floor hallway. "Are you talking to me?" she asked the white-haired man sitting behind her in his wheelchair.

He had a faint German accent and huge bags under his eyes. She put his age near sixty. He wore a light wool suit, had a blanket draped over his legs and a pair of canes laid across the arms of his chair. Powerful shoulders attested to the fact that he frequently used them.

"The elevator's on your right," he said in the same authoritative tone.

Rowen leaned against her bedroom door, studying him. "You must be Franz Becker."

He wheeled closer, his expression unpleasant. "You must be deaf. I said the elevator's this way."

"I heard you."

"Well?"

"Well what?" Pushing off from against the door, she bent over the back of his chair. "I'm not your servant, Mr. Becker," she whispered softly. "Ask me nicely and I might help you. Otherwise, you're on your own. Savvy?"

He wheeled around. A foggy light fell across his pouchy face. "And just who are you, my girl?"

"Well, I'm not your girl, that's for sure. My name is Rowen Hunter."

"Reggie's friend," he said in disgust.

"That's right." She smiled. "Reggie, who won't take kindly to being shouted awake at seven a.m."

Franz made an unflattering sound and motioned to the end of the wide hall. "Elevator," he repeated. When she didn't move, he added a resigned, "Please."

Satisfied, Rowen began to push. She glanced at Des's door in passing. Their rooms connected, but she'd stood firm in her resolve to keep her distance from the man. His teasing last night had affected her more than she cared to be affected. She'd thought for a minute he was going to kiss her in the downstairs hall, but then they'd heard that mysterious creak and the moment had vanished.

And speaking of creaks...

"You really should have these wheels oiled," she told Franz as they approached a set of carved walnut doors at the end of the corridor. "You could wake the dead with that noise."

"Cooper's an early riser," Franz responded without a trace of humor. "Be careful at the edge of the carpet," he snapped. "I've already been thrown into a wall once in my life. I don't need to have it happen a second time."

"You were thrown into a wall?"

"Thanks to your 'friend.' Open the doors." She waited purposely and again he relented. "Please."

Rowen patted his shoulder. "You're improving, Mr. Becker."

It was a tiny elevator, barely large enough to accommodate them, and as old as the manor itself from the look of it.

"Rather like entering a trap, isn't it?" Franz remarked.

"Cage door and all." Rowen secured the ornate gate and pressed the button marked 'Ground.' "Four floors," she noted in surprise. "This house must be enormous. Of course it was awfully dark when we arrived."

"And Almira's extremely frugal. No outdoor lights, and as few burning inside as possible."

The elevator jolted alarmingly, but at least it didn't plummet into the cellar. "How well do you know her, Mr. Becker?" Rowen asked.

"Franz. We met just over a year ago, on my first visit."

"So you and Harold were friends, then."

Franz sent her a pointed look. "He owed me."

The truth wasn't difficult to grasp. "I see. So Harold was making up for his grandson's mistakes."

"How do you make up for the loss of someone's legs?"

"I don't suppose you can. What happened, exactly?"

The man's features darkened. "Reggie hasn't told you?"

"It doesn't sound like something he'd want to brag about."

Franz wound his thick fingers around his canes. No doubt he wished it was Reggie's throat. "Your so-called friend caused me to catapult through the windshield of his car into the side of a cliff, that's what happened."

"Was he drunk?"

Franz snorted. "Only with his own importance. No, Reggie's never been one for drink. Clouds the mind, fuzzes the thinking, and Reggie's always thinking about something. Even at sixteen he was a thinker. Except when that punk in a supercharged Vauxhall challenged his brand-new Ferrari. Then he didn't think about anything but proving his own arrogant worth. He wanted to have the best, *be* the best, and to hell with anyone who got in his way. You're a walking testimony to that fact, I'm afraid."

Comments like that didn't faze Rowen in the slightest. She simply smiled and said, "No, I'm not."

The elevator shuddered to a halt, preventing further conversation. It was a shame because she'd wanted to get back to the subject of Almira Adams. Something about that woman unsettled her, yet for the life of her she couldn't decide what it was.

Fires burning throughout the manor barely took the chill off the October morning. Grateful for her russet stirrup pants, high boots and heavy, white cable-knit sweater that hung to midthigh, Rowen pushed Franz through the great hall, then down a short corridor to a marginally more cheerful dining room.

To her surprise, everyone except Richard was there, even Des, looking aggravatingly Bohemian in a pair of loose brown cords and an off-white cotton shirt that wasn't quite tucked into his waistband.

She had to remind herself that his lack of concern for details was more dangerous than amusing. Thank God his hair was all long curls, because it hadn't seen a brush today, Rowen was sure of that.

He stood at the sideboard, pouring coffee from an antique pot. When he saw her, he smiled broadly. "Morning, love," he greeted and gave her a big kiss on the cheek. "Going riding, are we?" Before she could respond, he draped an arm around her shoulders, and with a suitably courteous, "Hello, Franz," turned her toward a sullen-faced man across the table. "Rowen, meet my cousin, Cooper Forbes. Cooper, my fiancée, Rowen Hunter."

Franz made a rude sound. "Friend, huh?"

Rowen kicked Des lightly on the ankle. He responded by pulling her even tighter against him.

She gave up. "It's nice to meet you, Cooper," she said in a polite voice. "You must sleep very soundly," she added with a touch of sarcasm aimed at Almira who was gliding into the room in her black funeral dress and ugly black oxfords. "Reggie and I had a difficult time finding our rooms last night. No guide, you see. We almost stumbled into your bedroom by accident. Fortunately, Anna heard us blundering around and pointed us in the right direction."

Cooper had coarse dark hair, beady eyes and the suggestion of a five-o'clock shadow on his face. He also had what Rowen called a "mean" look, a surly brand of petulance that could frighten people in or out of dark alleys.

He'd been playing with a toothpick when she entered. Now he started breaking it into little pieces.

"How do you know which room is mine?" he asked Des in apparent agitation.

Anna sipped her orange juice. "I told them. I saw you leaving when Darcy and I came up."

"Leaving?" Des pulled out a chair for Rowen. "Where could you possibly have been going so late at night, Cooper?"

"Rat-hunting?" Richard suggested breezily.

He strolled through the archway wearing a blue blazer, gray pants and a paisley ascot. Completely pretentious, but at least he was smiling. Rowen watched him grin at Cooper's mutinous face.

"Still the Beau Brummel of the Forbes family, I see. You know, Cooper, thrift stores aren't the only places that sell clothes. And you might try something other than black for a change. You look as gloomy as Almira, but of course we can forgive her. She's in mourning for poor old Harold."

"Gilbert," Des corrected, sitting back cheerfully. "I don't think Almira's too broken up over *Harold's* death."

"No more than you appear to be, Reggie. Put it there," she directed Poole who'd struggled in with a loaded tray.

Des tipped his chair back farther, clearly enjoying himself. "Well, we all have our demons to deal with, I suppose. Where did you go last night, Cooper?" he pressed in the same breath, albeit in a less humorous tone.

Having destroyed the toothpick, Cooper turned his attention to his knife. "For a walk," he mumbled, which surprised Rowen. She would have expected him to tell Des to mind his own business.

Darcy shuddered. "You're a brave man, Cooper. I wouldn't go walking in the dark on this estate. Not so close to Halloween. Did you see all those witches last night? There must have been twenty of them in that one group alone."

"Thirteen," Rowen corrected. She took one look at the platter of slimy eggs and poked Des's ribs. "Let's go for a walk."

"What, and miss the scuttlebutt?" Richard settled himself between Darcy and Cooper. "Or has Poole already spilled the beans?"

Anna, drab in a brown sweater and pants, spread jam on her toast. "What beans, Richard?"

"About Peter Pettiston. His office was ransacked last night. Poor old Peter's in hospital with a concussion. Poole told me about it before I came in."

Des finished his coffee. "How did you find out about it, Poole?"

"From the policeman who patrols the docks," the man replied calmly.

"Ah." Des continued to watch him. "And when exactly did you receive this news?"

Unruffled, Poole carried on serving breakfast. "Last night," he said, not looking up. "I drove to the Ancient

Mariner. It's a bar near the water. It was last call when we noticed the commotion outside.''

Richard laughed. "I bet half the people there thought it was Blackstone's curse at work again.''

"You seem to know a lot about Midnight," Anna observed. "I thought you said you'd never been here before.''

Richard shrugged. "I haven't, but I've been to village pubs in England and Wales. There are local legends in every port and plenty of gullible souls who believe in them. You never know, maybe this *was* Blackstone's doing.''

Rowen seriously doubted that, but she didn't feel like debating the point right then. On the other hand, Peter Pettiston was Harold's lawyer, and offices weren't usually ransacked for no reason. And someone *had* murdered Harold Forbes less than a week ago.

"Was anything missing?" she asked Poole.

"Don't know, miss.''

"I doubt if anyone does," Franz said, scowling first at his eggs, then at Des. "These things take time to sort out.''

Shoving back his chair, Des added a wry, "So do murders, Mr. Becker." He took Rowen's hand. "It sounds to me like crime is on the increase here in Midnight.''

Cooper used his knife to scrape a piece of blackened toast. "In that case, cousin," he said, each thrust becoming more violent, "you'd better take care. Blackstone's curse isn't finished yet. And there are still a lot of days between now and Halloween.''

"THAT MAN'S a spook," Rowen declared once she and Des were outside. They'd stopped off upstairs for their raincoats before leaving by one of the side doors. "How's your head by the way?''

"Not bad. I don't bruise easily.''

Rowen resisted the urge to push his hair back and look for herself. "It was smart of you not to talk to Franz too much," she said, finishing a muffin swiped from the kitchen. "He's not a big fan of yours.''

Des squinted up at the clouds that hung threateningly over the surrounding woods. "Not a good sign," he murmured. "What did I do to him?''

"Shot him through the windshield of your new Ferrari into the side of a cliff."

"That was thoughtless of me."

"He thinks so. He says you were drag racing with someone in a souped-up Vauxhall. You were sixteen at the time. I gather you haven't seen him since." She eyed him up and down. "Fortunately."

Des smiled, still surveying the panorama of fall colors around them. "You're going to scold me about my clothes, aren't you?"

"I don't scold. Anyway, I can't imagine it would do much good." Tapping his arm, she pointed toward the top of a blackened building, visible through a patch of golden maples. "Is that the old Masque Factory?"

He nodded. "And that old mill and barn to our right must be the new one. Very atmospheric. Practically oozes New England charm."

"Maybe, but it's the ruin that's at the heart of Blackstone's curse."

A flurry of damp red leaves blew past them on the broad path that wound across the estate. There were dense areas of woods near the cliffs and on the other side of what Poole had called Cemetery Road. In fact, there were woods everywhere, all dark and suitably ominous, perfect for the season. Rowen wouldn't have been surprised to see gnomes lurking among the trees, doing whatever it was gnomes did to prepare for winter.

"I take it we're going to the old factory," she said as they passed the renovated mill.

Des shook the curls from his face. "Don't you want to see it?"

"Certainly. But you don't."

"No?" Again that enigmatic smile, directed at the burned-out structure ahead of them. "And just what is it I do want, Rowen?"

The question fell short of a verbal caress, but not by much. Rowen glanced at his profile, then changed her mind and looked away, unsure about this charade for the first time since she'd agreed to take part in it. Something about

Des's unconventional attitude unsettled her. More than that, it fascinated her.

It was an unusual reaction for her. Rowen had always prided herself on her ability to remain unaffected by men. She liked them and they liked her. It seldom got more complicated than that.

Absorbed in her thoughts, she didn't notice that Des had once again set an arm on her shoulders, not until he murmured a teasing, "Come on, Rowen, tell me. What do I want?" against her temple.

She reacted to his mouth on her skin with a shake of her hair. "Watch it, Des. We're not really engaged. And what you want is a cigarette."

He laughed, and kissed her forehead. "Very good."

She sensed something beneath his easy response but had no intention of pursuing it. Instead, she asked, "Do you think the lawyer's office being ransacked has anything to do with Harold's death?"

Des removed a cigarette and matches from his pocket. "It might. We still have to figure out who had a motive to murder him. Obviously, Franz could have wanted revenge."

"True, but it would be against you, not Harold."

"Haven't you heard the expression, kill two to cover one?" Des asked. "As for Almira's motive, I'm not sure yet."

"I am. She's a ghoul. So's your cousin Cooper. Darcy's a wimp, Richard's a playboy and Poole's hiding something. He's no more a fisherman than I am. Did I leave anyone out?"

"Only Harold's partner at the Masque Factory."

"That's right. Lester Ridgeway, the brooder."

"Ah!" Des stopped suddenly, his eyes widening. "Here's a thought. What if Jonah Blackstone had a child? And what if that child had a child and so on."

Rowen, who'd almost been yanked from her feet by his abrupt halt, steadied herself on his arm. "You mean whoever's using the curse might be one of Blackstone's descendants?"

"It's possible."

"Only remotely. Why start using the curse now?"

"Because until Harold moved here and rebuilt the Masque Factory, there was no one to use the curse against, and probably no reason to use it in any event."

"So what's the reason now?"

"Smuggling maybe."

"You said that last night. I still don't buy it. Midnight's too remote to be a viable port for smugglers, and in case you haven't looked out your bedroom window yet, those rocks at the bottom of the cliff are deadlier than anything I've seen in Devon or Cornwall or Yorkshire or..."

"I get the message, Rowen," Des interrupted. "Not a workable location. Just don't rule out my descendant-of-Blackstone theory. It's always possible we're dealing with a crazy person."

"Why would a crazy person ransack a lawyer's office?"

"We don't know there's any connection between that and Harold's death."

"True," she conceded. "But my instincts say there is. The timing's too convenient."

The old factory loomed before them now, a charred black dome surrounded by scorched pillars and gutted brick walls.

"I wonder if the police would tell us anything?" she mused. Before Des could respond, she pointed at the dome. "That must have been the core of the factory, the main workshop. Do you think we can go inside?"

"I don't see why not." Taking her hand, Des worked his way through the rubble. "If it wasn't safe, there'd be signs."

"Which Almira might have torn down. I wish I could figure out what it is about her that bothers me."

Since she couldn't, however, and since navigating the uneven ground was anything but easy, Rowen settled for absorbing the feel of the area.

Ravaged or not, the old Masque Factory had a haunting quality about it, something connected to her perception of eighteenth century Maine. Like the man beside her, Jonah Blackstone's face hovered in her mind. His features, as depicted in the portrait back at the manor, possessed an eerie, troubled aspect, yet they'd struck her as frighteningly sinister. Maybe he really had traded some part of himself for black powers.

The sky over the water had grown quite dark by the time they reached the dome. The front door stood open, wedged in place by time and the settling remains around it.

Des squeezed in first. Rowen followed, casting a last doubtful look at the clouds. She had only one uncontrollable fear, and it had nothing to do with wizards or curses or creepy men who made sawdust out of toothpicks. She was terrified of electrical storms, and the bank of clouds scudding along the coast had a definite aura of thunder and lightning about them.

With a shiver, she blocked the prospect from her mind and let her eyes adjust to the gloom.

It wasn't as dark as she would have expected, thanks in part to a gaping hole in the roof. There was a great deal of blackened wood and stone lying in heaps on the floor. There were also huge pieces of damaged equipment, although what they had been used for she couldn't guess. Low doorways and short staircases, most of them in ruins, led to multiple partitions filled with remnants of rusted machinery and tables long enough to hold two or three coffins.

The last was a morbid thought, but not unwarranted when Rowen considered that the factory's original product had been death masks.

"I feel like we're in a tomb," she said. "Look." She picked up a sooty piece of plaster. "This is probably a fragment of someone's mask. It might have been made by Jonah Blackstone himself."

"Mmm." Immersed in his own thoughts, Des lit a cigarette, then stood back to study a chain hanging on the far wall. "That's interesting," he said finally.

"Is it?" Rowen didn't look. The plaster pieces were much more fascinating to her. Some of them actually fit together.

It was odd, she reflected, that vandals hadn't destroyed all of this over the years. Unless, of course, they were too afraid of Blackstone's ghost to venture through the front door.

She heard a rattle of chains behind her, then Des wandered past. "Come on, Rowen," he said. "There are more stairs over here. They look like they might lead down to a cellar."

Dusting off her hands, she joined him. "I don't know," she said when they reached the bottom. "That door looks awfully old and heavy. I doubt if it..." She gave the iron ring a twist, then stood back and watched in amazement as it swung silently inward. "It opened!" she exclaimed. Suspicion replaced surprise in her mind. "Why did it open?"

Experimentally, Des swung the door back and forth.

"No squeaks," she observed. "Now that *is* interesting."

"Very." He indicated the top. "It's been leveled off. You can see where the burned wood's been scraped away."

"So, who would lubricate and level an apparently unimportant door inside an old ruin? Who and why?" She peered across the threshold. "There are no other staircases or doors, just four brick walls and a plank floor."

"All swept clean." Des eyed the cobwebbed ceiling. "Except up there."

Rowen ventured inside. "A storage room? No, that doesn't make sense. Too difficult to access."

"Maybe a tramp spent the night," Des remarked with a grin.

"A neat one who brought his own broom." A distant snap of wood brought Rowen's head up. "What was that?"

Des pressed a finger to his lips. He was up the stairs in two agile bounds, unusual for someone so tall. Rowen ran up behind him, staring over his shoulder at the source of the sound.

Menacing was the only word to describe the man who moved slowly past the hanging chain. Of sturdy build, he stood close to six feet tall, with straight dark hair, black eyes and a full mustache. His face was pockmarked, his hands were square and looked extremely strong.

"Whoever you are, come out," he said in a voice even more forbidding than his appearance.

He turned, and Rowen saw his right hand for the first time. "He has a gun," she breathed in Des's ear.

He also had exceptional hearing because she'd barely whispered the words, and neither she nor Des had moved.

The gun rose, pointing directly into the shadows where they stood.

"Out," he ordered coldly. He cocked the hammer with his thumb. "You've got three seconds before I start shooting."

Chapter Five

"No, don't do that. We were just having a look around." Des wasn't fond of responding to threats, but he was no fool, either. This man would shoot. He detached himself from the shadows, careful to stay in front of Rowen.

The gun didn't waver. "Who are you?" the man demanded.

"Who are *you?*" Rowen challenged, stepping out boldly from behind Des's arm.

"Lester Ridgeway."

"Harold's partner?" Summoning a pleasant smile, she extended her hand. "I'm Rowen Hunter. And this—" she gave Des a push to get him over his astonishment "—is Harold's grandson Reggie."

The man actually transferred the gun so he could shake Rowen's hand. However, not a flicker of friendliness registered on his dark face.

His appraisal of Des was swift and assessing. "I thought you'd be neater somehow."

"Did you?" Des smiled. "Well—" He looked meaningfully at the gun barrel, now pointed at his hip. Lester hesitated, then uncocked the hammer, tucking the weapon into his khaki waistband. "Thank you," Des said, maintaining his smile. "Who did you think we were?"

"Don't know, but I've seen things around here lately, before and after Harold's death. I'm not about to take chances."

"Shoot first and all that?" Des remarked with a mocking arch of his brows. He felt Rowen's elbow in his ribs and offered a more serious, "What kinds of things?"

"People who shouldn't be here. Nothing definite. Shadows for the most part, but they're not ghosts."

"More than one shadow?" Rowen asked.

Lester shrugged. "I just know someone's been messing around in here and they have no business doing it."

"It could be kids," Des suggested, wandering away to gaze up at the ceiling. "I don't think guns are the answer, do you?"

The man gave a rough imitation of a laugh. "Harold never told me you were a pacifist, Reggie. I'd have expected a more tyrannical attitude."

"Would you?"

"Reggie's not entirely what his reputation implies," Rowen inserted sweetly. "Tell me, Lester, when did you first notice these shadows?"

"Ten or twelve months ago."

"Did you tell Harold about them?"

"Harold figured it was kids, too. But I know the talk in town. Kids wouldn't come out here. The cemetery's as far out as anyone in Midnight will explore."

"Even on a dare?" Rowen asked.

His eyes were flat and unemotional. "Even then."

Des continued to inspect the ceiling. Except for the hole, it looked sound enough. Still, it was an odd design. He wondered if Jonah Blackstone had had a hand in the contruction. It was possible he'd used the dome shape to channel his so-called dark powers. Des had heard of similar cases in Scotland.

"How long have you been in Midnight, Lester?" he asked.

Hard eyes raked him up and down. "Two and a half years."

"How did you meet Harold?"

"He never told you?"

Des gave a short laugh. "My grandfather was a recluse, not to mention an eccentric. He told me what he had to, nothing more."

Lester glanced at Rowen, then followed Des's gaze to the ceiling. "We met in a bar in Midnight. He looked like a scruffy old sailor. We had a few beers and started talking."

"And that was two and a half years ago?" Rowen said.
"So Harold visited Midnight before he actually decided to move here and rebuild the Masque Factory."

"He made the decision to rebuild over the next six months, after he'd gone back to London. Then he contacted me and asked if I'd be interested in overseeing the construction. He figured on moving here sometime the following year, said it would take him that long to get his affairs in order. There was a lawsuit pending in Amsterdam and a fire in one of his Los Angeles buildings."

"I remember the fire," Rowen said.

"Ah, yes, the Los Angeles fire," Des lied, though he had no idea what Lester meant. "Go on."

Lester's flinty eyes came to rest on Des's face. Still no sign of warmth. "Harold had already hired old John Pettiston to take care of his personal legal matters and those connected to the Masque Factory. Old Pettiston drew up the agreement and the rest you know, or should, Reggie. You signed the agreement papers before Harold left London."

"I signed a lot of things before Harold left London," Des told him. He gave the man a veiled look. "Did you know about the Forbes family and Blackstone's curse before you met Harold?"

Lester snorted. "Everyone in Midnight knows about the Forbes family. It's the first thing you learn when you come to town. The Masque Factory in Midnight is where the Forbes empire was born. Now it's branched out, jewelry, antiques, art. Still, most people figured it was only a matter of time before someone came home."

"And were they pleased when someone did?" Rowen asked him.

"It stoked the legend," Lester said with a noncommittal shrug. "Really stoked it, I mean. As far as I can gather Blackstone's curse has always been big in Midnight. High season here is mid-September through All Souls' Day."

She smiled. "And how did Almira react to the news, do you know?"

"I doubt if she was happy about it. I can't speak for Gilbert."

"No one can anymore," Des said. "He died last year, didn't he? And I'll bet Almira's been calling it murder from day one. Harold worked her precious Gilbert to death, or something like that."

"Almira's not much of a talker," Lester said gruffly. "And Harold *was* a demanding man."

Hands in his raincoat pockets, Des examined a scorched brick wall. "Tell me, Lester, as a partner in the Masque Factory, aren't you worried about Blackstone's curse? If someone used it to kill Harold, what's to stop that same person from using it to kill you?"

He'd slipped with that, he could tell by the look Rowen shot him.

Lester's black eyes narrowed in suspicion. "What are you getting at, Reggie?"

"Nothing," Rowen said quickly. "Reggie's not clear on the curse, that's all."

"Sounds like he's pointing fingers, to me."

It took Des a moment to understand what Lester meant. When he did, he shook his head. "I wasn't accusing you, Lester, I was thinking about the conditions of the curse. Blackstone's letter condemned anyone whose name appeared on the Masque Factory ownership papers."

"What Reggie sometimes forgets, however, is that the curse only applies to members of the Forbes family," Rowen finished smoothly. "You have to give us both time to get the legend straight. We only arrived last night, and believe me, Almira's welcome was anything but enthusiastic. If that's how she treats guests, it's easy to understand why children never come out here."

She made a wide circle around the rubble-filled central chamber while Des did his best to hide his amusement. Lester's eyes were neither cold nor suspicious as they trailed Rowen about the room. Why should they be? With her dark hair tumbling over her shoulders, and those gorgeous, vaguely Latin features and long legs, what man wouldn't be riveted?

"I know I wouldn't venture into the domain of a vampire housekeeper who looks like she's wearing her own death mask," Rowen continued. "And speaking of masks..." She turned her charm on him. "Is the new factory ready to open?"

Lester seemed entranced for a moment, then roughly shook himself and nodded. "More or less. I have a few things to go over with you, Reggie, tomorrow or the next day if that's convenient."

Something told Des that Lester didn't care if it was convenient or not. True, the man had been talking openly enough, but there was no animation behind the words. At best, Des would call Lester's attitude distant, at worst—well, time and a little digging might supply that answer.

Rowen strolled over, presumably to ensure that he didn't make any more blunders, and Lester gazed up high on the walls. "It's getting a bit dangerous in here by the look of those old joists. I'd keep out if I were you." His eyes challenged Des. "No need to make things worse for yourself."

Now that sounded like a threat. "I can handle Blackstone's curse," Des said placidly. "Never doubt that, partner."

Lester's lips curled in a faintly sly smile. "That's what old Harold said—the night before he died."

"HE'S AN EX-CON," Rowen deduced when Lester was gone and she and Des were once more prowling the estate.

They walked past an empty marble pool, cracked now and covered with autumn leaves, the family crypt where Harold had refused to be buried, and on through a set of stone arches that bordered an extensive garden full of rose arbors, berry bushes and still more dead leaves.

Des lit a cigarette and looked backward through the tangle of his hair. "More like escaped con," he said with no trace of humor.

"Motive, Des," she reminded, letting the no-smoking rule slide, once more. They were out of range of the house, anyway. "Although," she reasoned, "as a partner in the

Masque Factory, Lester might stand to gain a great deal with both Reggie and Harold dead. We should check the ownership papers. Or I could call Reggie.''

''Reggie doesn't know anything,'' Des said. The humor was back in his voice, and for that Rowen was glad. His smile was so infectious that even with a Magnum aimed at their chests, she could stay calm. Well, calm to a point. For a moment, Lester's finger had seemed quite prepared to squeeze the trigger.

She picked up a red oak leaf. ''He's about forty-five, wouldn't you say?''

''Does it matter?''

''No, I'm just trying to keep it all straight. Darcy's thirty-seven and has his own electronics store in Green Bay. Anna's twenty-six . . .''

''Really?'' Des interrupted with a disbelieving chuckle. ''I thought she was forty at least.''

''It's her attitude. She's a sort of *young* fogy. My brother's like that.''

''You have a brother?''

''Last time I checked.''

''When was that?''

She counted backward. ''Seven years ago.''

Des stared at her. ''You haven't seen your brother for seven years?''

''I haven't *seen* him for ten. I told you, he's a fogy. We don't get along. He sells floor tiles in Albuquerque, has two bratty kids, whom I unfortunately *have* seen because his wife brought them to Los Angeles for a visit around the time I met Reggie—and why are we talking about Lance and his family, anyway? It's a very boring subject.''

''Lance and Rowen,'' Des mused. ''Sounds Arthurian.''

''Close. My mother's an English literature freak.'' Rowen's gaze swept the unkempt garden. ''She'd hate this country scene. She's an even bigger neat freak.''

''She must love Reggie.''

''Not really. She came to Los Angeles when my sister-in-law did. Reggie brought me home after the inquest. She was with him for five minutes and decided he was a pompous ass.''

"Your mother's a good judge of character."

"My mother was and still is a hippie, or a beatnik, or whatever you Bohemians were called between the fifties and sixties. You know," she said, switching topics midstream and indicating the untidy garden trellises, "all of these dead vines and fallen leaves remind me of a book I illustrated once, *The Magic Pumpkin*. I did it in art school, a Halloween kids' book written by a sweet old man from Brooklyn. The little girl in the story made a wish on a magic pumpkin seed and got whisked away to the Pumpkin Forest. You'd almost think the writer came from Midnight."

"Maybe he did." Des frowned. "What do you mean, 'you Bohemians'?"

"If you're thirty-eight, you know the term. Your chosen life-style was big right through the early seventies. And as long as we're back on the subject of age, how old is Cooper?"

With a laugh, Des let the matter drop. Eyes closed, he tipped his head back. "Thirty-five, I think, same as Reggie."

"What does he do, besides pull wings off butterflies?"

"He studies them. He's an entomologist."

"Creepy occupation. What about Richard?"

"Thirty-six and nothing."

"He doesn't work?"

"Not according to Reggie, although he's hardly a reliable source." Pausing, Des took a wild red rose between his fingers, sending her an engaging grin over his shoulder. "This would look pretty in your hair."

Rowen's resistant heart melted just a little. Something to do with the look on his face—and doubtless more than that if she were honest about her feelings. She didn't feel like being honest right then.

"You think red suits me?" she began. However, before she could take the rose, something long and straight and painfully sharp flew between them, slicing her arm as it careened past.

With a hissed breath she twisted her head around, crouching instinctively. "What was that?"

"Back here." Des had his hands on her before she finished her question. Together they tumbled behind an overgrown trellis. Des hovered over her, his body weight holding her down while Rowen struggled to get her bearings.

Her arm throbbed. She knew it was bleeding. But what had hit her? It couldn't have been a bullet, she wouldn't have seen that go by. Besides, who would be shooting at her?

"Des . . ."

"Shh."

She bit back a grunt of pain. "You're lying on my arm."

He shifted slightly, but his body still effectively pinned hers to the ground. "Don't move," he whispered.

She didn't intend to. She could see the thing now, embedded in the rose arbor behind them. It was an arrow—and whoever had shot it was crashing through the bushes.

A man's narrow craggy features emerged from a tangled thicket. Rowen recognized his sandy hair, his thin nose and close-set eyes. "Poole," she breathed, then reached up and tugged on the front of Des's shirt. "There," she said, watching apprehensively as the man wearing gardener's overalls and a pair of heavy gloves plucked the arrow from the trellis.

"Quiet," Des said, though only an idiot would have made a sound. The arrow had lodged itself deep in the wood. Poole had to give it two hard yanks to remove it. Even in pain, Rowen realized that it could just as easily be lodged in Des or herself.

Extricating himself from the weeds with difficulty, Poole held the arrow up like a knife. "Who's there?" he demanded, but he wasn't looking at them. His eyes were fixed on the garden path.

Rowen heard leaves crunching underfoot. The seconds crawled by. Breath held, she kept perfectly still. Then she saw Darcy, breathless and pale, stumble into sight and she relaxed.

"I'm so sorry," he apologized. He held up a bow. "That shot got away from me. I hope you're not hurt."

Poole continued to stare at him. It wasn't until Des stirred, rustling the underbrush as he climbed off Rowen that either man looked in their direction.

"Reggie!" Darcy exclaimed. "And Rowen. What are you two doing here?"

"Dodging arrows," Des said, not sounding pleased. He helped Rowen to her feet. He kept his fingers wrapped around her arm, inclining his head toward her. "Are you all right?"

"I don't think so," she said. The garden spun for a moment, then slowly settled.

He must have seen the tear in her coat. She doubted he could see the blood on the black fabric. In one deft motion, he tore the sleeve down and pushed aside the wool of her sweater.

Rowen saw the blood plainly. So did Poole. His face went white. The arrow slid from his fingers and landed in the dirt. "You're hurt," he whispered.

"Yes, I see that," she replied, feeling strangely detached. She would have made a horrible nurse, every doctor who'd ever stuck a needle in her said so.

"It really was an accident," Darcy mumbled, running his fingers through his pale brown hair. "Anna can tell you. We were shooting targets over by the oak trees . . ."

"It doesn't matter what you were shooting," Des said impatiently, tying a handkerchief around Rowen's numb right arm. His eyes took in her calm, pale features. "You're not going to faint, are you?"

She managed a weak smile. "I'm not sure. I've never been hit by an arrow before."

Poole backed away. "I'll get Almira," he said.

Oh, God, no, not that. Pressing a hand to her forehead, Rowen told herself to concentrate and stop being such a baby. It was only a scratch, nothing to get panicky over.

She lowered her eyes to the dirt, littered now with dead poplar and maple leaves. Something warm slid along her wrist beneath her sweater as Des finished tying the tourniquet. She shifted her gaze to him and focused on his beautiful mass of brown curls.

She wanted to touch his hair suddenly, and his face, but there was something warm and sticky trickling over the back of her hand. She felt it start to drip from the ends of her fingers. Her gaze dropped to the big maple leaf at her feet, a lovely shade of gold, now spattered with drops of red.

Her head swam in lazy circles. The black clouds along the coast seemed to sweep through her mind. I'm sorry, Des, she thought. Then she shut her eyes and let the blackness consume her.

IT WAS NIGHTTIME before the second letter could be composed. Electric candles on the walls gave off a luminous glow that pooled on the white paper. A careful hand began to write.

Dear Dr. Sayers,

It wasn't supposed to be this way, Rowen hurt and bleeding. She's asleep now in her bed while Reggie watches over her, pretending to care. But I know he doesn't really care, not Reggie, not unless he's worried that the arrow was intended for him. He would certainly care about that.

Maybe Blackstone's ghost directed it; someone made that suggestion at dinner. A ridiculous thought of course. Why would Blackstone want to hurt Rowen? No, like me, his ghost will be after Reggie.

Well, if it is, I hope I get there first. I won't be needing any ghostly help to eliminate Reggie. I won't be needing anything except my wonderful skull mask—the source of Blackstone's curse—and a chance to execute the second part of my plan.

Don't worry, I'm not out to get Rowen, Dr. Sayers. As I've told you many times, I really don't like to kill. I only want Reggie out of the way.

I've been prepared for quite some time now. But if in fact Jonah Blackstone should decide to rise from his grave afterward to thank me, I'd be most honored. To be honest, I'd like to meet this enigmatic ghost. We're very much alike, Blackstone and me. Both hungry for revenge. But I want to be the one to destroy Reggie. Blackstone will have to accept that. After all, it is only a few more days until Halloween.

Please rest assured,
A former patient

Chapter Six

Des watched Rowen's peaceful face. He sat back and stared at her asleep, the doctor's words echoing in his head.

"Twelve stitches and mild shock. She lost enough blood to affect her, but it's nothing serious."

Feet braced on the edge of the mattress, Des slouched in his chair and continued to stare. Nothing serious. She could be dead. That was extremely serious by his standards.

Darcy insisted it was an accident and Anna confirmed his story. Their denials meant nothing. Poole said he was sorry, he shouldn't have set up the targets in the garden. Almira said coldly that accidents could happen to anyone. And Cooper, well, he simply smiled and wandered off to his room.

A single bedside lamp threw soft streaks of gold light across the papered walls. Rowen looked pale and delicate in the huge canopied bed with its red velvet curtains and patterned spread. It was a garish room, they all were as far as Des was concerned, cluttered with ornate antique furniture and gloomy tapestries.

Maybe he was more superstitious than he cared to admit, but he was afraid to take his eyes off Rowen, as though she might dissolve if he didn't keep a constant watch. Or maybe he was hoping she would wake up.

Rubbing his eyes, Des sank deeper into his chair. The rain on the roof was a lulling background sound. He heard thunder in the distance, but it seemed to be moving away. Probably just as well. Every time it rumbled through the sky, Rowen stirred restlessly in her sleep.

Almira knocked and opened the door. Her cheeks were white, her lips bloodred, her eyes unfriendly. "I've left some food for you in the kitchen," she said. "Does Miss Hunter need anything?"

Des returned his gaze to Rowen's face. "If she does, I'll get it. Good night, Almira."

He heard the rustle of her black dress as she moved off.

A blast of rain and leaves blew against the window. He rubbed a hand across his forehead, recalling briefly the look on Franz Becker's face when he'd learned about the incident in the garden.

He'd glared accusingly at Des. "If there is a Blackstone's curse, Reggie, it will get you eventually. But in the meantime, you'll just jump aside the way you always do, and let someone else get hurt in your place. You don't care about anyone, do you, not even your fiancée."

Des had absorbed the words like blows, accepting them as if they'd been directed at him instead of Reggie. Rowen shouldn't be involved in this nightmare. He should get her the hell out of here before she wound up dead.

"So how's she doing?"

It was Anna who opened the door this time, still dressed in the same brown outfit she'd been wearing in the garden, clothes that made her look like part *of* the garden and matched her husband's brown suit perfectly.

Tweedledum and Tweedledee, Des thought, tapping his thumbnail in consideration on his lower teeth. But had they been trying to blend in? Eyes still locked on Rowen's face, he said, "She'll be fine. Don't!" His hand shot out to intercept Anna's.

She twisted free, clearly affronted. "I was only going to pull the covers up."

"I'll pull them up."

He could see her in his peripheral vision. He recognized the expression on her face. Suspicion.

"You're quite a paradox, Reggie." Clasping her hands, she strolled to the far side of the bed.

"Am I?" Des continued to run his thumbnail over his teeth, a habit Reggie didn't possess. He watched Rowen change positions. She wasn't sleeping very soundly. She didn't seem to like the thunder.

He felt Anna staring at him. "You're worried about her, aren't you?"

"Shouldn't I be?"

"I wasn't under the impression that you cared about anyone except yourself. I was also told that you're a natty dresser." She eyed his scruffy jeans, open shirt and bare feet. "Has your fiancée brought about this behavioral change, Reggie, or is there something you're not telling us?"

"If Darcy's the source of your information, you might bear in mind that we haven't seen each other for twenty-three years."

"People don't change their natures, Reggie. You were a spoiled kid, and we heard similar stories about you later."

"Did you?"

She started for the window. "Doesn't your reputation concern you?"

"Not especially."

He knew she was studying him but he didn't want to look away from the bed. Something about Rowen's features enchanted him. In this light they seemed almost translucent, pale but incredibly sensual.

"What's your scheme this time?" Anna asked in a shrewd voice.

"What makes you think I have one?"

"Because you always have a scheme, just like you've always hated Darcy, ever since he made you break that stupid mirror."

"What?" Des glanced up, then remembered Reggie's scathing childhood tale, and returned his gaze to Rowen's face. "Oh, that. I think you're making too much out of an accident."

"Am I?" Her voice was icy. "You told Darcy it meant seven years of bad luck. You said he'd pay for making you break it, and that if you were going to go through seven years of hell, then he was, too. You poisoned Harold's mind against him. Who was it Harold took to London as a child? Not Darcy. Who got cars and money and control of the old man's empire? Whose screwups got neatly covered up? Did

Franz Becker ever sue you for what you did to him? Of course not. Harold bought him off for you. And what about all those scams you and Harold ran over the years? Did anyone other than you and the old man ever profit from them?''

Dropping his feet to the floor, Des reached out to pull the sheet up over Rowen's bandaged arm. For a moment, his fingers strayed to her cheek. Cool, no fever.

''You're imagining things, Anna,'' he lied, settling back. ''We never ran any scams.''

''It was common knowledge within the family,'' she retorted scornfully. ''I checked.''

''No doubt you did.''

''What does that mean?''

''It means—'' he lifted ingenuous eyes to her spiteful face ''—that you're a greedy witch, just like Harold said you were. You resent the fact that there's money and property to be had but you're not going to have it. You married the Forbes name before you realized that marrying the name wasn't the same as marrying the money. Unless, of course, I die, in which case everything of Harold's that should come to me would then go to Darcy, Richard and Cooper.'' His smile contained no warmth. ''Does that about cover it?''

Her features hardened. She had a slight overbite and a receding chin. Somehow, those things together made her eyes seem larger than normal. She regarded him half lidded, like a snake trying to decide the best way to strike.

''You think you're clever, don't you?'' she said, arms folded across her chest. Thunder permeated the air. ''You're up to something, Reggie, I know you are.'' She headed for the door. ''It's a scheme of some sort, it must be. But I'll get to the bottom of it, rest assured. Assuming, of course, that Blackstone's curse doesn't get to you first.'' Pausing on the threshold, she summoned a frigid smile. ''Good night— cousin.''

''Bitch,'' Des murmured when the door clicked shut. He noticed Rowen moving and quickly leaned forward to take her hand. ''Oy, you awake?''

''Oy, yourself,'' she mumbled sleepily. ''I don't think I'd trust Anna if I were you.''

"You heard that, did you?"

"Part of it." She started to sit up. Des had to move to the side of the bed to stop her.

"The doctor said sleep," he said, brushing a strand of silky dark hair from her collarbone.

Her eyes shifted to the rain-streaked windows. "I can't. The thunder's keeping me awake."

"You don't like it?"

"I didn't say that."

The surge of protectiveness Des experienced didn't really surprise him. He'd known in Marrakech that Rowen was something special. What he wasn't quite sure of was how to deal with his feelings for her, or whether they even should be dealt with.

He'd never been one for relationships. You couldn't live the life-style he did or be the way he was, and expect other people to understand. If he'd learned one thing from old Harold it was that eccentrics were better off alone.

A closer rumble of thunder shook the manor. Rowen's fingers tightened on his. "Des?"

"What?"

"Would you..." Her words trailed off as she glanced hesitantly at the window. "Would you stay with me?"

He stared at her for a moment, then smiled and motioned her farther over with a subtle movement of his head. Stretching out behind her, he wrapped his arms around her waist and pulled her back against him.

It was torture, pure and simple, but worth every minute of it. Pushing her hair aside, Des buried his face in Rowen's neck and eased her closer.

Reggie was going to kill him for this.

WHEN SHE WOKE UP the next morning with Des's arm draped over her breast, Rowen knew exactly what she'd done, and why. What fascinated her was what she wanted to do about it. Not run and hide, or apologize for her fear. She wanted to press her breast into his hand and see where that action might lead. She wanted to roll over carefully and kiss him, but knew if she did that, she might not be able to stop. And she wasn't sure about sex with him.

Or would it be making love? Rowen wasn't altogether clear on her feelings for Des. Unfortunately, it never came down to a choice. The doctor barged in with his black bag and a "Good morning" loud enough to wake the dead.

Either Des had been awake all along or he was a fast riser. Before the doctor could set his bag down, he was up and bending over her, kissing her cheek. He looked wonderfully rumpled. "Enjoy yourself," he murmured, sliding from the bed. "I have to make a phone call."

To his banker, no doubt. He hadn't done it yesterday, and where Reggie and money were concerned, it was always wise to double-check.

Rowen moved her arm experimentally. There was only a twinge of pain.

"You're doing fine," the doctor confirmed several minutes later. "Keep the bandage on and stay out of the garden for a few days. It sounds like a dangerous place."

Poole, in the process of delivering a tray of coffee and toast to her door, heard the last remark and gave the doctor a resentful look. "It wasn't the garden that shot the arrow," he said tightly. For Rowen he managed a smile. "Good morning, Miss Hunter."

"So you're a butler again, are you?" she asked, while the doctor, disregarding Poole's miffed expression, repacked his bag. "Yesterday you were a gardener, the day before that a chauffeur. You must get awfully tired of changing hats."

"I beg your pardon?"

"Roles, assignments—you know, jobs. Never mind. How long have you been doing all of this?"

"Just over two years," he said, shooting the doctor a final irritated look. "Gilbert, Almira's husband, got me the job."

"And you were a fisherman before that?"

"I fished sometimes."

Definitely evasive, Rowen decided.

"If you'll excuse me," he said politely, "I have to help Almira with breakfast."

"Odd man," the doctor remarked when he was gone. "Terrible gardener. I don't think old Harold was too pleased with his work."

Rowen sipped her coffee. "Well, it can't be easy for him, can it? I mean, walking seems to be a chore in itself."

"At least he *can* walk," a voice at the door grumbled. Franz Becker rolled in. "And how are you feeling today, Rowen?"

"Better than yesterday."

"Where's Reggie?"

"He had to make a phone call."

"To do with money no doubt." He rolled closer, tapping the bed with a warning finger. "You mark my words, Rowen Hunter, that man's no good. Yesterday was only the beginning."

"Yesterday was an accident," Rowen maintained, refusing to acknowledge the fearful tremor that rippled down her spine. "It had nothing to do with Reggie."

"You're wrong!" Franz's fist struck the mattress. "Everything that happens from now on will have to do with Reggie. That's what Blackstone's curse is all about. Harold's dead. It's Reggie's turn next. I know that man, Rowen. Reggie Forbes isn't someone who intends to die alone."

A CLOUDY GRAY MORNING turned into a misty late afternoon. It took that long for Rowen to convince Des that she wasn't an invalid, and if he didn't want to see the new Masque Factory, then she'd go alone. He gave in.

As usual he was more Des than Reggie in his raincoat, hat and baggy pants. But maybe, she reflected, it was the lack of pretense that made the impersonation work. The more he could be himself the less chance there was that anyone would trip him up. Besides, none of the others seemed to know anything about a cousin named Desmond.

Partway across the grounds, Rowen spied Cooper lurking in the low mist of the garden, watching them.

"He's probably bug-hunting," Des said, but he changed sides with her even so.

Since her raincoat was ruined, Rowen was wearing a red jacket that hung halfway to her knees, a long black print skirt, black boots and gloves.

"Quite the Halloween picture," Anna had remarked as she and Des left the house. "Watch out for ghosts in the fog, you two. I hear this is Blackstone weather."

It was after four by the time they reached the converted mill and barn. The old Masque Factory sign swung from the eaves.

Lester and about ten other men and women were working inside. They all looked up, but no one seemed inclined to approach the new arrivals, which earned a quiet chuckle from Des.

"Reggie's reputation for warmth, no doubt."

Lester finally came over, his expression guarded. "Do you want me to show you around?"

"No thanks," Rowen said.

"Yes please," Des countered. She caught the amused gleam in his eyes when he explained, "Well, if I'm going to see the new factory, I want to know what I'm seeing."

What they saw was magic, something from another day and age. Stone and timber walls, carefully preserved, provided the setting for the well integrated displays, everything from traditional witches to antebellum hoop skirts to exquisitely crafted *Cats* costumes. And of course there were masks everywhere, Phantom, Harlequin and full-head. However, there wasn't a skull mask in sight, not even in the rear of the building where many of the original factory's death masks were housed.

"That's part of the legend, isn't it?" Des recalled as they wandered from room to room. "The skull mask is the only one never worn by anyone in Midnight."

"It's tradition," Lester agreed. "The factory won't even make skull masks for shipment elsewhere."

"That must be hard to explain to your out-of-state customers." Des stopped to examine a particularly malevolent head.

Lester shrugged. "Actually, it's a selling point. It arouses curiosity."

Des grinned. "Like a castle with a ghost?"

"Something like that."

Rowen wandered through the oak shelves. "So what would happen if someone did decide to wear a skull mask?"

"As far as I know, it's never happened."

"No perversity in Midnight, huh?" Des remarked. "I've forgotten a lot of the old story. Does anyone know what happened to the original skull mask, or where the safe room that supposedly housed it is located?"

Lester lounged against the wall. "The room was supposed to be hidden somewhere under the original factory."

"And no one's seen it for—how many years?"

"Over seventy," Rowen said. "The last time the skull mask was removed was in 1920. Three members of the Forbes family, all partners in the factory, died that year. The third one burned to death on Halloween night when the factory went up in flames. That's when the family left Midnight, isn't it, darling?"

Des smiled. "With just cause, wouldn't you say? What's on the upper levels, Lester?"

"The workrooms."

"Can we see them?"

Nodding reluctantly, Lester led them up a flight of wooden stairs to the second floor of the mill.

Again timber and stone prevailed. Even the machinery didn't seem out of place. There were alcoves and anterooms and costumes hanging from ceiling beams. Lester introduced them to a few of the people they encountered, but only when necessary, almost as if, Rowen reflected, he didn't expect Des, or rather Reggie, to be around long enough to get to know his employees.

For the moment one-third of the factory belonged to Reggie. It might be as much as two-thirds after Harold's will was read. More likely Harold's share would be divided between Reggie and Lester, but the fact remained that Lester didn't appear to appreciate his surviving partner's interest in the operation.

The fourth floor was in the process of being swept clean of dust and cobwebs. "We'll use this later for storage space," Lester informed them. "Right now, most everything's being kept in the old barn. We'll convert that area to more workrooms as our client list expands."

"Suitably ambitious," Des commented with a bore
glance at Rowen and a faint motion of his head. "I thin
we'll go and take a look at the barn."

In his work clothes and with that perpetually forbiddin
expression on his scarred face, Lester looked as though h
belonged on a chain gang. Clearly, he was tired of playin
tour guide. "Do you want me to show you the barn, too?
he asked woodenly.

Des struggled with a smile. "No thank you. We ca
manage."

"And the papers?"

"The what? Oh, the legal work." Des started for th
staircase. "Shouldn't we have a lawyer present?"

"Harold said you don't like dealing through lawyers."

"I don't," Des replied easily. "That doesn't mean the
aren't necessary sometimes."

"Well, Pettiston's still in the hospital."

"Then we can wait until he gets out."

Lester clomped down the stairs after them. "There ar
other papers that need going over, Reggie."

Des shook the hair back from his face. His hand went t
his raincoat pocket, presumably for a cigarette. Rowen in
tercepted it. "No," she said in a firm whisper.

"Well?" Lester asked.

"Later," Des said with a sigh. "Tomorrow maybe." H
lifted a meaningful eyebrow. "I do have a few other prob
lems right now."

A crooked smile touched Lester's mouth. "Curse prob
lems, Reggie? Or is it the season? I hear you're superst
tious."

It was a very good thing he'd said that. Rowen hadn
been paying attention. Apparently, neither had Des. Grat
bing his coat at the last second, she gave it a yank to sto
him.

"Ladder," she mouthed, indicating the rungs he'd ver
nearly walked under. "Go around it."

Pausing, Des looked up, gave a credible shudder an
walked around the outside. "I have a few superstitious ter
dencies," he agreed. He glanced back at Lester's shuttere

face, his own a mask. "I'm not sure I'd call Blackstone's curse a superstition, but I'd prefer to avoid dying."

"So you do think someone's using it, then."

"Don't you?"

"I think it's dangerous for you to be here. Someone murdered old Harold, that's a fact. That same person put a rubber death mask over his head. That spells curse to me."

"And if I die, you get the Masque Factory, is that right?"

Rowen watched closely. Lester's face went from cold to stony. "Yes," he said, jamming his hands into his pants' pockets. "It is. Does that spell motive in your eyes, Reggie?"

"It would spell motive in anyone's eyes, Lester. A lot of people would benefit from my death. I just want to know who they are."

Lester's black eyes narrowed. "In that case, you might want to take another look at your housekeeper. If you die, partner, she gets Midnight Manor. I heard her talking to Poole about it after her husband died. And by the way, I wouldn't rule out an alliance there if I were you. Almira might treat Poole like dirt, but that's exactly how she treated Gilbert, and like Poole, Gilbert obeyed her every command."

Des regarded him evenly. "Anything else?"

"You want it straight?"

"That would be nice."

Lester came to stand very close. "Get the hell out of Midnight before Halloween, Reggie." And turning on his heel, he strode from the mill, disappearing into the early-evening mist.

Chapter Seven

It was the most direct threat Des had received so far, and he'd received a few. He walked ahead of Rowen up a set of back stairs, then along a short corridor into the loft of the old barn where the two buildings connected.

"We could've followed him, you know," Rowen said, glancing over her shoulder.

"And been sitting ducks for another stray arrow? No thanks."

She caught his arm. "I think the arrow was an accident, Des. It would have been pretty obvious who the murderer was otherwise."

"Double bluff," Des muttered. "It's been done before." Louder he said, "What about the creaking door with no stairs behind it?"

"We don't know it was that door that creaked. It could have been Franz's wheelchair."

He sent her a dark look. "Stop being so reasonable. You're the one who almost got your arm sliced off yesterday." This time the shudder that ran through him was entirely real. "I don't like veiled threats. Where are we?" he interrupted himself impatiently.

"Trapped in a sea of boxes." Rowen forged a path through the maze. "This place has prosperity written all over it. Harold was good at that sort of thing. You never saw his antiques outlet in Los Angeles, but it was great. He lost most of his stock in the fire, which was a shame, but knowing Harold and Reggie, the insurance covered it."

"Mmm." Distracted, Des trailed along behind her, knowing it would be smarter to look at the crates than at her. But it wasn't nearly as much fun. His black mood hadn't lasted long enough to affect his enjoyment at watching the sway of her hair and skirt in front of him.

She stopped at the loft railing, peering over. "Not much down there." She sounded disappointed. "Just some old trunks, metal racks and lumber. I wonder if we can use the factory costumes for the Halloween parties?"

Des rested his forearms on the rail beside her. "What parties?"

"There's one in Midnight, a street party involving the whole town, and another here at the Masque Factory on Halloween night."

"Nice of Reggie to mention that."

"Oh, Reggie didn't tell me, I got it from Richard on the train. He knows a lot about the local traditions."

"I've noticed."

"On the other hand, he's the one legatee who doesn't seem to hate you."

"The key word being *seem*." Des eyed the sloping roof beams, sturdily built and free of cobwebs. "Poole," he murmured. "Now there's a puzzle."

"Why, because the garden's such a mess and this place is so neat and tidy. He takes care of both, you know."

Des grinned. "Very good, Rowen."

"Thank you." She continued to survey the lower level. "Maybe Poole prefers indoor cleaning to yard work. Maybe Harold had a soft spot for him. Or maybe Reggie did something to him and Harold was trying to make up for it. But then why would Poole lie and say he hurt himself fishing? I'm telling you, that man's no fisherman."

"You shouldn't judge by appearances."

"I'm not, I'm..." She caught his arm suddenly. "Des, look. The side door. It's Cooper."

"Creeping in."

Careful not to bump her sore arm, Des turned her toward the stairs. "Come on. Let's see what he's up to."

With Cooper on the far side of the barn, they were able to descend the staircase unnoticed. As soon as they reached the bottom, however, he began heading in their direction.

"Back here," Des said, pushing. "Behind these boxes."

"But I can't see..."

"Get down," he ordered through his teeth.

Rowen complied, glaring at him. Before he could stop her, she crawled to the edge of the stack. Des stayed put and kept his eyes on Cooper.

The man's small black eyes darted around the barn. He seemed to be scanning the trunks. Eventually, he stopped and laid his hands on the top of an old blue one. With a quick look behind him, he fumbled for a pick in his jacket pocket, inserted it into the lock and tipped the lid back.

A smile, eerie in its childlike simplicity, curved his lips. Des saw Rowen lean out for a better view. Confident she wouldn't scream, he reached over and caught the hem of her jacket, hauling her back.

She resisted mightily and he finally relented, joining her. "Why so intent?" he whispered, resting his chin on her head.

"It's a better vantage point. He's taking something out."

Stealing was a more appropriate word. Cooper's actions were those of a thief, swift and surreptitious. His eyes never stopped moving.

Whatever he removed, he set it down beside the trunk and carefully replaced the lid. Des felt Rowen stir, then saw her hand inch out to touch whatever it was.

The smile lingered on Cooper's lips as he picked up and cuddled his prize.

"A bolt of cloth?" Des said doubtfully to Rowen.

She nodded, rubbing her fingers. "Black velvet. Good quality. Reggie has a jacket made of similar material, and you know how picky he is about his clothes."

"Seems like an odd thing to steal, doesn't it?"

"For you or me, maybe. But Cooper's a very strange man." She eased herself up a little. "Where's he going? The door's the other way."

Des went up just far enough to see. "Maybe he isn't finished yet. Ah!" His eyes widened. "Scratch that. He's over by the wall."

"Doing what?"

He felt Rowen's hair against his cheek and smiled. "Walking through it."

ROWEN DIDN'T STOP to think. She only waited long enough for Cooper to get through the hidden panel, then she ran across the floor and caught it before it could close.

Either Cooper didn't notice or he knew he was being followed and panicked. There was no pressure from the other side and only a squeaking hinge to betray the cautious peek she took across the threshold.

Aware of Des behind her, she said simply, "No doorknob. There must be a hidden latch."

"You," Des said in a controlled voice, "are an idiot. Do you realize how dangerous that was?"

Defiantly, Rowen faced him. "Very dangerous, actually, But if you want to find out who murdered Harold, we'll have to do dangerous things."

"Why are you here, Rowen?"

"To watch you, of course."

"No, you're not. And stop pushing on the panel."

"Do you want Cooper to get away?"

"I want an answer."

She considered lying, but rejected the idea. Des was a very shrewd man, he'd see through a lie in a minute. She remained stubbornly silent instead and waited to see what he would make of that.

"You don't want Reggie, do you?" he said at last. His eyes darkened with mild suspicion. "Is he paying you to be here?"

She deserved that. Nevertheless, the fingers of her right hand curled into a fist. "I'm not going to tell you anything," she replied calmly, "so you might as well give up asking. What I do and why I do it is my business, not yours. Can we go now?"

He stared at her, but she could see he wasn't really angry.

"All right," he sighed. "I give up. But—" he caught her chin before she could look away "—only for now." And lowering his head, he set his mouth on hers.

She'd wanted him to kiss her. She hadn't expected it, though, and the shock of his action sent her mind into a spin.

Of course she should stop him. Then again, he was posing as her fiancé, what if someone was watching? Not that she really cared about spies, but his mouth on hers, now there was something she cared about very much.

It was only a kiss, and yet he was doing the strangest things to her, making her hot and shaky and altogether hungry for more of him.

He probably hadn't intended to do more than brush her lips with his, but it wasn't working out that way. His tongue slid over her teeth, pushing deeper into her mouth. She felt her fingers in his hair and his breath on her face.

Sexy. She hadn't consciously associated that word with him, but she did now. So much for caution and distant attraction, she was lost in an emotional welter too wide-ranging to understand.

Des was neither rough nor gentle with her. Well, maybe he was a little more rough than gentle, and his hands on her body were far from chaste, but it was only what she wanted. In fact, it wasn't enough.

That disturbing thought brought her slowly back to reality. "Des." Pulling her mouth free, she squirmed in his arms.

He lifted his head slightly. She should probably be insulted by the spark of amusement in his eyes. She wasn't.

"This isn't a good idea," she said a little breathlessly.

"Isn't it?"

"You're no help," she grumbled. "Let me go."

His reluctance was evident. So was the smile that hovered on his lips. But there was something beneath that smile, a glimmer of desire he made no attempt to hide.

"This was a mistake," she said, taking a purposeful step back from him.

"Was it?"

"Well, wasn't it?"

The smile he could no longer contain emphasized the beauty of his cheekbones. Oh, God, yes, he really was frighteningly sexy. She might be well out of her depth with this man.

With a subtle sideways motion of his head, Des indicated the panel. "Come on," he said, his words and that one small action easing the tension. "Let's see where Cooper went."

THE TUNNELS UNDER the estate were dark and cobwebbed and dangerously rutted. The man fell twice trying to walk in a straight line. God help him if he ever needed to hurry.

Well, he shouldn't ever need to, so it probably wouldn't matter. For the moment, he was an observer of Blackstone's curse. All he had to do was watch and wait and let the curse unfold.

Currently, he watched the pair who descended into the tunnels. He couldn't help beaming at the irony of the situation. They would never figure it out. How could you apply rules to a madman's curse?

"Oh, Jonah Blackstone," he whispered into the darkness. "You're going to be my salvation." Then he laughed again and melted into the shadows. Let the curse do its damnedest.

THE MAIN TUNNEL spread out in two directions from the barn. One led toward the house, the other away from it. Into the old Masque Factory, Des figured, and Rowen tended to agree. They started for the manor.

She wasn't certain if she saw Cooper in the shadows ahead of them or not. She saw something, she was sure of that, but given the state of decay down here, it could have been a rat.

"Why would he steal a bolt of black velvet?" she wondered out loud as they made their way over the uneven ground.

"I have a better question," Des said, running the flashlight he'd found on a shelf behind the panel across the old brick walls. "How did he know this passageway was here?"

IT WAS AN INTRIGUING remark. How *had* Cooper come to know about the hidden passageway? The more Rowen thought about it, the more the question set her nerves on edge.

There was something malevolent about all of this. She wished she understood what her instincts were trying to tell her, but the feeling was so nebulous that it was impossible to define.

The eerie sensation haunted her while she showered and dressed for dinner. Of course there were two perfectly logical answers to how Cooper had knowledge of the tunnels. Either he'd been there before, or he'd been snooping around for the past few days. But that still didn't explain her mounting unease.

Fortunately, Rowen didn't see Cooper again until they were all gathered for dinner in the great hall. Candles fluttered on the polished table, unearthly lighting for an unearthly collection of people. Almira glided in with a passable meal of roast chicken and rice. Cooper stared as if it were roast blackbird.

"He doesn't eat meat," Richard stage-whispered to Rowen across the table. "Something to do with a childhood nightmare."

"What kind of a nightmare, Cooper?" Anna asked, cutting her chicken.

He blinked at his empty plate. "I ate—something."

Richard grinned. "Did that something walk upright?"

Darcy grimaced. "Is this really a suitable topic for dinner conversation?"

"It's suitable for Reggie," Franz said from his wheelchair. He raised his wineglass. "You're a cannibal of sorts, aren't you?"

Des was very good at bland looks. "Am I?" he countered.

Rowen kicked his ankle when he would have reached for the wine bottle. "Not tonight, darling," she said under her breath.

"What?" Anna asked in quick suspicion.

Rowen smiled. "Reggie was going to pour me some wine. I told him I didn't want any. Would you like to change seats with Richard so you can hear our private conversations better?''

Anna's lips compressed. Cooper's eyes moved to the layer of white mist outside the window. ''I used to go hunting in the fog,'' he said in a strained but perfectly audible voice.

''Change the subject,'' Des advised Rowen in an undertone.

''You're walking a little better tonight, Poole,'' she remarked pleasantly. ''The fog must agree with you.''

''I'm wearing a back brace,'' he admitted.

''It belonged to my husband,'' Almira said with a wintry look at Des.

''So you've kept his belongings then,'' Des noted.

''Some of them.'' She glided out, her oxfords making no sound on the partially carpeted floor.

''Spooky lady,'' Richard said, chuckling. ''What are you staring at, Cooper? Blackstone's ghost in the fog?''

''I thought I saw a dog,'' Cooper revealed, his gaze riveted to the window. ''Harold had a dog, Reggie. Do you remember? It didn't like me.''

''I wonder why?'' Franz refilled his glass. ''More wine anyone?''

Darcy accepted the offer. ''What happened to this dog of Harold's?''

''I killed it.'' Cooper gave a light laugh at the shocked looks he received. ''I had to, didn't I, Reggie?''

''Did you?'' Des replied with a vague smile.

''It was old and sick. You couldn't shoot it, even though it would have been the kindest thing to do. I called you a coward for that.''

''I call this a gruesome conversation,'' Richard interjected with an attempt at cheerfulness. ''Shall I make a toast or something before we're forced to hear the gory details?''

Anna nodded. ''Please do.''

Rowen saw Cooper's agitated fingers curl around the edge of the table. ''Reggie didn't like being called a coward,'' he remarked tightly. ''He ran straight to Harold and told him what I'd done. But you didn't mention the part about the dog being sick, did you, cousin? And Harold wouldn't listen to me. I was a freak. I collected bugs!''

Anna made a distasteful face. "If you don't mind, I'd rather not get into this."

That made two of them. Setting her napkin on the table, Rowen stood. "Reggie, can I talk to you, please?"

Cooper offered a strained little smile. "Yes, you talk to him, Rowen. Make him tell you about all the horrible things he's done. But then you'd better stand well away from him, because Blackstone's curse is going to make mincemeat out of your lover. Look it up, any of you who don't believe. Jonah Blackstone always wins."

"LOOK IT UP," Rowen repeated, pacing restlessly. "Look it up where?" She gave Des's arm a passing smack. "You knew about Cooper, didn't you? Collects bugs—that man's not weird, he's sick."

"He's been in treatment," Des told her, rubbing his forehead. "Several years' worth, I gather."

They were outside on a rear balcony above the kitchen. The wrought-iron railing was choked with dormant vines. The night air was thick with mist and smelled of burning leaves.

"Treatment doesn't seem to have helped him," Rowen said. "So what do we know about him? He's familiar with the underground tunnels, he stole a bolt of black velvet and he predicted that Blackstone's curse was going to make mincemeat out of you."

"Reggie."

"Same difference for now. He also said that we should look it up, which indicates that there's a documented history of the curse. But who would have documented this legend?"

Des sent her a vague grin. "A fanciful Forbes? There have been a few, you know."

Rowen watched a misty gold leaf flutter to the ground. "I suppose we could check the library. But according to Poole, it's enormous, disordered and uncataloged."

Des looked down as the kitchen door below swung open, nodding toward Almira and Poole who emerged together.

A mild start passed through Rowen's body when Almira handed Poole a large carving knife.

"No bruises," the housekeeper ordered. "And leave a bit on the end for me to work with. I might use it to hold soup on Halloween."

For a brief moment, Rowen had a vision of a skull being used to serve soup, then she shook herself. Almira had to be talking about a pumpkin.

The butcher's knife glinted in the misty light from the kitchen. "You won't tell anyone, will you?" Poole asked.

The housekeeper shrugged. "I mind my own business. Besides, he's seen the grounds. When the will's read, the decision will be up to him, won't it?"

"Maybe," the butler cum gardener allowed. "Of course, his decision depends on what happens with the curse, doesn't it?"

Almira's smile was distant. "Precisely. Now run along, Poole, and bring me back a big one."

Des gave Rowen a push and at the same time cleared his throat. "Good evening," he said, smiling down at the startled pair. "We were just enjoying the fresh air. *What* depends on the curse, Poole?" he asked without a pause.

Rowen wasn't sure she wanted to descend. However, short of digging in her heels, she couldn't stop Des from propelling her down the stairs to the small stone patio.

"I see you number eavesdropping among your talents," Almira commented stonily.

"Sometimes." Des slid Poole a sideways glance. "You haven't answered my question. What depends on the curse?"

Poole's thin fingers tightened on the knife handle. Rowen could see a number of scars on his wrists. She couldn't quite establish what kind of scars they were.

"Your grandfather felt I wasn't doing my job properly," he confessed in a halting voice. "He thought I needed help. I told him I didn't."

"Ah." Des smiled. "In other words, he threatened to fire you."

"No, he didn't," Poole denied swiftly.

"He never came right out and said it," Almira amended with a glance at the man's craggy face. "Don't glare at me, Poole. Reggie's not stupid. He can see the condition of the grounds. Besides, he's looking for suspects, someone on whom he can pin his grandfather's murder.''

"I thought you minded your own business,'' Poole charged with a flash of hostility.

"I am.'' Her dark eyes sought out Rowen's. "This one's ready to convict me, and I suspect she wields a great deal of influence with her fiancé. I'm protecting my interests, so to speak. We all have some reason for wanting Reggie and/or Harold dead. I want them to know that.''

"Well,'' Rowen said, arching an ingenuous eyebrow, "we could always fall back on the ghost-of-Jonah-Blackstone theory, couldn't we?''

Poole continued to clutch the knife, but apparently Des didn't see that as an immediate threat. He walked around the housekeeper, pausing behind her left shoulder to remark, "I bet you know all about Blackstone's curse, don't you? Tell us about it. For example, how many members of the Forbes family have allegedly died as a result of it? When did they die? What years, specifically? And how did the skull mask play into their deaths?''

Hands clasped, she stared past Poole into the shadows of the garden.

"It began with Jonah Blackstone's death,'' she said stiffly. "William and Edmund Forbes were partners with Jonah in the Masque Factory. Jonah was a peculiar man, a loner, creative but dark. Some said wicked. In time, William and Edmund began to question his sanity. Some people thought he was a wizard, others said he was crazy. He'd made a skull mask that he seemed very fond of. It was the first mask ever to be produced at the factory. It became his personal treasure. It seemed fitting somehow that when William and Edmund killed him, his skull mask should become the vessel for his soul.''

"Rubbish,'' Des scoffed. His gaze on her profile hardened. "Give us facts, Almira, not superstitious gossip.''

She refused to look at him. "I'd have thought a superstitious man like you would appreciate the occult aspects of the legend.''

He smiled. "Would you? What happened after William and Edmund killed Blackstone?''

"The letter Jonah had written prior to his death was delivered to them. He said he'd foreseen their plot and would now have his revenge."

Rowen leaned against a sturdy wooden table. "In other words, he eavesdropped, then wrote the letter in case he couldn't prevent them from murdering him."

"If you wish." Almira shrugged. "In any case, William and Edmund buried the cursed mask with Jonah and went about their business. By the following Halloween, both men were dead."

"And as prophesied in Blackstone's letter," Poole interjected, "they both died horribly."

"So where is this letter now?" Rowen asked.

"I wouldn't know," Almira replied. "Shall I go on?"

"Please," Rowen said.

"William and Edmund's four sons took over the Masque Factory after their fathers died. One year later, they were dead as well. The fourth one died on Halloween night, burned to death in the old guest cottage."

"Where's that?" Rowen asked.

"Beyond the family crypt," Poole pointed through the garden. He'd finally lowered the knife, but his attitude toward Almira was still one of minor resentment. "Lester lives there now."

"Does he?" Des murmured. "How convenient. Go on, Almira."

"After the second set of deaths, the skull mask was dug up and a diviner was called in. He recommended the construction of a safe room, a sanctified chamber, and said that the mask should be locked inside. Once there, the mask's power would be nullified."

Rowen wanted to move this story along. It was getting very cold, and she was only wearing a black knit dress. "So they built the room and put the mask inside, and everything was fine until...?"

"Fifty-two years later. In 1843 a Forbes rationalist decided to remove the skull and thereby disprove the curse."

"Was he one of the owners of the factory?" Des asked, coming to lean against the table next to Rowen.

"Yes."

"And he died," Rowen assumed.

"Within the year. The man, his brother and their cousin. Again, the last one was killed on Halloween night. Naturally, the skull mask was returned to the safe room."

The chill that swept across Rowen's skin wasn't entirely due to the falling temperature. "How many more times did this happen?"

"It happened in 1913 and for the last time in 1921. That's the year the original factory burned. Nobody's seen the skull mask since."

"So we're supposed to believe that someone's unearthed it and is now using it to his or her advantage." Eyes on the ground, Des shook his head, smiling slightly. "I don't think so, Almira."

"Neither do I," Almira said tartly. "No one uses Blackstone's curse. It might use someone, but no human can control dark powers."

"Oh, damn, she believes in it," Rowen murmured to Des.

Poole turned the knife over in his hands. "You don't believe, do you?" he said roughly. His eyes met Des's. "Even with your grandfather dead and the Masque Factory about to reopen, you think it can't be real. You would, you know, if you lived here for even a few months. Especially in the fall. That's when his ghost is at its most powerful. A lot of people think Blackstone's spirit haunts both the ruin and the guest cottage."

Rowen inched closer to Des for warmth. "Is that where Blackstone lived, in the old cottage?"

"For a time," Almira said. "Poole stayed in the new cottage briefly, before Lester decided he wanted it."

"And did you see any ghosts?" Des inquired, apparently amused by all of this.

Poole looked away, into the swirling fog. "I don't know what I saw. Sometimes I heard things." His chuckle was uneasy. "Maybe it was Blackstone turning in his grave."

"More likely it was rats in the tunnel," Des said flatly.

Almira's head came up. "You know about the tunnels?"

"It seems to be common knowledge," Rowen said, straightening from the table. "Cooper could probably give us all a guided tour. Now if you'll excuse me, I'm freezing. I'm going upstairs to take a nice hot bath.''

''It is cold tonight,'' Poole agreed in a distracted tone. ''I'll get your pumpkin, Almira.''

To Rowen's surprise, as she began climbing the stairs, she caught a glimpse of a man's outline hovering just inside the glass balcony doors. He must have been listening to them because he backed quickly away, dissolving silently into the shadows of the second-floor sitting room. Unfortunately for him, he didn't vanish fast enough for Rowen to miss the flash of his blond hair.

She hesitated. Richard? But why would he want to hear Almira's story about Blackstone's curse? He already seemed to know it backward. Still, except for Poole, he was the only person at the manor with blond hair. Unless . . .

Rowen frowned, her thoughts taking a somewhat darker turn. What if the hair she'd glimpsed had been white rather than blond? Franz Becker had white hair. He was also crippled—she raised considering eyes to the empty doorway—wasn't he?

Chapter Eight

It started to rain at midnight. Des watched the downpour from a chair near his bedroom window.

Pouring himself a glass of whiskey from a bottle he'd found downstairs, he contemplated the blackened outline of the Masque Factory visible through the trees. He also considered what Rowen had told him about seeing someone at the balcony doors, a man with blond hair. Or white, she'd added with a meaningful parting look.

She'd gone to take her bath, while Des had gone in search of a drink and a cold shower, not necessarily in that order.

Lightning flashed beyond the ruin. He wondered if Rowen could see it, then shoved all thoughts of her away and concentrated on the old factory. According to Almira, the tunnels that ran under it were falling apart. Only a fool would try to traverse them now.

Des laid his head back, sipping his drink. Maybe he was a fool. Her certainly didn't trust Almira. She stood to inherit the manor if Reggie died. And it seemed she and Poole shared certain confidences. They could be working together.

Sighing, he closed his eyes. He didn't hear anything except the pelt of rain until Rowen's hair brushed his cheek.

"Come to any profound conclusions yet?" she teased.

He controlled a start, smiling down at his glass as she walked around him to lean against the windowsill. The room was dark, illuminated only by a fire and the distant lightning. She glanced at the crooked forks, then turned determinedly away from them.

"Well?" she asked again.

"Well, I don't know." He raised the glass to his lips but didn't drink. She was wearing a short silk robe, white with pastel roses on it, and her feet were bare. "I think you're right about Almira. She is cold. I'd say she reminded me of a female impersonator, but you'd probably start screaming at me."

Rowen grinned. "A female vampire impersonator. And she wears men's shoes. They're way too big for her."

Des nodded, sliding veiled eyes down her long legs.

"I wonder what Gilbert was like?" Rowen mused, although she was watching him.

"Probably a prat. Do you want some of this?"

Surprisingly, she took the glass he offered and drained it.

"I don't like thunderstorms," she explained, handing it back.

Des rearranged himself to a less uncomfortable position in the chair. "Tell me about this eavesdropper you saw," he invited.

"There's nothing to tell. I only saw his hair and only caught a glimpse of that. It could have been Franz. It's possible that he, like Reggie's cousin, stands to inherit a larger share of Harold's fortune if Reggie isn't alive to collect. But we won't know that until the will is read, and that won't happen until the murder is solved—assuming Mr. Pettiston can locate the will."

Des, who'd been trying not to stare at her breasts, suddenly sat bolt upright, his eyes fastened on the window.

"What?" She turned to look.

"There's someone out there, running across the lawn toward the marble pool." He stood, leaning over her from behind and pointing. "Do you see him?"

"No—yes! He's running toward the Masque Factory not the pool. Where are you going?"

Des didn't answer. He already had his shoes on and was reaching into the closet for one of Reggie's Harris tweed jackets.

"Wait a minute." Rowen caught his arm. "You can't go chasing phantoms all over the estate in the middle of the night. It could be dangerous."

"I know." He flipped out the jacket collar and kissed her startled lips. "I'll be careful."

"Idiot," he heard her mutter in his wake. "It's probably only Lester."

Possibly, Des reflected, taking the stairs in three long strides. But why would Lester go to the factory at midnight? Why wear black and hug the shadows in order to get there?

No, this person was up to something. And for a hundred thousand pounds Des was willing to take a risk or two.

A strong, gusting wind blew rain in his eyes, blinding him. He could no longer see the figure, but it must have gone into the factory.

His clothes and hair were soaked by the time he reached the front door. He tried the handle and felt it give.

"Convenient," he murmured, hesitating.

He opened the door, anyway, setting his suspicions aside but not discarding them. Experience had taught him that when something was too easy it had usually been set up that way.

He entered the old mill cautiously, waiting on the threshold until his eyes adjusted to the scattering of night-lights.

A sharp flash of lightning outside helped to reorient him. Three steps led down into a large room riddled with support beams and costume displays. Staircase on the right, smaller rooms at the back, death masks on exhibit just beyond the rear door.

He moved forward quietly, shoving the sopping hair from his eyes. His instincts told him there was someone here, lurking in the shadows. Waiting to do what? Shoot him? That wasn't a violent death, at least not violent in the sense that Jonah Blackstone would have intended.

He was strong enough to put up a good fight, so it was doubtful he would be jumped, and knives also seemed unlikely. A blade was too fast—although that carving knife Poole had been holding tonight could no doubt do a nasty job of hacking a body apart.

Curiosity spurred him on. He sensed madness in this nightmare.

The mannequins dressed in Masque Factory costumes looked eerily human in the pale wash of light, a river of faceless people with white waxy skin and no blood.

Des moved toward the center of the room. The exhibit beneath the staircase was better lighted than the others. He walked over to it, his eyes probing the shadows. Nothing stirred. There were only his wet footsteps on the plank floor and the drum of wind and rain against the windows and walls.

Another pallid mannequin loomed before him. It wore a cape and red gloves. Dracula? Des raised his eyes to the face—and felt his teeth clench in an automatic response.

This mannequin wasn't faceless. It had a bony leering set of features seen everywhere on Halloween. Everywhere except Midnight, Maine.

He halted ten feet away, staring at it, listening.

The sound came, as he'd somehow known it would, a papery thin chuckle that betrayed no gender and seemed to emanate from the foundations of the factory itself.

He stood absolutely still, his eyes lifting, though he didn't move his head. The chuckle died. Lightning flickered across the display mask. A rubber skull, Des suspected. It looked malleable which made sense since it would doubtless need to fit over his head.

"Where are you?" he said, still not moving.

No answer.

"This won't work, you know. The police aren't stupid. They know there isn't any curse."

The chuckle came again. Rain and wind pelted the eaves. The Masque Factory sign outside creaked ominously. He heard thunder now, but nothing closer than that. Only the killer's soft chuckle, an eerie thread of sound that managed to be louder than the storm.

"I am the personification of Blackstone's curse, Reggie Forbes," the person behind it whispered to him. "Tonight, I bring you death."

THE SECOND-LEVEL landing circled the large central room below. A grid work of beams, crawlways and light fixtures stretched across the space just under the ceiling. Rowen, having lost Des halfway across the grounds, was crouched now at the junction between the mill and the barn, very near that shadowy grid.

She heard the murderer's threat as clearly as if it had been spoken in her ear, but with the thunder disrupting her senses, she couldn't pinpoint his location. Somewhere in the nearby rafters, maybe out on one of the crawlways.

She forced her frozen muscles to carry her forward. A clap of thunder set her teeth on edge but she overcame her terror and crept up to the railing.

A tiny movement deep within the shadows confirmed her worst fear. The figure was huddled on the crawlway.

Lightning streaked through the window. The movement had ceased, but now she saw the knife blade with horrifying clarity. It was sawing through a piece of thick rope.

Rowen's palms went clammy. One of the light fixtures, a huge brass-and-wood affair, vibrated ever so slightly as the rope began to fray. A few more slashes of the blade and there would be no rope.

She lowered her eyes. "Des," she whispered. Then at a more desperate pitch, she cried, "Look out! The lights!"

She could only pray he moved in time. With a whoosh like a guillotine blade, the fixture plunged downward, smashing to the plank floor and breaking into a thousand glittering pieces.

The figure on the crawlway gave a violent jerk, in response to her cry. Rowen heard its snarl of reaction and saw the knife blade flash.

But he didn't come for her. Knife in hand, he crawled with more speed than grace to the other side of the mill and tumbled through the railing.

Rowen's response was automatic. She pried her fingers from the rough balustrade bars and raced for the stairs, almost pitching headlong in her haste. A door slammed in the distance. "Des!" she shouted, her concern for him momentarily blotting out her fear of thunderstorms.

A close flicker of lightning revealed the fallen fixture, but she still couldn't see him. "Des!" she called again, this time more urgently. "Please answer me."

From the darkness a pair of hands snaked out to grip her arms. Rowen stifled a scream and twisted around prepared to shove her knee into her attacker's groin.

"It's all right, it's me," Des said before her eyes could focus. "Which way did he go?"

Rowen pointed. "I heard a door slam. He's long gone by now."

"I wouldn't count on that." She felt his lips brush her forehead. "Stay here."

Never one for taking orders, Rowen gave her nerves a moment to steady, then ran after him, up the stairs and around the landing to the far side.

"Gone?" she asked when she caught him.

Pushing the damp curls from his eyes, Des nodded. "Yes."

She indicated the rigging. "He had a knife. I saw him cutting the rope that held the light fixture up... Hey, wait a minute, what are you doing now?"

He was already out on the crawlway. "Ropes don't hold up lights, Rowen," he said over his shoulder.

"I know that. Which means this attempt on your life was planned well in advance." She grabbed hold of his wet tweed jacket. "Don't go out there, Des."

He looked back at her with a quick smile. "Just stand guard for a minute, okay? I want to see what's left of the wires."

Reluctantly, Rowen released him. Struggling with him would be riskier than simply letting him have his look.

The thunder crept closer, rattling the glass in the windows and sending a panicky tremor along her spine. Shivering, she closed her eyes.

"Pretend it's a train going by," Des suggested from the darkness of the crawlway. He was kneeling where the phantom figure had been moments before, examining wires in the weak light from the second-floor landing. "Were you left alone in a thunderstorm?" he continued in that same calm voice.

"Not exactly."

She hunched her shoulders as another loud peal rocked the floorboards. The train thing didn't work for very long.

Within seconds she was back to bone-chilling terror and the memory of woods and a cave and her brother shrieking louder than the wind on the mountain.

Swallowing her fright, she forced herself to walk back and forth in front of the grid. Des had almost been killed tonight by someone dressed in black and wielding a large knife. She needed to concentrate on that.

Poole had been carrying a large knife earlier tonight. Was it the same one? Rowen didn't think so, but there was no way to be sure. There was also no way to tell if the person using it had been male or female. An amorphous shape at best, its whispered threat had been indistinguishable to her ears.

So much for detailed observation, but then details tended to elude her when terror intruded.

It had been the same with the fire she'd witnessed in Los Angeles. The rain hadn't bothered her in the slightest. But there'd been thunder that night as well, great furious cracks of it. She'd been lucky to notice anything at all.

"Hurry up, Des," she whispered through gritted teeth.

"Got it." He emerged from the crawlway on cue, hopping effortlessly over the railing. Taking care not to touch her stitches, he rubbed her chilled arms. "You ready to go?"

Back into the storm? Rowen flinched inwardly, but nodded. "What did you get?" she inquired belatedly.

"An idea of how the fixture was rigged. The cables and wires were sheared, the bolts removed, the rope tied to a beam with a double knot. Nothing fancy."

"In other words, anyone could've done it."

"Correct."

"Well, I'm reassured," Rowen said with forced sarcasm. She headed for the stairs. "The murderer's real. I saw him, we both heard him, yet neither of us knows who he is, or if he might in fact be a she."

"Right again."

She kept her gaze on the storm. "You're taking this awfully calmly, Des."

"No more than you are."

"I'm not calm, and besides, the killer's not after me."

"You didn't shout my name when you warned me about the lights falling."

"I shouted it afterward."

"He was gone by then."

"That's what I tried to tell you downstairs."

"You're missing the point, Rowen."

"No, I'm not. You admire my fortitude. I'm flattered. But as I keep pointing out, I'm not the target of this so-called curse." She let him pull her sideways at the bottom of the stairs. "Where are we going now...? My God, what's that doing here?" Both things came out in one breath. Rowen stared at the ghastly skull mask in front of her, then reached out an experimental finger to touch it. "Rubber," she murmured. "Just like the one they found on Harold, I'll bet. So what do we do? Take it to the police?"

"No."

"I didn't think so." She couldn't resist a sigh. "All right, we keep it. What do we do with it? Wear it to dinner tomorrow night and see if it spooks anyone? Personally, I don't think it will. Whoever's behind this won't be easily unnerved."

Des slipped the mask off, tucking it into his pocket. "Whoever's behind this, Rowen, is mad."

"You can't be sure of that."

"No, but I've learned to trust my instincts. Blackstone's curse is handy. It predicts a violent death. I think our murderer relishes the violence almost as much as the idea of the kill."

Thunder shook the windows. Rowen's fists clenched in her pockets, but she refused to let her fear show. Des had already seen too much. "In that case," she said, her composure hanging by a thread, "Cooper would seem to be our most likely suspect."

Des's eyes were intent on hers. "Are you all right?"

He was too close, his body too tall and warm and tempting. "No," she said, meeting his gaze. "But I will be. I always am."

He didn't understand. She didn't expect him to. His hands came up to touch her, but this time she evaded him, stepping back. "Don't," she said. "You'll only complicate things."

A shrewd light glimmered deep in his eyes. "Things are already complicated, Rowen."

"Not emotionally they aren't."

"No?"

"No." Yet even as she made the denial, Rowen realized with a sudden sense of doom that she was lying. Like it or not, her emotions were deeply involved.

Shaken, she glanced at the fallen fixture, reliving the dreadful moment when the murderer's knife had slashed the rope. And for the second time that night, she forgot all about the thunder crashing around her.

ROWEN ALMOST TRIPPED over Franz thirty minutes later. He was rolling through the darkness toward his bedroom. "Be careful," he snapped, then realized it was her and in a less sour tone asked, "Where's our mutual friend?"

"Downstairs," she replied. Smoking a cigarette and staring at a rubber mask, she added to herself. Her fingers found the light switch inside his room and instantly a dozen electric candles flickered to life. She looked down at the man in his wheelchair, frowning in surprise. "Why are you wet?"

He looked irritated. "Why are *you* wet?"

"I've been out."

"So have I."

"Really." Rowen smiled but made no further comment.

"You were with Reggie, I assume," Franz remarked after a protracted silence.

"We love walking in the rain."

"Do you love walking in the lightning, too?"

"It makes life more exciting that way," she lied. "Did you go into the garden, Mr. Becker?"

His expression altered ever-so-slightly, mistrust and maybe a trace of guilt crowding in. "As a matter of fact, I did."

"In the lightning?"

"As you say, it makes life more exciting. Now, if you'll excuse me, it's time I went to bed."

"Of course."

Standing back, Rowen let him roll into his room, then she reached out to close the door for him. Before she did, she dropped her gaze deliberately to his feet.

"If you leave your shoes in the hall, I'm sure Poole will take them to be cleaned."

"What?" Franz looked quickly down.

"Mud," Rowen said succinctly. "That's the trouble with rain, isn't it? It makes the ground so messy." She summoned a pleasant smile. "Good night, Mr. Becker."

"Good night," he said evenly.

But he knew what she'd seen. As she left, Rowen saw his fingers digging into the arms of his wheelchair. His dry, mud-free wheelchair.

THE THIRD LETTER couldn't be started until well into the night. Gloved and tightly clenched, the hand finally began to write.

Dear Dr. Sayers,

You told me I must learn to deal with my anger. You showed me how to do it. But I'm angry now, and I don't know how to let it out.

I want him dead. I don't want her dead, but she's very smart, and she interfered tonight with my plan. Why did she do that? Does she love him? I can't believe she could, although I see something in her eyes when she looks at him. Maybe she only wants his money. She couldn't really want him, could she?

I don't care how he's acting here, the truth is he's a slimy, two-faced bastard who would do anything to get what he wants. He's evil and a thief. He took everything from me, my life that was and all it could have been. I hate him for that.

Do you think it was fated for Rowen to interfere tonight? Did Blackstone make her follow Reggie to the Masque Factory? Maybe he did. And yet, Jonah Blackstone wants Reggie dead, too. We're confederates, Jonah and I, two minds with one goal: kill Reggie.

Just writing his name, I can feel it suddenly coming

over me again, that uncontrollable rage. My hand is shaking as you can see. I must close now and take deep breaths. I must go to bed. I must think. I must bring Blackstone's curse to bear on Reggie Forbes.

Rest assured, I remain,
A former patient

Chapter Nine

"Down here is where the real work's done. This is where we make the masks, some by hand, others not. The quality depends on the customer's specific requirements. Am I boring you with this, Reggie?"

"Not at all," Des lied as Lester led him through a labyrinth of arcane machinery in the well lighted basement.

Clearly, Lester didn't believe him. "You look bored as hell."

"Do I?" Des smiled cheerfully. "Well."

"We could always go over the paperwork."

"Or you could tell me about last night's accident," Des suggested. "Something to do with a falling light fixture, wasn't it?"

Lester shrugged. "You heard the talk, did you? What can I say? This morning we found that both entrances had been forced open, the one in the mill and the one in the barn. That spells vandalism to me. Malicious mischief, I believe the police call it."

"I'm sure they do," Des agreed. "I call it an unlikely coincidence."

Lester's black eyes narrowed. "Unlikely in what way?"

"Harold was murdered recently. Now someone's broken into the factory intent on causing damage. Did this sort of thing happen before he died?"

"Not that I know of."

"But it has now. Doesn't the timing strike you as odd?"

Lester's stocky body stiffened. "Why all this concern for a few hundred dollars' worth of damage? We're insured."

The last word had a taunting edge that Des knew he was expected to pursue. "Meaning?" he obliged.

"You've suffered bigger losses and not given a damn about them."

"Or so you've heard." Des started back through the sea of gleaming machinery, forcing Lester to follow. "I wouldn't assume that everything I'd heard was true if I were you."

Lester gave a coarse laugh. "Fine words, Reggie, but I know about the theft in Brussels six years ago. Diamonds, wasn't it? All insured. A pity they never resurfaced, but you and Harold came out all right. Then there was that fire in L.A. a few years back. Such a pity that all those antiques were destroyed. And the paintings, don't forget those. Wasn't there a Picasso or two among them?"

"Was there?"

"You don't remember? Now that is convenient."

"We were talking about a break-in," Des reminded him. "Here, last night." His expression was stony. "Have you called the police?"

"They've been notified."

"What do they think?"

"Not a damned thing. They're still trying to figure out who clobbered Peter Pettiston the other night. As for Harold's murder, well, if you're waiting for them to crack that case, don't bother. The chief's about as sharp as a broken pencil, and there's nothing better under him."

"Sounds like a fine force."

"It suited Harold."

"Ah, I see." Des surveyed the humming machinery. "Running a scam here at the factory, are we?"

"No, but I got the strong impression that Harold was expecting you to come up with one."

Des smiled, stuffing his hands in his pants' pockets. "Too bad he'll never know. What do you expect, Lester?"

"Same as you. To make money."

"From the factory?"

"Where else?"

Des arched a shrewd eyebrow. "Harold's will, maybe?"

"What the hell kind of crack is that?" Lester's outraged demand caused several curious heads to turn.

Des ignored them. "Oh, a reasonable one, I think. If you know me the way you claim to, you wouldn't find it uncharacteristic."

The gloves were off. Lester glared at him. "You are a bastard, aren't you?"

"I can be. I don't like threats, Lester, and I like accidents even less."

"That light fixture..."

Anger flashed in Des's eyes. "I don't give a bloody damn about that fixture. I'm talking about the arrow that almost hit Rowen."

"What's that got to do with me? Your cousin shot it. Go abuse him."

"Darcy's not clever enough to plot a murder."

"But I am, is that what you're saying?"

Lester's fists were clenched. Des knew he could hold his own in a fight, but a brawl at this point would accomplish nothing. What he needed was proof—and to make sure that Rowen didn't get caught in the crossfire.

Keeping his hands in his pockets and his expression benign, he leaned against the cellar railing. "I'm not saying anything, Lester, except that I don't intend to be the victim of a phony curse."

"You're sure it's phony, are you?"

"Until I meet Blackstone's ghost personally, yes."

Slowly, Lester relaxed. "Then I suggest you start looking for him, Reggie, because he's here. One way or another, Jonah Blackstone's come back to Midnight. He got old Harold. And I'd be willing to bet that he'll get you before Halloween is over."

ROWEN LOVED Halloween. She loved trick or treat, and carving pumpkins into jack-o'-lanterns, and eating miniature Hershey bars from a bag. She didn't love cooking or pandering to the whims of a domineering housekeeper who today had been transformed into a cross between Vampira and Mussolini.

It was small consolation that Anna had been recruited for the same tedious work. Pies and bread needed to be baked. Stews needed to be cooked and that meant vegetables needed to be cleaned and chopped, and big black pots had to be washed and filled.

"Harold planned on a big turnout at the factory's Halloween party," Almira said from her supervisory station in the middle of the old-fashioned kitchen. "I'm sure the numbers won't change with his death. Put the carrots on the hearth for now," she directed Poole. "Rowen, bring the brown bowls in from the pantry. Anna, find out how much room is left in the basement freezer."

Richard chose that moment to stick his head through the door. "Morning, ladies."

"Afternoon," Rowen retorted. "I'd go play with Darcy in Harold's workshop if I were you."

Richard looked puzzled. "What's he doing out there?"

"Making a knife rack," Anna told him.

His golden eyebrows came together. "Funny thing to make. Ah, well, I've had my morning meditation. I'll see if I can find him. Have fun, you two."

Rowen murmured a disgruntled goodbye as she headed for the pantry. So Darcy was making a knife rack. Why, she wondered? And where was Cooper? She'd seen him at breakfast, staring at the black clouds bunching up over the cliffs, but since then there'd been no sign of him. As for Des, she was better off not thinking about him at all. At least not in the disturbing way she'd thought of him most of last night.

Squeezing past a stack of baskets, Rowen slipped through an anteroom and into the shadowy pantry. There must be something wrong with her, she decided, surveying the jam-packed oak shelves. Here she had the wonderful discovery of a wet and muddy Franz sitting in a dry wheelchair to ponder, and all she could do was picture Des's face and wonder if the strong attraction she felt for him might be mutual.

Truthfully, though, it went deeper than attraction, and that was the discovery that really unsettled her. What did she expect from him? What did he want from her?

"Probably a night in bed and a cigarette afterward," she muttered, locating the elusive earthenware bowls on the top shelf.

For a few dusty moments, she had to concentrate on climbing up and removing the bowls without banging her sore arm, but once she'd managed that tricky feat, she was right back to Des and her twisted, inescapable feelings for him.

Her Reeboks made no sound on the stone floor. From the kitchen she caught the sound of hushed voices, Almira's and Poole's. Halting, she clutched the bowls to her chest. Eavesdropping would certainly take her mind off Des. Cautiously, she peered through the anteroom to the kitchen.

Poole's craggy features looked strained. "You said I could trust you," he accused Almira, no doubt referring to the remarks she'd made last night—something about Harold not being happy with his work, Rowen recalled.

"You deliberately put suspicion on me," he continued. "Why?"

"I told you why, Poole." She began slicing celery on a board. "They're looking for motives, and I'm not going to be the only person on their suspect list."

"So you betrayed my trust in order to have company on that list. You never told the police anything."

"Chief Parkhurst is a self-serving idiot who attends séances and talks to his mother's ghost twice a week. He thinks either one of Harold's nephews snuck into town and killed him, or Jonah Blackstone came up from the grave to do it. There was no need for me to tell him anything about anyone. And actually—" she carried on with her methodical chopping "—you should be thanking me for not telling Reggie all that I could have about you."

Poole's wiry shoulders tensed. "What do you mean?"

"I did some checking on you when you showed up here two years ago asking my Gilbert for work. You said you were a drifter, but I said that a man with your infirmities wouldn't simply drift into Midnight. There must be a reason behind it. I said you had it in for old Harold, but Gilbert didn't believe me. So I went through some of Harold's papers, things he'd brought with him from London. I also went through back issues of our town newspaper and the *New York Times* in the library. It didn't take long for my suspicions to pan out."

Poole's knuckles were chalk white around the edge of the counter. "I had no reason to want Harold dead," he denied quietly.

"No?" Eyes on the cutting board, Almira smiled. "Well unfortunately, Poole, the *Midnight Chronicle* used to follow old Harold's business ventures quite closely, probably because he was such a recluse. There were no pictures to identify him or his closest associates—but his deals, now those were another matter. We heard about thefts and fires and mergers and even a couple of corporate takeovers. One of those takeovers happened four years ago in London, and involved a large shipbuilding firm. This firm had an outlet in Boston. Harold and Reggie, in their usual ruthless fashion, managed to get hold of the parent company and promptly closed down the Boston outlet. Several hundred people wound up out of work because of that. I found the employees' names on a company roster in Harold's study. One of those names was Poole."

"My name's hardly unusual," Poole retorted stiffly.

"No, it isn't," Almira agreed. "And of course, you're free to disprove my theory anytime. But it will require proof, and since I think you and the shipbuilding Poole are one and the same man, I have a feeling you won't be producing any."

"I'm not the Poole you're talking about," the grounds keeper maintained.

"As you wish. I didn't mention that particular suspicion to Reggie, anyway, did I, so it really doesn't matter. I'd have no reason to betray your secret, Poole," she said. Her eyes came up. "Unless, of course, I were backed into a corner."

"Almira, listen to me," Poole began in something akin to desperation.

"Quiet," she ordered. "I hear Anna on the stairs."

Rowen came out of her trance then. Giving her head a shake, she marched into the kitchen, deposited the bowls on the table and announced to anyone who cared, "I'm tired of crawling around on dusty shelves. I'm going into town for lunch."

Almira looked displeased but didn't argue. Poole gave no indication that he even heard her. Anna emerged from the cellar, draped in cobwebs and said, "Your freezer is an antique. It needs defrosting. There's about two square feet of space left—and who mentioned lunch?"

"I did," Rowen said, pushing through the door.

"In Midnight? How will you get there?"

"Harold had a Land Rover. Reggie said I could use it anytime."

Anna caught up to her, brushing off her maroon pants and sweater. "So Reggie automatically assumes that Harold's Land Rover is his now, does he?"

Wanting to change out of her old jeans, Rowen worked her way through a series of corridors to the front staircase. "I think almost everything in the house will be Reggie's in the end," she answered abstractedly. "Have you seen Franz today?"

"Not since breakfast."

"What about Cooper?"

"I have no idea." Anna clutched a handful of Rowen's shirt, halting her in the great hall. "Why all the questions?"

Rowen stared at her. "I think the answer's fairly obvious, don't you?"

"Fairly," Anna agreed. "But I'm curious. What's your angle in all of this?"

"Do you mean why am I here?"

"Yes."

"I want to make sure that Reggie doesn't get killed by whoever murdered Harold. Now let go of me, please. I'm hungry, and I don't like being cross-examined."

"You do like money, though, don't you?" Anna trailed her up the stairs.

"No more than you do, I imagine."

"You went out last night in the rain. First Reggie, then you. You both went to the Masque Factory."

"I know where we went, Anna."

"But you're not going to tell me why."

Maybe you already know, Rowen thought, glancing at her. "No," she said over her shoulder, "I'm not."

She continued up the stairs.

Unfortunately, Anna wasn't prepared to be shaken off. She was standing by the front door thirty minutes later when Rowen, showered and dressed in fresh jeans, her red jacket and a pair of black ankle boots, returned.

"I thought I'd drive into town with you," she said flatly. "The Land Rover's parked in the old stable. I got the keys from Almira. She says it's starting to rain. We can use these umbrellas I found."

"You don't miss much, do you?" Rowen said, peering out at the blackened clouds, which so far contained no thunder.

"Not much." Anna's brown eyes confronted Rowen's. "I saw Reggie from my bedroom window while I was changing. He and Richard were getting into an old gray car."

Rowen sensed something behind the remark, as Anna had doubtless intended. "Yes?" she said.

"Well, correct me if I'm wrong, but Reggie is still highly superstitious, isn't he?"

"Meaning?"

Anna's tone sharpened. "I have a very good view from my window. Good enough to see Lester's big black cat walk right in front of Reggie while he was getting into the car. And do you know, Rowen, that your fiancé didn't even flinch?"

DES MANAGED to lose Richard on the vast expanse of the Midnight docks that extended from one end of the coastal New England town to the other.

Trading barbs with Lester that morning had made him irritable. Going over papers that meant nothing to him while eating a desktop lunch of sandwiches and milk had been worse. He had a blinding headache and an urgent desire to board the first train out of Midnight.

Except that he wouldn't leave without Rowen, and she wouldn't leave until Harold's will was read and so on.

Des settled for a respite instead, time alone in town, and if he got lucky, a cigarette and beer into the bargain.

He managed both in the Ancient Mariner, a small warehouse of a bar down on the water. The atmosphere was pleasantly nautical, the air thick with smoke, the lighting subdued but adequate. A mixture of people drifted in and out.

Des chose a back table. In the mirror over the bar, he caught a glimpse of his rumpled clothes and hair and grinned, shaking the mop of brown curls from his eyes as he made his way to the table.

He wasn't sure how he found the poker game or why he decided to join it. The stakes were low, the players gruff but honest, the talk centered on fish, women and Blackstone's bloody curse.

"So you're Reggie Forbes," an old fossil of a fisherman remarked during the fifth game. "You're not what I expected. Your hands have done some work."

"Some," Des acknowledged, lighting a fresh cigarette and accepting another glass of dark beer.

"What did you make of old Harold's death?" another man asked.

"Murder," Des corrected. "It wasn't a curse that killed him if that's what you mean."

"A lot of folks hereabouts would argue that with you," an Irishman named Jon said. "I'll raise fifty."

He meant cents. No one was going to get rich today, Des reflected humorously.

"Jonah Blackstone was a character, you know," Jon continued, lighting his pipe. "They say he was eight foot tall if he was an inch."

"A slight exaggeration, I suspect," Des murmured.

"Maybe. He was a wicked bastard, that's for sure. Walked with a limp, but they say it didn't slow him down at all. It was his eyes you had to watch out for. Pure silver, they were, and cold enough to freeze you in your tracks."

Des regarded the man through the smoke from his cigarette. "So why did Blackstone let William and Edmund Forbes kill him?"

"No one knows. Could be he believed in fate. He knew he was going to die sure enough. He wrote his curse letter almost a month before your ancestors killed him. Some say he wrote it before the idea of murder even occurred to old William and Edmund."

"I doubt that," Des said. He nudged another fifty cents into the pot. "Murders take time to plan."

"You'd know that, would you?" Jon asked.

Des sent him a tolerantly amused look. "I read a lot of mysteries."

"You don't believe in Blackstone at all, do you?" an elf of a fisherman inquired.

"To a point. What became of his letter, does anyone know?"

Jon cackled. "Don't you?"

"Let me put it another way, has anyone ever seen it?"

"Sure," the elf said. "William and Edmund."

"I see." Des sat back, leaning his chair against the wall and grinning as he raised his beer glass. "No one's ever seen Blackstone's letter or his skull mask, but you all still think his ghost killed Harold."

"It's no joke, boy," a man who looked older than the real Ancient Mariner stated solemnly. "I knew your grandpa. We used to talk sometimes. He didn't know I knew who he was, but I did. He figured old Jonah just might have had something going with the devil. That's not to say he believed in the curse outright, but I suspect he did a little private digging around the ruin."

Des studied the man thoughtfully. "What makes you say that?"

"Saw it," the man told him. "My place is up on a knoll overlooking the old factory. Sometimes I used to see a man going through the rubble at night."

"What makes you think it was Harold?"

The old man snorted. "Who else would it be?"

Any number of people that Des could think of. "Do you know if he found anything?" He kept the question casual but the man merely shrugged.

"Doubt it. He never told me if he did. That safe room was underground, you know. The entrance to it probably got destroyed when the factory burned. 'Course, we're all assuming that the mask was there to be found."

"Meaning?" Des said.

"Meaning," Jon took over, the mischief in his lined face not quite disguising his belief in the curse. "Someone else could've found it years ago and he's been keeping it hidden ever since, waiting for a Forbes to move back into Midnight Manor and rebuild the Masque Factory.''

"So Blackstone's curse only works when the Masque Factory's in operation,'' Des clarified, lighting a new cigarette.

"That's what they say.'' Jon held up the deck of cards. "One more game?''

Des started to nod, then he caught sight of a woman heading purposefully toward their table, and immediately settled his chair back on all four legs. "Oops.''

"What is it?'' The elf followed his gaze, his eyes brightening when he spied Rowen. "Very nice,'' he murmured. "Your girlfriend, Reggie?''

"My fiancée,'' Des told them, smiling.

Rowen's expression was a mixture of exasperation and suppressed amusement. Des took one last drag from his cigarette and started to put it out. Then he saw Richard behind Rowen and knew he was in trouble.

Turning his head, he coughed the smoke from his lungs, shoved the ashtray in Jon's direction and stood, all in one motion.

He'd had too many glasses of beer, he knew it the moment he got to his feet. He wasn't drunk, but he could feel the alcohol in his bloodstream.

Rowen rounded the table and took his hand. "Ready to go?'' she asked cheerfully.

"I've just been waiting for you.''

"And drinking beer and playing poker,'' Richard noted, chuckling. "You've lightened up some, Reg. Did you win?''

"I broke even.''

"Why don't you take his place, Richard?'' Rowen suggested.

"Yes, why don't you do that?'' Des nodded at his empty chair.

Richard sighed, patting the pockets of his blazer. "No money, I'm afraid.''

"Take Reggie's,'' Rowen offered. She pulled on Des's hand. "You don't mind, do you?'' she said. Before he could answer, she added a bright, "Good, let's go then. Good-bye, gentlemen."

Obediently, Des let her lead him out of the bar. Once they were on the rainy dock, he leaned over her shoulder. "You're going to yell at me, aren't you?"

"No, I'm going to kill you." She stomped an angry foot in a puddle. "How dare you go off and have a good time and leave me stuck in that mausoleum with a housekeeper from hell."

Ignoring the rain that seeped through his clothing, Des frowned. "You're mad because I left you with Almira, not because..." He motioned toward the bar.

"Well, yes, I'm mad about that, too," she said, not sounding it. "But I understand why you did it. And the people around here don't really know you, so no one's likely to ask a lot of questions. Unless—" her shrewd gaze shifted to the bar "—unless they say something they shouldn't to Richard. What did you talk about in there?"

"Blackstone's curse mostly." Des's lips curved into a smile. "Could we please use that umbrella you're holding?"

"I should let you drown," she retorted but there was no rancor in her tone. "Better yet, I should have opened it inside. It's bad luck, you know."

"Is it?"

"And speaking of bad luck, you let a black cat walk right in front of you this afternoon. Anna saw it. She found that very suspicious."

"Tell her I crossed myself afterward."

"Reggie's not religious."

"Then tell her my mind was on the ten million papers that Lester insisted we go over at the factory and I didn't see the cat."

"That's more or less what I did tell her."

They began walking along the docks toward town. Rowen regarded the puddles beneath her feet rather than the colorful shops lining the pier.

"I think Anna's starting to wonder about you," she said at length, "and she strikes me as someone who knows how to dig up information. She might find out about the switch.''

''While she's here? I doubt it.''

''I don't. All it would take is a few phone calls. I think I'll call Reggie and see if there's anything he can do to stop her. He said he'd be in Boston if we needed him.''

For some reason, Des didn't like the idea of her phoning Reggie. Not because he didn't think it would work, but because he didn't want Rowen turning to Reggie for anything.

Still, Anna's curiosity could become a problem, and he wasn't exactly helping matters by dismissing minor details like black cats, cigarettes and afternoon poker games that Reggie would never have condescended to join.

Des looked at Rowen, resisting a sudden urge to stop her on the sidewalk, push her under an awning and kiss the hell out of her. That was frustration and too much beer talking. And maybe the sight of her long legs in the faded jeans she wore.

''So did those fishermen in the bar tell you anything new about Blackstone's curse?'' Rowen asked.

They were walking past a stark-looking house not far from the village green. Scorched figures on the trees outside indicated something of a Halloween nature, though Des suspected he wouldn't want to pursue the meaning of the markings themselves.

Rowen followed his gaze to the shaded windows. ''That's the coven house,'' she told him, confirming his suspicions. ''Anna told me all about it. After he left the guest house at Midnight Manor, Jonah Blackstone went to live there. It's kind of a shrine to him now. No one stays there.''

Des smiled knowingly. ''Haunted, of course?''

''Probably. Anna says it's full of locked rooms that no one's ever dared break into.''

''No one?'' He found that hard to believe.

''According to Anna, and she got her information from Almira who seems to be knowledgeable on a variety of different subjects. Including one Terrance Poole.''

Des had dropped back a pace to watch her walk. When she glanced over her shoulder, he raised his eyes, probably not hiding a thing. "What about Poole?" he asked.

"Do you want to have coffee or something?" she suggested.

"That depends on what 'or something' is."

"Not what you'd like it to be, I'm sure. However..." She turned to face him, her eyes sparkling slightly in the murky afternoon light. "If you're good, and if you don't try to kiss me, or smile at me so that I have to look at those gorgeous cheekbones of yours, if you stay on your side of the table and don't stare at me too hard or too long, I might..." She paused, drawing the last word out. Then suddenly, her expression changed and she reached up to press her mouth against his. The unexpected action startled him.

"Might what?" he managed to ask when she stood back.

Shoving her hands into her pockets, she grinned. "Let you have a cigarette, of course."

THEY PROBABLY didn't realize that he could pick locks or that he'd followed them from the pier and watched them as they looked at Jonah Blackstone's old house. They would never guess that he'd made that house his murder-plotting headquarters here in Midnight.

The man let himself in through the back door and went straight to the locked cellar. Nothing had been disturbed. The witches, hundreds of them by the sound of their plodding feet, trudged through the house nightly, but none ever attempted to force a lock or came anywhere near the cellar.

Many people thought that Blackstone had slept down here. Some believed his ghost still did.

The man shook himself. The plan was the important thing. It had to be executed before midnight on Halloween. Peter Pettiston wasn't out of hospital yet, which was good, but his office was a fortress now. No chance of another search.

Running a weary hand across his forehead, he tried to think. He had so much on his mind these days, and sleep had been elusive lately. He found himself drifting occasionally, wondering if he'd covered all the angles, wondering if together they might not be a match for him.

No, surely not. He had too many things working in his favor. True, the plan with the skull mask at the factory last night had failed, but there would be other opportunities—wouldn't there?

A measure of edginess crept in. What if he was wrong? Time could be running out. Maybe he shouldn't wait.

He glanced at the ceiling. There were no witches upstairs at the moment. He could slip out unnoticed and probably catch up with them.

Yes, that's what he'd do. Be a shadow in the rain. Be his own Jonah Blackstone returned. Kill the curse that had plagued him for far too long.

Chapter Ten

"So Poole has a motive for wanting both Harold and Reggie dead, Almira's keeping secrets, Lester's threatened me openly, Franz might be able to walk, and my 'cousins' not only want Harold's money, they also hate me for reasons of their own."

Des finished off his coffee in The Cove, a seaside café decorated in a graveyard motif for Halloween. The waiters wore capes, the waitresses wore cobwebbed shrouds, the walls had been hung with murals of fog-covered headstones, like something out of a horror movie. The effect was convincingly eerie, and overdone. Rowen loved it. She only wished she could keep her eyes off Des long enough to appreciate it.

"It seems to me that everyone at the manor wants Reggie dead," she said, cupping her chin in her hands. "Except for Richard. I don't think he cares enough about money to kill for it, and Reggie doesn't appear to have done anything nasty to him."

"Not that we know of." Reaching over, Des speared the last bite of her chocolate cheesecake and popped it in his mouth. "You ready to go?"

"Sure. How? I left the keys to the Land Rover with Anna and told her to leave whenever she wanted to."

"You were that certain you'd find me, huh?"

"Pretty certain." She glanced out the window. "It's stopped raining. I suppose we could walk along the beach under the cliffs."

Which would be an incredibly stupid thing to do, Rowen conceded silently, given her growing attraction for this man, but she had a tendency toward recklessness, and what could a two-mile walk hurt?

Her mind wisely refused to answer that question. Des agreed to the idea, and they left the café.

With an effort, Rowen steered their conversation to Blackstone's curse and for a time got her mind off her feelings for Des. Unfortunately, he had a long, easy stride that she enjoyed watching, and his hair today was a mass of rumpled curls that fell in his eyes and down over his collar. The smile that hovered on the corners of his mouth made her sigh and think of sex, and sex was a thought she simply didn't know how to fight. Maybe if she thought about the attempt on Des's life last night instead . . .

A shiver ran through her and she jammed her hands into her pockets. "One of the men you met today *thought* he saw Harold digging in the ruin," she recalled, her eyes on the ocean swells, "but he wasn't sure it was Harold, right?"

"Right. Add to that the fact that he lives on a knoll a good half mile from the old factory and that he's at least ninety years old and wears glasses, I'd say it could have been anyone digging there."

"It's also possible that the skull mask was found a long time ago, assuming there really is a skull mask."

Des slid her a sly sideways look. "Oh, there's a mask. It's the rest of the story I question."

He was walking on her right near the water when his eyes suddenly left her face and rose to the high cliffs. She twisted her head around. "What?"

He continued to search the rough peaks. "Nothing. I thought I saw something but it's gone now."

"Famous last words," Rowen murmured.

He laughed, lowering his gaze to her face. "You're not your usual cheerful self this afternoon. Are you still mad at me for deserting you?"

"No, I'm worried that . . ." She hesitated. "I'm not sure what exactly. Maybe that reality is a lot more frightening than its conceptualization. I've never witnessed an attempted murder before."

"You witnessed a fire."

"But I didn't see anyone die." She frowned. "Although someone did die that night. A woman, Grace Mitchell. They said she was having an affair with Reggie."

"'They' certainly get around."

Rowen grinned. "Well, they were only guessing about Reggie. He denied the affair, and in the end no one could swear to having actually seen them together."

Des glanced at the cliff again. "What was this Grace person doing in the building that night? I assume it was quite late."

"I don't know why she was there, and yes, it was late. But she wasn't alone. Her husband, Val, was with her. Well, not when she died, although he went into the building before the fire started. Two security guards checked him in. Val worked in the corporate offices downtown. The consensus is that he'd heard the rumor about his wife and Reggie, followed her to the store planning to confront them and wound up accidentally causing the fire."

Des arched a doubtful eyebrow. "Accidentally?"

"As far as anyone knows. The only thing they're sure of is that Grace died, her husband got away and Reggie was nowhere near the place when it happened."

"Lucky Reggie."

"I think so. Grace's husband didn't have the same luck. Three of us saw him run out of the building into the alley."

"And what were three of you doing standing around in an alley?"

"We weren't in the alley, we were at the other end of it, and it really wasn't an alley as such. It was a small street that opened into the parking lot. We'd been to *The Rocky Horror Picture Show* and . . ."

"Really?" he interrupted in apparent delight. "You do things like that?"

"I prefer it to sitting around in my rocking chair all night," she said with mild sarcasm. "Anyway, we went for a drink afterward, but only one, so we were still considered credible witnesses. On our way to my car, we saw a man duck out of the building. He kept looking over his shoulder. He didn't see us, but of course he was busy dodging construction equipment—scaffolding ladders, pieces of plywood, paint cans, glass. He really didn't have a chance to see much of anything. When he'd cleared all the equipment, he headed straight for the parking lot, got into his car and took off."

"Did you see the car?"

She nodded. "It didn't help. He drove home, grabbed some clothes, ditched the car and was gone by the time the police arrived. No one's seen him since."

"Are they sure his wife died in the fire?"

"Pretty sure. There were a couple of scorched bones left and the fire fighters found her wedding ring. Like her husband, she'd been checked into the building, so I'd say she probably died. It was an awfully hot fire in spite of the rain. There wasn't much left really except ashes."

"Interesting story," Des mused. "I wonder . . ."

"If her husband's out there somewhere and blames Reggie for his wife's death?" Rowen nudged his arm with her shoulder. "Come on, Des, don't you think this curse business is complicated enough without adding an irate phantom husband to the list?"

"What did he look like?"

"He had dark hair."

"Was he tall or short?"

"Average height, average build. Average man actually."

"When did this fire happen?"

"Three years ago."

Des's expression became speculative. "Lester showed up here two and half years ago."

"And Poole showed up two years ago."

"Poole doesn't have dark hair."

"He could have dyed it. Besides, Lester has muscles like an ox. Average to my mind is more along the lines of Darcy and Cooper, both of whom are insipid human beings, but neither of whom is likely to be an impostor."

"I'm an impostor, Rowen," Des reminded her. "Why not one of Reggie's cousins?"

"Because there are pictures of Reggie's cousins. There are hardly any pictures of Reggie, at least not after he went through puberty." Rowen paused, knitting her forehead as his eyes rose to the cliffs again. "What are you looking at?" she demanded, not seeing anything except rocks and a bank of ominous black clouds. And then...

She spotted it at the same instant Des did, the person dressed all in black who materialized on the edge of the high rocks. He had something in his hands and Rowen's instincts warned her it wasn't a bow and arrow.

A shot rang out, whizzing past her head and impacting in the cold sand. She felt Des's hands hauling her sideways, although he needn't have bothered. Fear didn't tend to paralyze her, not if it meant she might be killed.

They stumbled across the sand, ducking as more bullets flew by. There was an overturned rowboat beached near the base of the cliff. Rowen clambered over the rotting hulk ahead of Des, and for a moment lay prostrate while her mind tried to assimilate what was happening.

"Keep down," Des said through his teeth, pushing on her head when she raised it.

"I can't breathe with my face in the sand. Where is he?"

"Same place as before."

She took a cautious look, her heart pounding, her mouth dry with fear. "It isn't safe here," she hissed. "He can work his way along the cliff and have a clear shot at us from above."

"Let's just hope he doesn't figure that out."

Two bullets struck the side of the old boat.

Des squinted upward through his hair. "It's a deserted spot, but he can't keep shooting indefinitely. Someone's bound to notice."

"Who?" Rowen forced her panic down with a blend of self-will and prayer. Every muscle in her body ached from not moving. "There's only the cemetery behind him, and dead people can't hear." She broke off as three more bullets embedded themselves in the boat. Then her breath caught in her throat and she grabbed Des's arm. "I think he's figured it out," she hissed. "He's coming this way."

The figure moved relentlessly toward them, slowed by the rocky terrain but resolute in his intent. He'd be within striking range in a few minutes and Rowen couldn't see anyplace else for them to hide. Except maybe in the water.

"Des," she whispered, her wide eyes locked on the ocean. "There are fishing boats out on the point. If we could swim..."

He gave a distracted nod of understanding. Still watching the figure, he asked, "Can you wriggle around and reach into my right boot?"

"For what?"

"My gun."

Rowen went limp with relief. "Thank God."

"Thank Him when we're out of this mess," Des said, peering over the top of the rowboat. "Where did he go?"

Rowen hated to think. Terrified, she crept along the sand, tugged his pant leg up and extracted the gun.

Were they in the murderer's sights yet, she wondered, but didn't waste time looking. She needed to stay calm and think—and pray that Des had enough bullets to cover them until they reached the sanctuary of the water. Because he'd never hit the figure from here. She doubted that even a sharpshooter could manage that.

She crawled back up beside him. "Where is he?"

"Coming up to a bunch of boulders." Des took the gun and checked it. Then he set a hand on the back of her neck and worked himself up just high enough that he'd be able to get in front of her quickly.

Rowen waited. Her heart slammed against her ribs; her breath formed a painful knot in her chest. The ocean seemed miles away instead of yards, the fishing boats were even more remote. But it was either run or get shot, and Rowen was too much of a survivor to die without a fight.

"Okay, go!"

Des's voice was a hiss in her ear. Using her terror as a catapult, Rowen scrambled to her feet and raced across the wet sand. She wanted to look back and see what was happening, but knew that would be suicidal, to say nothing of what might happen to Des if she slowed and he slammed into her.

She heard him firing and then the answering retort of the rifle. High-powered, she judged, splashing through the first few feet of water. Only then did she risk a backward glance.

She knew Des had squeezed off his last shot. Now the figure was taking aim.

"Hurry," she shouted, and Des turned, tucking the gun into his waistband. She heard him plunge into the water after her.

There'd been no time to shed clothing or shoes. Rowen felt the encumbering drag of wet material. It would sap her strength very quickly, but stopping would be certain death until they were out of the shooter's range, whatever that might be.

She sensed rather than saw Des beside her. As for the fishing boats on the point, she had no idea if they were still there. Hopefully they'd be at anchor, but she wasn't counting on it.

The saltwater, usually buoyant, kept hitting her in the face. She was exhausted already and the suction from below seemed to grow stronger with each stroke she took.

Rowen struggled on, refusing to give up, fueled as much by stubbornness and anger as by fear. Skull masks flashed through her mind, then the husk of the old Masque Factory. A hazy picture of Reggie's face solidified and ultimately became Des. The water washed over her, her arms and legs went numb, her muscles had long since gone weak from exhaustion.

She didn't know where it came from, only that it appeared out of the ocean mist—a great patchwork troller looming before her.

Ragged nets materialized and then she heard men's voices. Des was close behind her, telling her to go left. "Swim to the ladder, Rowen."

She obeyed, her frozen fingers catching the lowest rung and clinging tightly. Even dead-tired, however, she couldn't resist glancing back at the distant cliffs.

It didn't surprise her that the figure was gone. He must have realized he couldn't hit them over such a vast distance. They were safe enough. For now.

And yet, even as several pairs of hands reached down to haul her on board, it occurred to Rowen to wonder about the person who appeared to be using Blackstone's curse to commit murder. She had no part in the curse. Why had the killer been shooting at her?

It wasn't a large troller after all, just a small boat with a captain and two puzzled crewmen. They probably thought she and Des were crazy, swimming fully clothed on a rainy late-October day and requesting to be let off at the dock below Midnight Manor rather than in town.

Luckily for them, the captain was an obliging man, disinclined to ask a lot of questions.

"Not that we could have answered them," Rowen remarked once they were safe and sound on the tiny estate dock. She stared through her sopping hair, first at the roughly cut stone steps that zigzagged up the side of the cliff, then at Des's unrevealing face. "You know, whoever that person back there was, it's unlikely he was shooting at me. You should have let me cover you."

Shoving the hair from his eyes, Des rubbed his forehead. "Don't count on it, Rowen. I think whoever was shooting would have been more than willing to go through you to get to me."

"Not if he planned to use Blackstone's curse to cloud your death, he wouldn't." The dock swayed precariously beneath them as they headed for the rock face. "Come to think of it, death by shooting's not a particularly brutal way to go. People get shot every day. Blackstone wanted his victims to suffer, or so the legend claims."

"Maybe our killer's abandoned the curse," Des suggested, squinting at what seemed like nine million steps awaiting them.

Sighing, Rowen took his hand and pulled him forward. "God, what a horrible day this has been."

Des leaned over her from behind, setting his cheek momentarily against hers. "Horrible," he agreed with the faintest trace of humor, "and not over yet." He indicated the top of the cliff. "Someone up there isn't going to be very happy to see us."

"I SEE YOU got caught in the rain," Almira said unnecessarily as Rowen and Des came into the kitchen through the back door.

"You'd think that, wouldn't you?" Des countered. "Have you been here all afternoon?"

"Of course." She stared as if challenging him to dispute her statement, which meant she was probably lying but confident he'd never be able to prove it.

"I don't suppose Poole or anyone was with you," Rowen said, undaunted.

The housekeeper's head lifted another notch. "I was alone."

Rowen summoned a perfunctory smile. "I see. Well, if you'll excuse us, Almira, we'll go and change." Pausing in the doorway, she added a casual, "By the way, do you know where the others are?"

"I have no idea," Almira said and promptly turned her back on them.

"Well, that was no help," Des remarked once they were safely out of the kitchen. "Afternoon, Cooper," he added in the direction of a large shadow in the entry hall.

The man within it stirred, then reluctantly emerged. "Is it raining again?" he asked, looking oddly pleased by their bedraggled appearance.

"No," Rowen said pleasantly. "What are you hiding behind your back?"

"A jar."

"Of what?"

Des shook his head but it was too late. A nervous giggle bubbled from Cooper's lips. He stepped forward, bringing the jar out and offering it to her.

She didn't flinch. "Spiders," she said calmly. "How charming."

"And flies." He took another step and while she didn't retreat, Des felt her tighten against him. "My pets have to eat, you know."

Before Cooper could stop him, Des reached out and snatched the jar away, inspecting it. "Where did you collect these, cousin?"

Cooper blinked. "In the garden. And in the woods."

"On the way to or from town?"

"How did you know I went to town?" Cooper demanded.

"Lucky guess." Des held the jar over the marble floor, his intent clear. "Did you just get back?"

Cooper stared in desperation. "No. I came back for lunch. Five or six hours ago."

"And went out spider-hunting afterward." Rowen assumed.

"Yes."

"Near the cemetery, I'll bet, huh?"

"I—don't remember."

Yes he did, Des thought, but Cooper wasn't stupid enough to admit it. For all his slimy, sick tendencies, Cooper was a clever man. Maybe more clever than anyone suspected. He gave the bug jar back.

A moment later, the elevator doors opened and Franz came out. He treated them to a sour look but didn't stop to chat. In a loud squeak of wheels, he rolled away toward the drawing room.

"No mud on his shoes today," Rowen observed as they climbed the wide stone staircase, leaving Cooper to retreat into his shadowy corner. "I think Reggie was right. Weirdos and perverts, that's what these people are. You're lucky not to be related to... Oh, hello," she greeted. "When did you get back?"

Anna stood at the top of the stairs, wearing the ugliest green-and-brown print dress Des had ever seen. The damp curtain of her hair hung limply around her face.

"Harold's useless Land Rover stalled twice on the road from town," she announced as if it were Rowen's fault. "I had to get out and jiggle the battery connections to get it going again."

"How clever of you," Rowen said, passing her. "We had a less enjoyable return journey. Someone was shooting at us."

"What?"

"With a rifle," Des added, enjoying himself. "Fortunately, whoever it was needs lessons in marksmanship."

Anna looked vaguely sick, although her voice came out steadily enough. "What kind of a rifle?"

That stopped Rowen. She backtracked, her eyes flicking to Anna's white-knuckled fists. "We didn't catch the make. Is it important?"

"Not especially."

"Then why ask?" Des said, closing in. "Where's Darcy?"

"In our room, of course."

"Where was he earlier?" Rowen pressed from behind her shoulder.

"That's none of your business."

"Yes it is," Des said. For some reason, his smile seemed to disturb her. Or was it Darcy's whereabouts this afternoon that made the ends of her hair quiver? "Where was he?"

"We could always ask Darcy," Rowen observed.

Anna glared at her. "If you must know, he was on the shooting range."

"Ah. And where's the shooting range?" Des asked.

"On Cemetery Road, near the outskirts of Midnight. He went there after lunch. After you and I left," she added with a poisonous look at Rowen.

Rowen wasn't cowed. "And before that, he was in Harold's workshop making a knife rack."

"What are you getting at?" Anna retorted angrily.

"Oh, come on, Anna," Des prompted. "You're not stupid. Surely you can understand our curiosity."

"You'd be curious yourself if you'd had a sniper firing bullets at you," Rowen added. "It's not a lot of fun."

"Darcy was skeet-shooting," Anna maintained, stiff-lipped. "I'm sure there were witnesses. He rented his rifle at the range."

"Of course he did," Des said, moving past her and motioning to Rowen.

"You can check at the range if you want to," Anna called after them.

"In which case I'm sure we needn't bother," Rowen murmured with a glance at Des. "But it's still an interesting discovery, don't you think?"

"That person on the cliff was using a high-powered rifle, Rowen," he reminded her.

"I know. But Anna's admission does prove one thing."

"Which is?"

"Cousin Darcy knows how to shoot."

Chapter Eleven

Rowen insisted that Des dress properly for dinner that night. She went through the clothes that Reggie had given him and tossed her selections on the bed.

"Gray wool pants, black boots, white shirt, burgundy velvet jacket, burgundy-and-gray tie. And," she added, opening his bureau drawer, "a brush for that unholy tangle of hair." She turned, forestalling his objection. "Anna's already suspicious of you. If we hadn't started attacking Darcy this afternoon, she probably would have started attacking you. 'Why didn't you have a fit when you saw that black cat? Why don't all your clothes have designer labels? What was the Forbes Corporation's net profit last year? How many companies do you own? Why are you so much nicer than you were as a child?'" She widened her eyes to emphasize her point. "Get the picture?"

He knew better than to laugh. Instead, he zeroed in on one of her sample questions. "So I'm nicer than Reggie, am I?"

"I didn't say that." She handed him the brush. "Here. Make yourself presentable. I have to get dressed." A look of uncertainty crossed her face. "And I should phone Reggie."

Des threw the brush on the bed, advancing on her. "There's nothing Reggie can do," he said, "and nothing Anna could dig up fast enough to make a difference."

Rowen stood her ground while he closed in on her, challenging him with her eyes. "Why don't you want me to call?"

Des set his hands on her arms. "No reason," he lied. "Why are you trembling?"

"I'm not."

"Yes you are."

She took a deep breath but her composure didn't falter. "Let go of me, Des," she said calmly.

He slid his gaze to the V of her coral silk robe and the lightly tanned skin of her collarbone. "Why?"

"Because I said so."

"I'm not holding you, Rowen."

She lifted her chin a fraction. "Seduction doesn't have to be physical. Why are you doing this?"

His fingers caressed the silky flesh of her upper arms; his eyes strayed to her breasts. "Guess," he suggested softly.

She didn't move a muscle. "I don't want you, you know that, don't you?"

He smiled. "Do I?"

"Stop it, Des." Now she did pull away, her expression momentarily cross. "I'm not a toy for you to play with. I came here to help Reggie, and because—well, never mind. The point is I don't like being surreptitiously seduced, which is exactly what you've been doing ever since we got here. And what makes it worse is that you're enjoying yourself."

He fixed his gaze on her face. "It isn't a crime to enjoy yourself, Rowen. And you were going to say that you were bored, weren't you? That's the real reason you came to Midnight. You have a low threshold for boredom." He approached her as he spoke. He knew it was her pride refusing to let her retreat. "Reggie's fine," he continued, "but you don't really want him. You don't even really want his money, although there are probably plenty of people who assume you do and don't blame you in the slightest. From what I can tell, my cousin's no prize. None of us are, actually."

He towered over her now, but she still didn't back away. "You're not a Forbes, Des," was all she said. "You're no part of them."

He stared down at her. "No denials, Rowen? No cries of outrage for all my assumptions?"

"No."

Simply stated, and in the back of Des's mind comprehension began to glimmer. Not enough to make sense, but he had a feeling that something inside her corresponded strongly to a part of him. He had an obscure, restless side to his nature, one that had kept him from settling into a two-car, two-kid, nine-to-five job, barbecue-on-the-weekends life-style. Some people called it selfishness. Des tended to think of it as fear. In Rowen's case, he wasn't sure what it might be.

A slow, knowing grin curved her lips as the welter of thoughts slid through his mind. "Are you trying to figure me out?" she asked, not sounding the least bit upset. "I wouldn't bother if I were you. I'm not complicated. I don't want the things that most people want, and I see no point in pretending that I do. In fact, I think that kind of self-delusion is dangerous. I know too many people who've done the accepted thing and wound up miserable afterward. Miserable and stuck, because you can't 'undo' a child even if you were heartless enough to want to."

Des frowned. "How did children get into this?"

"I'm not sure," she said, hesitating.

He ran a hand around the back of her neck, his thumb stroking the silky warm skin of her throat. "I am," he murmured. "About this, anyway." And lowering his head, he covered her mouth with his.

THE SENSATIONS that raced through her were both frightening and immediate.

He had no business kissing her, opening his mouth over hers and forcing her to respond. Except that he wasn't forcing her to do anything, wasn't even imprisoning her with his hands. All she had to do was twist her head to one side and step away.

Instead, her fingers found his waistband, running under his untucked shirt and exploring the smooth skin of his back. He teased her with his lips and tongue but there was a certain rough urgency mixed in that Rowen recognized instantly. It was the same thing she felt. And for the life of her, she didn't know how to deal with it.

Heat like liquid fire suffused her body. She felt hot, startled and excited all at the same time. She felt the hardness of his arousal pressing into her stomach and wanted to bring her hands around and unzip his fly. She wanted so many things that she almost said, "to hell with reason," and gave in to her desires.

But where sex was concerned, Rowen was never, never reckless, and this man spelled danger to her in capital letters.

She held on to the threads of that resolve, moving her hands up instead of around, knowing she should stop yet unable to do it.

Her body responded as his did, betraying her completely. His mouth slid over her lips, dampening them, creating just the right amount of friction to send hot tremors up her spine and down into her belly.

Her nipples were hard against his chest. She slid her hands over his deceptively broad shoulders, curling her fingers into his hair. He had such beautiful hair, such a wonderful mouth; she might never be able to push him away.

Thank God, she didn't have to make a choice.

The sudden hammering on Des's door was an imperative clamor, loud enough to wake a zombie let alone intrude on an ill-advised kiss.

"What?" Des demanded when the noise persisted.

"It's Darcy," a distressed voice called from the other side. "Can I come in?"

In spite of her relief, Rowen hesitated, part of her wanting very badly for Darcy to go away. But she knew better than to tempt fate. Nodding at Des, who looked thoroughly irritated by the interruption, she let her arms fall to her sides. She didn't release her pent-up breath until he was halfway to the door.

"Yes, Darcy, what is it?" he said, resting his elbows on the jamb and rubbing his eye. He sounded more weary now than annoyed, and Rowen turned away, fanning her flushed skin with her hand.

"Hello, Rowen," Darcy greeted, evidently embarrassed.

"What do you want?" Des repeated, forestalling her response.

"I was wondering if you'd seen Anna. She went downstairs an hour ago, and now I can't find her."

Rowen pushed aside the damask curtain. It was pouring out, pitch-black and windy. "I doubt if she's out there," she said over her shoulder. "Why did she go downstairs?"

"I'm not sure. I heard her say something about wanting to see someone, but I was in the shower, so I couldn't hear very well."

"Anna, the rear-window sentry," Rowen murmured to Des who gave a short silent laugh. Darcy appeared not to notice.

"I thought maybe you could help me look through the house," he said, fidgeting with his hands. "It's not like Anna to disappear."

Rowen glanced at the clothes on Des's bed. If he handled this properly, he'd have a perfect excuse not to dress for dinner.

"Of course we'll help," she said, which seemed to relieve Darcy enormously.

"I'm sure Richard and Poole will, too," he said. "That'll make five of us searching for her. Maybe she got locked in the cellar."

Rowen doubted it. Anna liked to spy from her bedroom window. Rain or no, if she'd seen something interesting, she would have braved the elements and gone after it.

"Curiosity killed the cat," Rowen said to herself, once Des and Darcy had left.

Shedding her robe, she reached for a pair of jeans and a red shirt. There was rain gear in the laundry room, she'd seen it there this morning. Five minutes later, she was downstairs, tugging on an oversize yellow slicker. Then she remembered the sniper on the cliffs and decided she'd be a fool to wander off alone.

She found Lester standing in front of the fire in the great hall, wearing a black raincoat and muddy boots. "What's going on?" he demanded when he spotted her.

"Anna's missing. We're about to go looking for her. Have you seen Reggie?"

Lester's lip curled into a sneer. "Behind you."

Des entered the hall with Richard, who was definitely not dressed for a night in the rain. His pants were a blend of silk and wool, his jacket a rich black velvet. Rowen wondered idly where he got the money to accommodate his lavish tastes. Everyone knew he didn't work.

"Almira's checking the cellar, and Poole's going through the east wing," Des revealed. He grinned slightly at Rowen's bright, baggy attire. "No one knows where Franz and Cooper are." He raised inquiring eyes to Lester's face. "Come to help us, have you?"

"I came for dinner," Lester snarled, "and to bring you some more files. We open in a few days, in case you've forgotten."

If he'd hoped to get a rise with that remark, his plan failed miserably. Des merely smiled and made an imperceptible motion at Rowen with his head. She preceded him to the shadows at the rear of the room.

"I saw Lester coming out of Harold's study a few minutes ago," he said quietly. "He walked over to the front door, put his boots back on and came in here."

"How devious of him." Rowen glanced up. "Should we look?"

She needn't have asked really. Lester had no business being in Harold's study and he certainly had no business sneaking in. His actions said it all. He'd been looking for something.

"The question is, did he find it?" she wondered out loud minutes later when she and Des were behind the locked double doors of Harold's ground-floor study.

Des switched on a pair of old-fashioned floor lamps. "Probably not. He didn't look too happy." He surveyed the room. "This place is worse than the rest of the house. It reminds me of a medieval library."

"Not quite that bad." Rowen ran her fingers over a dusty bookshelf crammed with American classics, Latin prose and British poetry. "I don't think any of this stuff's been moved recently. The desk's probably our best bet."

"Or the safe."

Rowen watched as Des swung a small oil painting of a dying man away from the wall. "Morbid picture. Who painted it?"

"Gwydon Byron, no relation to the poet. It's eighteenth century. Quite valuable."

"So, obviously Lester didn't sneak in here to deal artwork." Rowen began rummaging through the Edwardian desk. Her nose wrinkled in disgust. "God, it's no wonder Harold needed Reggie to run things. I've never seen such a mess. There are papers here dating back ten years, and Harold wasn't here anywhere near that long."

"Must have been a pack rat."

Des went to work on the wall safe. Within ninety seconds, he'd cracked the combination. "Anything?" she asked, moving on to a new drawer.

"Letters and deeds." He withdrew a bundle of envelopes tied up with red string, then frowned and looked deeper inside. "Ah, and a floater."

"A what?"

"An envelope on its own." She heard the rustle of thick paper, followed by a deep chuckle. "So it is real," he said softly.

"What is?"

"Blackstone's letter. Here."

He set it down so she could see the stark handwriting. The letter, written in black ink, was smudged in places, but still legible. "If you understand ancient Egyptian, that is," she noted, pushing back her hair. "I can't read a word of this. How do you know its Blackstone's letter?"

He sent her a humorous look. "I read ancient Egyptian."

"How handy. What language is it, really?"

Smiling, he picked up the paper.

"English. Written backward."

"The devil's prose." Rowen returned to her own task. "Can you read it?"

"I could if I had a mirror. I'll take it upstairs and..." He paused as she shook out a piece of paper. "Did you find something?"

"It's part of a letter." Flipping the stationery over, she glanced at the reverse side. "Or rather, it's a carbon copy of part of a letter. Handwritten. I don't know who it was written to, but most of his other correspondence is typed."

"Quiet," he said, holding up his hand.

Rowen lifted her head. "What is it?"

Des's eyes focused on the door. She heard it then, the experimental rattle of handles. Someone was trying to get in.

Raising a finger to his lips, Des slipped both letters into his pocket and motioned for Rowen to join him. She switched off the floor lamp and crept across the carpet to where Des waited behind the left door. When she reached him, he switched off the second lamp and pulled her tightly against his body.

Distracting though that was, Rowen still caught the grunt of frustration from the other side. The handles rattled again, then it sounded as though a foot kicked the base.

Breath held, Rowen waited for the intruder to hurl his full weight at the doors. It was a man, the grunt had proved that much, and the doors, though strong, had feeble enough latches.

Again an irritated foot struck the bottom, but for some reason, the larger assault never came. Instead, an eerie little giggle filtered through the crack.

"I know you're in there," a familiar voice sang out in an unnerving falsetto. "I saw you go in."

"Cooper!" Rowen recoiled involuntarily.

The handles jiggled. Cooper's voice grew muffled. "Come and see me, pretty lady. Let me put you with your prey."

"What's he talking about?" Rowen whispered too softly for anyone but Des to hear.

He shook his head, clearly not understanding any better than she did.

"I'll put you in my special jar," Cooper continued. It sounded as though his mouth was pressed up against the door. "Just you and Reggie, together. And then we'll see how great he is. You'll eat him, and he'll be sorry. Better than sorry, he'll be dead. You kill Reggie the fly, pretty lady, and Jonah Blackstone will kill Reggie the man. And Halloween will be a celebration for all of us.''

IT TOOK every scrap of courage Rowen possessed not to run and hide behind the desk when Des finally eased the study doors open.

''It's all right, he's gone,'' he said over his shoulder.

''Completely gone,'' Rowen added, shuddering. ''He's mad, Des, you do realize that.''

Nodding, he mouthed the word, ''Later,'' to her and closed the doors behind them just as Richard came through the archway from the great hall.

''Ah, there you are. We thought you'd deserted us. No sign of her?''

''None,'' Rowen answered. She allowed herself one last fearful look back, then shoved the spooky incident from her mind.

As they started into the great hall, Des nudged her arm lightly, nodding at the coatrack inside the front door.

''Anna's raincoat's missing from the peg,'' he said with a quick glance out from under his curls at Darcy. ''She must have seen something or someone and gone to investigate.''

''Well, her room does overlook the garden, and the family tomb, and the old pool and the cliffs,'' Rowen recalled.

Des ran a hand through his hair, holding it off his face. ''Would it do any good for me to suggest that you stay here and help Almira and Poole search the manor?'' he asked.

''Not much.'' As he took her hand, Rowen noticed that Des was wearing another of Reggie's expensive wool jackets together with his own baggy cords and shirt. The man was determined to destroy his forced wardrobe piece by piece.

It took ten minutes for everyone to decide which part of the estate he or she wanted to search. As far as Rowen was concerned, discussion was a waste of time. No one would stick to a designated area, anyway. Someone as surly as Lester might not search at all. He'd probably go outside, get a little wetter, then come back in and lie through his teeth about where he'd looked.

She and Des exited the manor through the kitchen door. Des held the flashlight while Rowen combed the overgrown garden, including the vegetable and pumpkin patches.

Rain washed over her in icy, wind-driven sheets. It was a hellish night, custom-made for...

She cringed inwardly as the first inevitable peal of thunder rumbled over the water. Des glanced swiftly back at her. "Are you all right?"

She managed a faint nod. "Where next?"

"The marble pool."

Rowen's feet refused to move. More thunder sounded beyond the cliffs. She saw flashlights bobbing at various points around the estate, then saw a razor-thin bolt of lightning fork to the ground somewhere near town.

Setting his hands on her shoulders, Des turned her toward the manor. "Go inside, Rowen," he said patiently.

"But..."

"Don't argue. Come on, I'll take you back."

It was the betrayal of her body more than Des's words that made her temper rise. She wriggled out from under his hands. "I can go myself," she said in a controlled voice. "It's only a few yards, and there are at least a dozen lights burning in the windows."

He didn't say a word, just gave her a little shove.

He couldn't know it, of course, but that tiny push sent her right back into her childhood. It was the cave all over again, her brother screaming in terror, shoving her out into the storm. *"You have to get our gear, Rowen. You have to! We'll freeze if you don't."*

Rowen blocked the memory. At the same time, she tried to block the sound of the thunder. It was getting closer, but she'd almost reached the house. Her fingers found the doorknob. She *had* reached the house.

Breathing a shaky sigh of relief, she darted inside, leaning her weight on the heavy door until the latch clicked shut.

The stone walls muffled the storm, but she could still hear the thunder. Her brother's screams rushed back again—a single terrified shriek, cut off before it could fully develop.

Rowen's head came up sharply. Her brother's screams hadn't been cut off. And they hadn't come from a distance.

That last cry hadn't been in her mind. It was new and alarmingly real. And it had come from the direction of the water.

SOMETHING WHITE and vaguely luminous flapped like a ghostly arm between the rocks at the edge of the cliff. Des caught sight of it seconds after he heard the scream.

"Anna?" he shouted into the wind. There was no response. Cupping his hands to his mouth, he tried again. "Anna!"

The wind was a gale on the high rocks, the darkness virtually impenetrable even with a flashlight. Head bent against the storm, he started for the edge.

The arm continued to flap wildly. Except that it wasn't an arm. His flashlight beam showed a long strip of material, probably a scarf.

Had Anna been wearing a scarf? Had she followed someone out here, and then wound up trapped herself?

Des made his way to the boulders, his senses as alert as they could be under these conditions. A wall of rain blinded him, the wind buffeted him from behind. And the prospect of a setup hovered in his mind.

He was considering a discreet approach when he picked up another sound. It had a pathetic edge to it, like the bleat of a lamb. Like the scream before it, he couldn't quite tell where it came from.

"Anna?" he called. The wind carried her name away.

Through the slanting rain, he saw a hand creep up from behind one of the rocks. It groped for the scarf and finally found it.

"Help me," a weak voice cried.

Des knew better than to rush blindly on. You didn't survive in Marrakech or on the London docks by blundering stupidly into a trap. On the other hand, if it was Anna back there, she could be seriously injured.

He moved cautiously through the rough boulders, always keeping one eye on the cliff. The wind slammed against his spine, blowing strands of wet hair in his face.

It didn't help that half of his mind was on the thunder crashing around him and how Rowen might be reacting to it at the manor. Assuming she was still at the manor.

The scarf flapped before him, but the hand clutching it had vanished.

"Bloody hell," Des swore through his teeth.

Poised, he considered his options. There weren't any, really. He had to take the chance.

One agile jump brought him off the rock and onto the lip of the cliff. Reaching out, he closed his fingers on the scarf and yanked it free.

Far too easy, his mind warned. But as quickly as that thought occurred to him, a gloved hand snaked out of the shadows to ensnare his wrist.

While the grip wasn't especially brutal, Des's instincts told him it wasn't the grip of an injured person. He'd been set up, and the piece of wood that collided painfully with his left shoulder merely emphasized the fact.

The murderer's fingers clamped to his wrist held fast. Ducking, Des brought his arm around and intercepted the branch, jerking it loose midswing. But he was off-balance, and now his attacker's other hand was free. It lashed out, catching him in the throat. With a guttural roar, the person behind the rock surged up out of the darkness.

Everything happened in a split second. Des saw a flash of white and a set of bared teeth leering at him. He heard a concentrated howl, then felt himself tipping sideways.

He couldn't stop any of it, couldn't hope to regain his balance in time. With a mighty thrust, the figure knocked him backward, shoving him over the edge of the cliff.

Des had a sense of nothing beneath him except air, of endless darkness rushing past. He was tumbling through a wet, black void, pitching downward to the rocks and the pounding waves. Falling to his death in a cold, watery grave.

Chapter Twelve

"No!" Rowen skidded to a halt, screaming the denial out loud as she saw Des tumble from the cliff.

She ran for the rocks, not stopping to consider the consequences. She couldn't believe he was gone. Maybe he'd grabbed hold of something, a jutting piece of rock or a bush, a vine strong enough to support his weight until he could climb back up.

The person who had pushed him heard her scream. He swung his head around in surprise. Even through the driving rain, Rowen could see the blurred, bony lines of the skull mask he wore.

"You bastard," she cried, although she knew he'd never hear her above the roar of the storm.

The figure straightened abruptly, then hopped down behind the rocks. Preparing to do what? Ambush her? If he succeeded, she wouldn't be able to help Des.

Rowen switched directions, making for the water. Scrambling up onto a flat boulder, she dropped down on her stomach and shone the flashlight at the spot where Des had gone over.

There was no sign of him, only darkness and the ceaseless crashing of the surf below.

A violent crack of thunder shook the ground, shooting through Rowen's nerves. "Des!" she cried, then crawled right to the edge and shone the light again. "Des!"

Desperately, she swung the flashlight around in a wide arc. The beam caught a movement. The murderer was no longer hidden behind the rock, he was—gone.

She didn't waste time wondering why the killer had run. She'd seen him duck into the woods. He must be confident that Des, or as he saw it, Reggie, was dead.

Well, he wasn't. Rowen refused to believe that. Slipping and sliding, she clawed her way over the boulders to the point where she'd seen him fall. It was very near the steps they'd climbed today. Maybe he'd caught hold of one of them and...

No. That was stupid. And impossible. Her flashlight revealed nothing, no trace of him at all.

But that didn't mean anything.

Setting her jaw, Rowen located the steps, and started down, clutching at bits of stone and weed as she went. Lightning illuminated the stormy coastline, throwing the cliffs and ocean into bold relief. How many sailing ships had been wrecked on these rocks, she wondered, her teeth chattering with fear and cold? How many dead Pilgrims and fishermen?

But those people hadn't died falling from the cliff. And the water was deep at the base. The captain who'd rescued them today had told them that. A person might survive the fall, if he was very, very lucky.

The thunder crashed through her, but she wouldn't stop, wouldn't give up hope.

It took forever to navigate the slippery steps. The dock at the bottom was even more treacherous. It pitched and tossed beneath her, threatening to fling her into the water with each wave that slammed over it.

Exhausted, Rowen dropped to her knees. "Des!" she cried, shaking the wet hair from her eyes. "Where are you?"

Everything looked black and blurred. The lightning helped, but it was always accompanied by claps of thunder. Rowen felt numb mentally and physically. Yet for all her fear, she still couldn't give up hope.

Her eyes searched the waves. "Des, please," she whispered, then gasped as something brushed her hand. It wasn't water, it felt like someone's fingers.

She bent over, almost toppling from the dock in the process, and finally saw it, a hand groping for the edge.

"Des!" Hastily she grabbed hold of his wrist, pulling as hard as she could. His head emerged, then his other hand. He located the dock and hauled himself up. Rowen wrapped her fingers around his jacket, not letting go until he was beside her.

He sat there, panting for breath, unable to speak for several minutes. Rowen didn't care. She threw her arms around his neck and hugged him with something akin to desperation. "I knew you were alive," she whispered, turning her face into his sopping hair. "I knew it!"

She glanced uncertainly at the cliffs above—and prayed the murderer didn't know it, too.

DES FELT as though he'd been put through a meat grinder. He wasn't sure how Rowen got him back to the manor, or who was there when they arrived. All he wanted to do was fall into bed and sleep for a month.

Halfway up the stairs he remembered the letters he'd taken from Harold's study, the ones he'd put in his jacket pocket. He pulled them out and gave them to Rowen.

"Actually, Blackstone's letter will be fine," she revealed, opening his bedroom door. "Once it dries out in front of the fire, that is. As for this other one—well, we'll see." He felt her eyes on his face. "Are you sure you're not hurt?"

"Only sore," he said. "And tired."

"And lucky."

She began stripping off his wet clothes. Des let her do it. If he was really lucky, she'd climb into bed with him and wrap her warm body around his chilled, wet one.

"No one downstairs has an alibi," she said, unbuttoning his shirt. "It could have been any of them out there. Except for Anna, I guess. You said whoever pushed you seemed strong?"

"Pretty strong," Des agreed. "Still, I wouldn't rule out Almira."

"I never do."

His answering laugh stuck in his throat when Rowen's hands started tugging at his belt. He wrapped his fingers firmly around hers. "Not unless you're feeling adventuresome," he said.

She didn't pretend to misunderstand. With the same composure she displayed in all things, she reached over and switched on his bedside lamp. Then suddenly jumped back against his chest.

"What?" It took his bleary eyes too long to focus. She'd already gone from being startled to glaring at it—whatever it was.

"The bastard," she declared in an angry whisper. "One of them did this, Des."

"This" being some kind of a sick private joke, he assumed. He was wrong.

"Oh God," he sighed when he saw the thing. He closed his eyes, the pounding in his head a match for the fury of the storm.

Another rubber skull mask lay on his pillow, like a disembodied head. Its empty black eye sockets stared blankly up at him.

It was Death lying there, the same twisted form of death that had stalked and ultimately ensnared Harold. It wasn't going to go away, not until its job was finished.

"It *is* Blackstone's curse," Rowen stated. "The murderer hasn't abandoned it." Despite her bravado, she took a backward step, pressing herself against him. "This killer's sick, Des, really sick. I think you should get out of here."

"I should," Des agreed. Picking up the mask, he studied it obliquely. "But I'm not going to. It's personal now, Rowen. It's arrows and falling light fixtures, and bullets and being shoved into the ocean. I want to know who's behind this, and I want to know why."

THERE WAS SOLITUDE in this dark underground room. Clear thought was possible here—well, most of the time. Tonight for some reason, weariness seemed to have replaced clarity. Maybe another letter would help.

Gloved hands began the task of composing the fourth letter.

Dear Dr. Sayers,

I can't believe I failed again. It was easy to kill Harold. Why does Reggie's death have to be so difficult?

He fell, I saw him go over. I know she couldn't have saved him. He was long gone by the time she showed up, and yet he's still alive.

I wish Rowen wouldn't keep interfering. If she doesn't stop, I'll start to think that she loves him, even though I know she can't. It's impossible, Doctor. Reggie's slimy and selfish—and you know, the more I think about it, the more I'm convinced that she's just leading him on. Of course! What she really wants to do is help me kill him.

That must be it. I should have realized. She hates him as much as the rest of us. Oh, but then it's all very complicated, and I have to be so careful not to be seen.

I thought I had been spotted earlier tonight, but it turned out all right. I wonder if she thought she was seeing Blackstone's ghost? It's possible, you know. People keep saying he'll be back. Maybe on Halloween he'll appear to me and we can talk.

Now where was I? Oh yes, I was telling you about my growing list of failures and how upsetting they're becoming. I do my breathing exercises regularly, Dr. Sayers. I'll do them again in a few minutes to clear my mind. Then I'll sit down and make a new plan. I won't let failure deter me. I have Blackstone's skull mask in my possession. Together we'll be invincible.

How unfortunate for poor Reggie Forbes.

Rest assured as always,
A former patient

"THERE'S NO SIGN of her at all," Richard revealed late the following afternoon.

The police had come and gone, Darcy was a nervous wreck and everyone else was wandering around the manor looking cross and/or guilty.

Rowen came into the drawing room searching for Des. She had the dried letters in her pocket. With Richard there, however, and Cooper sitting ramrod-straight in the corner, she was disinclined to show them.

Rubbing her arms, she crossed to the long narrow window, avoided a suit of armor and pushed aside a corn-husk wreath. "Fog," she said flatly, looking out. "It's getting thicker by the minute. Are the police going to search the grounds again?"

"They already have." Franz rolled in and went straight to the carved rosewood bar. "They didn't find a thing. So, Reggie, how are you feeling today? Rowen told us you fell off the dock last night."

To save time and energy, Rowen had lied. The killer knew what had happened. No one else needed to know.

"Did she?" Des, typically rumpled in army green pants and a dark orange shirt, studied Franz from under his tangle of curls, a deceptively pleasant smile curving his lips. "Well, I'm fine now, thank you."

"Dangerous days," Richard said in a theatrical tone. "No light of truth shines in Midnight." He frowned. "You have to wonder where Anna could have gotten to. Oh well, I'm sure she'll turn up eventually. Drink, Reggie? Rowen?"

Des, like a good boy, shook his head, while Rowen went to perch on the arm of his chair. Giving his arm a tap, she indicated the folded letters in her pocket. "I think I might have found something."

He nodded but offered no response as Darcy dragged himself into the room.

His thin face was lined with worry. "Oh God," he moaned. "What if he killed my Anna?"

Franz snorted and poured a large brandy. "Why would God want to kill Anna? He might want Reggie's head on a platter, but..."

"I don't think Darcy meant that God killed her," Rowen said, not especially impressed by Franz's glib attitude. "I imagine he was referring to the person who murdered Harold."

"Either that or Blackstone's ghost," Richard said from behind the bar.

Like Franz, his lack of concern seemed rather heartless to Rowen, but then who was she to judge? Richard had never made a pretense of caring for Anna. Maybe he felt a display of emotion would be hypocritical.

The giggle that erupted from the corner made her skin crawl. "I think Blackstone took her," Cooper said softly. "Don't you, Reggie?"

Des sent Rowen an eloquent look. "Why would Jonah Blackstone kill her, Cooper?" he countered evenly. "I thought he wanted me."

Cooper's smile had a cunning edge to it. "Maybe he's holding her for ransom."

"Ransom!" Darcy groaned, burying his head in his hands. "I hadn't thought of that. What if she's been kidnapped? I don't have any money. How could I pay?"

"Oh, I'm sure Cousin Reggie would pay a ransom for you," Richard said in a sly voice.

Rowen leaned against the wall. "The thread of another possible scheme is added to an already complicated web," she murmured to Des.

"Fake a kidnapping in order to get money out of me?" He gave his head an imperceptible shake. "As Reggie I'm not that soft a touch."

"True." She glanced up, a movement in the corner catching her eye. "Why are you plucking your sleeve, Cooper?" she asked.

He stopped instantly, his fingers still pinching the shiny gabardine of his black jacket. "No reason." He blinked. "Where's Almira?"

"Who cares?" Richard drained his glass of sherry and poured another. "Darcy, stop moaning and try to think."

"I am thinking," Darcy said miserably. "It's all I've been doing all night."

So had Rowen, although her thoughts hadn't been centered on Anna. She slid her eyes to Des, resisting a sudden impulse to run her fingers through his tousled hair.

"It's been one awful thing after another for us," Darcy went on. "Anna's mother died last June, and her grandmother before that. A close friend of ours was killed in a bus crash eighteen months ago, Anna's best friend died in a fire, two of our dogs had to be put down..."

Franz cut him off with a sour, "We get the picture, Darcy." His pouchy eyes glittered with malice. "Of course, I'd help you look if I could, but this weather's murder on my spinal injury."

How tactful of him to put it that way, Rowen reflected. Standing and walking over to Darcy, she patted him on the back. "It'll be all right," she promised. "No one has any reason to hurt her."

He raised his head. "That's a point. Even Blackstone wouldn't harm an innocent bystander."

Another giggle issued from the corner. "Don't be too sure, Darcy," Cooper said, grinning like a spooky court jester. "I think Blackstone would go after anyone who posed even the slightest threat to the fulfillment of his curse."

"I DON'T WANT to talk about Cooper," Des declared twenty minutes later as he and Rowen walked across the foggy estate grounds. "Tell me about your discovery instead."

"Don't be rude," she retorted, "and stop walking so fast. I can't keep up."

He glanced at her short black skirt and matching lace-up high-heeled shoes that were not meant for hiking, and smiled. "All right. I did drag you out here, didn't I? Do you want to go back?"

"No, I want to know why you dragged me out here."

"To talk."

"In the fog? With a murderer running around and full darkness only fifteen minutes away?"

"More like fifty," he said. "Besides, we're safe enough in this weather. You can't aim at a target you can't see, and we're nowhere near the water."

The air smelled of pine and burning leaves, not a trace of brine. Even so, the tendrils of moist, clammy air that flowed over Rowen's face brought a shiver to her skin. She buttoned her jacket all the way up and shoved her hands into her pockets. "You may be right," she agreed. "But I still think we should have stayed with the others. They were drinking. Who knows what one of them might have accidentally said."

"Unless the murderer happens to be Lester, Almira or Poole. None of them were there."

"True. Well, to answer your earlier question, my discovery has to do with the carbon copy of that partial letter I found in Harold's study." She pulled the wrinkled paper from her pocket as they passed the mist-shrouded marble pool. "I don't know who it was written to, but it's signed, H.F., which I think is how Harold used to sign his personal correspondence."

"So it's a personal letter." Des squinted at the badly smudged carbon. "I can't read this."

"You can read parts of it," Rowen contradicted patiently. She indicated two blurred words.

Des held the letter at arm's length, then brought it closer. "'Insurance—freak'?"

"Or 'fraud,'" Rowen suggested over his shoulder. But that was just a little too close for her peace of mind. Deliberately, she stepped back. "I think he's talking about insurance fraud, Des. Then a couple of lines farther down, he says 'can't—something—murder.'"

"Looks like 'condemn.'"

"Or 'condone'? And that word at the top looks like 'payment.' Right below it is the word 'fire.'"

"Or 'fine.'"

"Well, maybe. But over here he's written, 'drastic solution' and 'divorce.'"

Des furrowed his brow. "'Divorce' or 'diverse,' Rowen. I think you might be stretching a few of these smudges to suit your own purpose.'

Careful to keep a discreet distance between them, she fixed her gaze on the trees, ghostly outlines in the darkening fog. "It's possible," she admitted, taking the page back. "But I've been thinking about it. The only fire I know of was that one in Los Angeles three years ago, the one in which Grace Mitchell died."

"So?"

"So, her husband worked for the Forbes Corporation at the time. And we know he was in the building the night of the fire." At his blank look, she made an impatient sound.

"Well, don't you see? Val Mitchell could have been up to something with Harold."

"You mean, Harold paid Val to set the antique store on fire?"

At his skeptical tone, Rowen sighed, huddling deeper into her jacket rather than moving closer to Des as she would have preferred. "It's possible," she insisted. "The only glitch being that Harold didn't expect Grace to be inside. That might be what Harold meant when he wrote 'can't condone murder.' Val found Grace in the building that night and, believing that she was having an affair with Reggie, decided to kill her. Thus the phrase, 'drastic solution.'"

A smile Rowen didn't need to see split Des's face. "That's very good," he congratulated her. "Utter fantasy, but good."

Since she couldn't reasonably argue the fantasy angle, Rowen dipped her head and smiled back. "I try. Still, you have to admit, Val could have gone in and confronted Grace. No, wait." She caught his sleeve as another idea occurred to her. "Maybe he killed Grace, *then* set fire to the building." She paused, frowning. "Except that would be stupid, wouldn't it? Val checked in with security. If he'd been planning to set fire to the place all along, he would have snuck in, wouldn't he?"

"Unless he was a particularly stupid arsonist."

"Don't be smug," she warned, releasing his sleeve. "I'm trying to make some kind of sense out of all this."

Draping an arm that didn't feel entirely casual about her shoulders, Des leaned down to whisper a conspiratorial, "What about this then? Maybe Val Mitchell was supposed to go into the building that night and discover that the store had been robbed."

"When in fact certain items had only been moved?" Rowen smiled, but her mind was more focused on his arm around her than on his idea. "I suppose that would work," she agreed. She forced herself to concentrate. "Instead of a fake robbery, however," she theorized, "Val discovered his wife. He thought she was waiting for her lover, they fought and he killed her. He either accidentally or deliberately set fire to the building, then he panicked, ran out, drove home, threw a few things in a suitcase and disappeared.''

Amusement shimmered in Des's eyes, eyes that were regarding her at much too close a range. ''And here I thought you didn't want to complicate things by adding a phantom husband to the suspect list.''

''Well, it is only a theory,'' she reminded him. And a pretty wild one at that, her brain added. On the other hand, she wasn't thinking with her usual clarity right then. His fault entirely, of course. And yet... ''You know, it's funny,'' she mused, biting her lip. ''Something about that night has always bothered me. It's like I've overlooked an important detail.'' She shook her head, and this time forced herself to step out from under his arm. ''Oh, well. Don't forget, there's also Poole's motive to consider.''

Des made no move to recapture her. But he smiled, damn him. He knew. ''Revenge for a layoff from a shipbuilding company? It's not a bad motive.''

''He's also infirm. I don't know when that happened, but any kind of a construction job would probably be out of the question for him now. For all we know, he might blame his condition on Harold and Reggie. As for Almira, well, I went into the kitchen this afternoon and heard her talking.''

''So?''

''There wasn't anyone with her.''

''Really?'' Des grinned in delight. She wished he wouldn't do that. ''What was she saying?''

''Something about being tired of constantly having to pick up clothes from the bathroom floor. Then she got snappy and said, 'I'd appreciate it if you wouldn't tramp around in my kitchen with mud on your shoes', and finally, 'Please stop leaving bits of paper in your shirt pocket. It makes a mess in the dryer.' ''

''Odd,'' Des remarked, his expression thoughtful. ''Anything else?''

''Nope. She saw me and shut up. Where are we going?''

''Nowhere in particular. Why?''

The ground cover of bright leaves and pine needles had grown slippery underfoot. Rowen clutched Des's arm to avoid falling. "Because I think we're very close to the old Masque Factory."

"Are we?" He took her hand, steadying her. "We've walked a long way." He stopped suddenly and lifted his head. "There's a light."

"In the ruin?" Rowen caught her balance, squinting through the fog and encroaching darkness. "I don't... No, wait, you're right."

"Shh." Des covered her mouth. "Listen. Do you hear something?"

She stood absolutely still, then finally nodded. Actually, the sound was perfectly audible. If they hadn't been talking, she would have noticed it some time ago.

"It sounds like someone's searching through the rubble," she said, puzzled. "For what, though? The skull mask?"

Giving his head a faint shake, Des urged her forward.

Fallen leaves muffled the sound of their approach; the thickening fog obscured them from sight. They followed the glow to the doorway, then slipped quietly inside.

A kerosene lamp burned on one of the rotting wooden tables. Rowen had expected the banging to emanate from the empty room they'd discovered the other day, but instead it seemed to come from the back.

"Come on," Des said. He sounded like a kid playing explorer. "Let's see who it is."

They were almost three-quarters of the way to the rear wall when the noise ceased.

They moved even more quietly after that. Ahead of them a door creaked, followed by an ominous groan of decaying wood.

The last noise sounded like a floorboard to Rowen. Stopping, she caught Des's sleeve and gave it a warning tug. "It's too dangerous," she whispered.

Des nodded. "Stay here. I'll be right back."

"Idiot," she muttered. "That's not the answer I wanted."

He continued advancing. Which meant of course that she had to go after him. Des was the kind of person who let curiosity rule reason. Well, so did she, Rowen conceded, but at least she had the odd moment of rational thought. Like now for instance.

She proceeded, regardless, through the shadows of a disintegrating doorway to a room with a raised trapdoor. A set of stone steps led to the tunnels. The person making the noise must have gone down there. Rowen couldn't see any other way for him to have gotten out.

Taking a quick look down, Des began to descend. Rowen sighed and did the same.

It didn't look like a very secure passageway to her. The earth was damp and stony. She saw evidence of several minor cave-ins. But she'd been right, this was part of the tunnel system. Doubtless it would take them right back to the manor.

The air smelled musty, like mold and old dirt. She stayed close to Des, not making a sound. Where had the noise-maker gone? Was he halfway back to the manor by now?

A shiver ran up her spine. Her skin felt chilled all over.

Des reached back for her hand. "Look," he said, motioning with his head at a wall of earth, wood and rock directly in front of them.

She peered over his shoulder. The tunnel was completely blocked. "So where's that light coming from?" she wondered out loud.

They had no flashlights and yet they could see. Well, more or less. There were still a number of shadows.

She located a burning kerosene lamp in a niche behind a large stone. "I don't think I like this," she began, then snatched her head around as a loud rumble suddenly filled the tunnel.

"Des, look out!" she cried, hauling him sideways.

From above, a shower of earth and stone poured down. Together they stumbled backward, out of the deadly cascade. Rowen stared, terrified, her heart pumping in her chest.

The tunnel was collapsing in their wake, and there was nothing they could do to stop it. Nothing except stand and watch as their only route to the surface vanished.

COUGHING AT the dust thrown up by the falling earth, the man on the steps inspected his clever trap.

They'd never be able to dig their way out, not without tools and a lot more time than they would have. The air wouldn't last long in there. Not that either of them would panic, but human beings must breathe, it was a physical law.

Waving at the dust, he checked his watch. He estimated at most three or four hours of air available to them.

So there it was, his problems neatly solved. Reggie Forbes would be discovered dead—if he was discovered at all, that is—gone to join old Harold in hell.

With a satisfied nod, the man brushed off his gloved hands and started up the steps. Sheer bad luck had intervened on the cliffs last night. This was a better way, well-rounded and complete. Not even a snake could wriggle out of this one.

He let the trapdoor fall closed. Halloween was going to be the best day of his life. His new, completely revitalized life.

He let his laughter ring out in the darkened ruin. Maybe to honor the ghost, he should change his name to Jonah Blackstone.

Chapter Thirteen

Rowen wasn't talking, wasn't moving, scarcely seemed to be breathing at this point. With his back pressed against the wall, Des pulled her closer, setting her head gently on his shoulder and hooking his leg over hers. He kept his arms wrapped around her rib cage, wanting to feel her heart beat, needing to feel it.

"How long has it been?" she asked softly, surprising him.

He turned his face into her hair, loving the scent of it. "Almost three hours."

She looked down. "Your hands are a mess."

"So are yours."

"Well, my gloves are, anyway." She rested her head against his shoulder. Her eyes rose to the ceiling. "The lamp's almost out. There's not much air left, is there? We didn't get anywhere with our digging, I can't think straight anymore, and even in those moments when I can, I wind up thinking about you."

His lips curved on her temple. "Maybe you're confusing me with Reggie."

"Not possible. You're completely different animals. Reggie's a charming rat. You're a big, sexy wolf. You have the cunning of a fox, and the reflexes and curiosity of a cat. Not to mention the nine lives," she added with a trace of sarcasm. "By contrast, whoever made the tunnel collapse is a vicious, cold-blooded snake. Cooper was right. The murderer would have killed everyone in the house just to get you. He probably killed Anna, too."

Des gave her a squeeze. "Stop being so morbid. We're not dead yet, and we have no idea what happened to Anna."

"Stop being so morbid, he says," Rowen echoed with a sigh. "I'll bet you've been in a hundred situations just like this, haven't you? Life on the edge and all that." She turned to face him. Her mouth was only a few inches from his. All he had to do was lower his head.

He did it slowly, a faint smile touching his lips. This hesitation was unlike him, and Rowen was more than capable of pushing him away even in her weakened state.

That she didn't push or even object surprised him slightly. Her mouth moved softly, almost inquisitively over his, as if she was afraid of missing something. A last kiss, maybe?

Sliding a hand around her neck, he urged her closer, heard her moan gently in her throat and closed his eyes. Regret washed through him as he raised his head to look at her.

She had a dreamy expression on her face. "That felt like a goodbye kiss to me, Des."

"Did it? I must be losing my touch."

"You have a very weird sense of humor," she said in a hazy tone. As she turned back around, her body shifted between his legs, her backside rubbing him in exactly the right—or rather the wrong—spot. He hissed back a tight breath against an exquisite stab of pain. Suffocation might be bearable if he could make love to Rowen first.

Ah, but they weren't going to suffocate, he reminded himself, weren't going to die, not just like that. It was too ignominious a fate for either of them.

"Ignominious and peaceful," Rowen added.

Des rubbed his forehead against her shoulder. "Was I talking out loud?"

"A little. But this isn't awful, you know."

"I beg your pardon?"

"Suffocation. It isn't an awful death."

"At the risk of sounding like an alarmist, aren't you taking this rather calmly?" he said into her jacket.

She pulled her legs up, wrapping her arms around her knees. "When I was nine years old, my brother Lance and I went on a Y-organized camping trip to the San Juans. My idiot brother took a dare from another boy—you know, to see who had enough nerve to ditch the counselor during a hike and return to camp last. Unfortunately, my brother had absolutely no nerve, so he dragged me along with him. We might have been okay except that a hornet chased him, which meant that I had to chase my brother, and we wound up lost. It got late and eventually started to rain, one of those big summer thunderstorms. We found a cave and hid in it, but Lance got panicky. He was sure we were going to die.''

"How old was he?" Des asked.

"Thirteen."

"And you were nine."

She nodded. "Anyway, after a few hours of listening to his hysterics, I got scared, too, so scared that when he shoved me out of the cave and told me I had to get our gear, I panicked myself. But I knew I couldn't let him see it, because he would have gotten even worse. So I hid my fear, went out into the storm, found our stuff and came back. Now every time I hear thunder, I remember that night. And every time I get scared, I keep it inside and pretend to be calm."

Des felt a twist of emotion in his stomach followed by a full-blown feeling of anger for her brother. Hugging her from behind, he murmured, "Poor Rowen. All of that, and now this."

"I walked into this, Des," she said, relaxing against him. He accepted it for the token of trust it was and tightened his arms around her. "It's funny," she continued, "but I always wanted to be a private detective, the Richard Diamond–Sam Spade type, with a cluttered office in a broken-down part of town." She stopped talking and lifted her head. "What's that noise? It sounds like tapping."

It sounded like scraping to Des. He listened for several long seconds, then gave her a gentle push. "It's coming from the other side of the cave-in."

She didn't need any urging. Unfortunately, movement required an effort now. Des's body felt lead-weighted. He was cold, too, bitterly cold, and tired.

Dropping to her knees in front of the wall, Rowen threw a loose stone at it. "Is anyone there?" she called.

"Rowen?" Richard's voice came to them, badly muffled. The scraping proceeded with renewed vigor. "Reggie? Are you both there?"

"Yes," Des answered. He wedged out another rock with the last of his depleted strength.

"They're alive," he heard Richard shout.

Poole added a relieved, "Tell Almira to call the doctor."

It took almost twenty minutes for the first shovel to break through. "That's done it," Lester's unemotional voice declared.

Richard's face, dirt-streaked and cheerful, appeared at the hole. "You still with us?"

"Barely," Des said.

"Right. Well, we'll have you out in a jiffy. Dig right here, Lester. They only need to be able to crawl out." He glanced back. "Ah, good. Here's Poole with blankets and hot coffee. That'll do the trick. Careful, Lester, that ceiling's not exactly stable."

Five minutes later, they were on the other side.

"Thank you," Des said simply.

"Thank Poole," Lester retorted, jamming his shovel into a pile of loose dirt. "He was burning leaves by the crypt and saw you come in here."

"The ruin's a dangerous place," Poole said in a subdued voice.

"As I think I mentioned before," Lester added, glaring at Des. "Are you all right?" he asked Rowen.

"Fine. Thank you, Poole, and all of you. We were almost out of air."

"I heard a noise," Poole explained as he gathered up the shovels. "The dust was still billowing when I came in."

"Did you see anyone leave?" Des asked him.

Poole frowned, then looked at his feet. "I'm not sure."

Des left it to Rowen to press, "What did you see, Poole?" She touched his arm. "Was it a man?"

He wouldn't look up. "I don't know. I thought it was someone. But he was there and gone so quickly I couldn't tell. It was like . . ."

"Like what?" Richard prompted, serious for once.

Poole's shoulders hunched. "It was like he disappeared. Like he was never there." He raised uncertain eyes to the circle of faces around him. "Almost like he was a ghost."

THANK GOD FOR the diversion of Midnight's Halloween street party, Rowen decided. It took her mind off death and ghosts and curses and the horror that had been seeping into her bones ever since her arrival in the small New England community.

It didn't take her mind off Des but then she had a feeling nothing would do that. Not even a belated phone call to Reggie the night after the cave-in.

Heavy rain played havoc with the Midnight phone system. After a number of clicks and pauses, however, she finally got through to his Boston apartment.

"What do you mean, Anna's disappeared?" he demanded. "People don't just vanish. She probably ditched Darcy for someone better."

Disgusted, Rowen stared at the receiver. "You really are a bastard, Reggie, you know that, don't you?"

His chuckle reached her across the static-filled line. "A wealthy bastard, Rowen. Has Pettiston been able to cut any red tape yet to try to push the old man's will's through?"

Rowen sighed and explained about the lawyer's "accident."

"In other words, the answer is no," Reggie translated flatly. "Damned nuisance, I knew this would all screw up the minute I lost my lucky rabbit's foot."

Surely he meant his rat's foot. Rowen managed a sweet "Des is fine if you're interested. No thanks to whoever killed Harold, but so far, you're still alive."

"You needn't sound so disapproving," Reggie retorted "It isn't like you. Besides, you knew what you were getting into when you went to Midnight."

"Yes, I did," she agreed. "Would you like a progress report, or would you rather I waited until the will's been read?"

"You're sounding hostile again."

"Must be a bad connection."

"What's gotten into you, Rowen?" His tone was laced with impatience. "Is it Des? Is he driving you crazy? He isn't messing up, is he? Smoking, drinking..."

"Letting black cats walk in front of him."

"What!"

"Nothing. I was going to ask you to erase him, so to speak, from the family history, but now that Anna's gone missing, there's not much danger of anyone discovering his identity."

"That bastard's going to jinx me," Reggie muttered. "I can feel it. For God's sake, Rowen, don't let him break any mirrors."

"You mean like Darcy did when you were kids? You're really not very popular around here, Reggie. If I were you, I'd work on that. Unless of course you feel that inheriting Harold's money will buy you respect."

His chuckle had a bitter edge despite the increasing static. "It bought you, my dear," he said softly.

Rowen gritted her teeth but didn't snap at him or deny a thing. Self-delusion was not part of her character, and real or not, she knew the impression she'd given.

She felt depressed when she hung up, another aspect of her character that seldom surfaced. It must be all the near brushes with death. It couldn't have anything to do with Des—could it?

She avoided that question over the next few blessedly attack-free days, concentrating instead on watching Almira and Cooper, her two top suspects, and Franz, a lesser one. It helped enormously that Des was busy with Lester and the impending reopening of the Masque Factory.

It didn't help to learn that on the evening of the cave-in, the gathering in the drawing room had broken up moments after she and Des left the house. That meant the person who'd collapsed the tunnel could have been any of them. Again.

The morning of the street party dawned cool and misty with the smell of wood smoke thick in the air. There was still no word from the police concerning Anna, and nothing of startling significance to be learned from deciphering Jonah Blackstone's letter.

"Except he sounded like a maniac," she mumbled under her breath as she pushed through the kitchen door.

She'd come looking for food. What she found was Almira having another conversation with no one while she laced up her oversize oxfords. Rowen caught the words, ". . . came here and ruined everything," before the housekeeper raised her head and spied her in the doorway.

"Am I interrupting?" she asked, not moving.

Almira's foot hit the floor with a thud. She wore her usual vampire makeup and red lipstick, a long black dress and a black wool jacket that was miles too big for her.

"What do you want?" she said coldly.

Rowen held her ground on the threshold. "A piece of bread."

"Help yourself. I have more pies to bake for the collation."

"Have our costumes been sent over from the Masque Factory yet?" Rowen asked, giving her a wide berth.

Richard strolled through the back door in time to hear the question. "They're in the great hall, love," he said. "Ah, bread. Mind if I make cinnamon toast, Almira?" He didn't wait for an answer, simply turned to grin at Rowen. "Reggie at the factory again?"

A light giggle warned her of Cooper's arrival. She moved toward the table, nodding. "How's Darcy doing?"

"Bearing up. He thinks it's rotten of us to go out celebrating the autumn harvest, or whatever Halloween's all about, with Anna missing, but I say, why sit around and brood? Who knows, maybe we'll pick up a valuable lead on the streets."

"I think the witches have her." Cooper, a garment bag slung over his shoulder, was a statue in the shadowy doorway. The slits of his eyes traveled to Rowen's face. "Don't you?"

She shook her head silently, watching him.

"Well, if they do—" Richard sprinkled cinnamon sugar on a piece of buttered bread "—they'll probably be holding her at Blackstone's old house. They say that evil is drawn to that place like a magnet." His eyes sparkled. "In which case, I'm surprised Reggie isn't stuck to the walls, although

I don't suppose Blackstone would be too happy about finding him there, seeing as Reggie's one of the cursees, so to speak.''

Cooper knelt on the stone hearth and began playing with a piece of scorched wood. When he set the garment bag down, Rowen noticed the label: Midnight Tailor Shop.

''What's that?'' she asked him.

He touched it almost reverently. ''It's for tonight. Very elegant.'' He offered her an artless sideways look. ''Does Reggie believe in Blackstone's ghost?''

She started for the door with her slice of bread. ''Not enough to believe that it could cause a tunnel roof to collapse. That would require a human touch, don't you think?''

''Maybe it would,'' Cooper said, his strong fingers tightening on the blackened wood. The resulting snap echoed sharply through the kitchen, bringing a chill to Rowen's skin. His slitty eyes came up, shining eerily in the muted light. ''But did it ever occur to you, pretty lady, that Blackstone's ghost might have taken possession of one of us?''

DES LIKED his costume, a bearded pirate with a long black cape, black boots and an eye patch. He liked Rowen's even better, Oliver Twist in tight knee breeches, ankle boots, a hunter green pea jacket and a green cap. She looked delicious, especially with the added touch of soot smudges across her cheeks.

''I don't see how people can wear those horrible head masks,'' she said as they wandered toward the crowded village green. ''Maybe that's why the Masque Factory decided to get into making costumes, too.''

He shook his hair from his face. ''Let's not talk about the Masque Factory, okay? It's all I've heard for three straight days.''

''Would you rather talk about Blackstone's letter? I wrote it all out. You were right about the mirror by the way. It was written backward, and beautifully penned at that.''

Des glanced at the costumed people converging on the green. A curtain of mist drifted down the streets, but it was a light coating. On the bandstand, a local group played

"The Monster Mash." There were orange-and-black stalls everywhere he looked, and of course the usual assortment of ghosts, goblins, witches and vampires. It was a typical Halloween scene, harmless enough if you didn't happen to notice the stark lines of the coven house, or the forty-plus figures standing outside it, looking on in silence.

"They're going to have a séance to contact Blackstone's ghost," Rowen said, following Des's gaze. "I wonder if we could sneak in."

"We could try."

She grinned. "I wasn't serious. Here." She tapped his arm. "Read the letter."

Des halted under a mist-shrouded lamp, skimming the copied version of the curse.

I, Jonah Blackstone, reveal herein that I have known of your plot to murder me for some time. You have no conception of what you do. You have no conception of me. Dark powers stir at my command. My soul will not rest until justice has been meted out, justice as I deem it and for such a period of time as I see fit. You will pay for your acts of treachery, you and all of your descendants whose names shall ever appear on the documents of ownership at the Masque Factory. I look forward to your deaths, my partners, your most violent and brutal deaths. For none of you will die quickly or without great pain. These things I promise you . . .

Rowen peered over his shoulder. "Cheery, huh? And do you know that in spite of getting soaked, the ink was hardly smudged at all?"

"Indelible?"

"Apparently. He wanted that letter to last." She nodded ahead of them at one of the homestyle food stands. "There's Franz. I think he's supposed to be an inquisitor. Darcy refused to leave the manor, but Richard's coming as Jack the Ripper and I saw Almira earlier, dressed as Vampira."

"Naturally."

"Poole is Mr. Hyde. Cooper wouldn't tell anyone what his costume was, but I saw his garment bag today. There was something black in it, so I figure he'll either be Jonah Blackstone or a giant spider. Or maybe a combination of the two. I'm not sure about Lester."

"Longshoreman."

She wrinkled her nose. "That's not very original."

"He doesn't strike me as an original person."

"No, I suppose not." She looked around. "You know this is awfully wholesome stuff, unless you count the massing witches at the coven house, and even they're only standing around looking evil. Why don't we go down to the docks? Richard says there's a lot of atmosphere down there."

"And privacy?" Des suggested. He'd moved up behind her. Now he set his hands on her arms, and his lips against her cap.

It was a deliberate tease, but for one deliciously enticing moment, she swayed against him, her backside pressing into his lower body. Then she caught herself and pulled away. "No," she protested, albeit in a vaguely breathless voice. She wasn't quite able to face him, he noticed with more frustration than humor. "I can't—I won't—I don't want to get any more involved with you than I already am, Des. I told you that before. We're two different people." She sounded angry, defiant, on the verge of desperation. "It almost chokes you to put on a tie, and I swear you're allergic to silk."

"Which you like," he said softly.

"No—yes." She held up her hand when he would have pursued her indecision. "No, don't. You're making me crazy and that's the last thing I want. I go out with men like Reggie because they're easy for me to deal with."

"Men *like* Reggie, Rowen?"

"Stop it, Des."

"Do you love him?"

She opened her mouth to answer, then closed it again. "Well, it's not as if I'm using him," she defended herself. Her head came up. "I like to do different things. My ideas intrigue him. And it's no hardship jetting off to Monte

Carlo for a party on the company yacht. It's a failing of mine, I enjoy moments of extravagance.''

"Sables and diamonds, too?"

Turning, she started for the docks. "No, not fur. I love animals. And I don't care for diamonds. I just want to do what I want to do, and I don't want to have to explain it to anyone.''

"So why are you explaining it to me?"

She spun around. "Because I think I'm falling..." Clamping her mouth shut, she let her eyes stray to the overflowing village green. An acrobat and two ghosts brushed past them. "Never mind," she said finally. "Let's just say it would be wrong for us to be involved. There's too much danger here, anyway. One lapse, Des, and you could wind up dead." She raised her eyes to his. "I don't want anything to happen to you."

It wasn't the admission he wanted from her; nevertheless, Des let the subject slide. Being in love didn't suit him any more than it suited her. The prospect of settling down made him restless. To stay in one place—no, he couldn't do that. And to work at one job...

He shuddered, bridging the gap between them. "All right," he agreed. "You win." On impulse, he reached out, trapping her chin between his thumb and fingers and setting his lips on hers. "For the moment."

THE FOG ON the Midnight docks disturbed the man who was concealed in the shadows behind the Ancient Mariner. He slipped one costume over another—just in case—placed a mask on his head and temporarily tucked another inside his pocket.

The people down here were a different breed from those congregating in the common. There were no families on the docks. These were the serious Halloween celebrants, floating around in the mist, performing all sorts of arcane rituals, dancing to weird music and generally making his skin crawl. Even their laughter disrupted his senses. It was too unrestrained, the feeling too offbeat and grotesque for his taste.

He wasn't sure why, since he was the danger and they were simply revelers, but it was. He'd seen their type before, smoking God-knew-what, and drinking too much wine at dimly lighted outdoor restaurants. These particular people happened to be talking about Blackstone's curse, but it was the same wherever you went.

Clinging to the shadows, he joined the flow of the passing crowd. The Midnight witches would hold the first of three Halloween séances tonight. He'd heard them from the cellar when he'd stopped at the coven house. They'd been chanting like zombies, willing Blackstone back over. Creepy heathens, why couldn't they turn their minds to his cause instead?

It upset him to think about his failure in the tunnel. That meddlesome idiot Poole had had no business interfering. Why did fate always have to favor the wrong side?

The man sighed, then tensed again as he spotted his victims. Bored with the fun and games already, were they? It didn't surprise him. Bobbing for apples was hardly their style.

A chance, he thought, his hand caressing the dagger under his robe. That's all he needed. A quick thrust and it would be done.

"Come on, Blackstone," he whispered to the misty night air. "Help me put an end to your curse. And to mine."

Chapter Fourteen

The alley behind the shadowy dockside shops bore a strik-ing resemblance to the silent werewolf movie Rowen had watched in bed last night. Damp, foggy and dark. She sa-vored the delicious shiver that swept through her as she tried to pinpoint the source of the ghastly music barely audible from here.

"It's like stepping into a world of evil spirits," she said to Des, who hadn't really spoken since they'd left the main streets. "I love it, but something tells me it's not smart for us to be roaming around alone in dark alleys."

Des glanced behind them. "We weren't alone thirty sec-onds ago. Where did everyone go?"

"Maybe the fog absorbed them." She didn't object when he took the opportunity to light a cigarette. "You've been waiting to do that all night, haven't you?"

He inhaled deeply, dropping his head back in a gesture of pure enjoyment. "Yes."

"Now I suppose you'll want a drink."

"Love one." His eyes sparkled. "Are the bars open?"

"I don't think so, but some of the smaller cafés are." She caught a movement in her peripheral vision, looked around, then did a startled double take. "Des, it's someone wearing a skull mask!"

His reaction was instantaneous. "He's seen us." Grip-ping her shoulders, he held her in place when she would have followed him. "Forget heroics, Rowen. I'll go after our masked friend, you get a policeman. There should be one down by the water."

He was gone before Rowen could protest or even warn him to be careful. For a moment, she stared into the fog where both he and the person in the skull mask had vanished. Then she shook herself. Find a policeman.

Running in breeches and ankle boots was easy. Knowing which direction to run proved difficult. The docks creaked all around her, a sound distorted by fog and the distant sound of laughter. The combination swirled around her head, bringing to mind a vision of partying ghosts.

Rowen paused to get her bearings. Where was the laughter coming from? To her right, she decided, and started toward it.

Tendrils of mist, like disembodied arms, enfolded her. She heard the music again, some kind of flute weaving a mysterious spell in the night.

A foreboding shiver swept through her. There should be people here. But it seemed that everyone had vanished. She was alone among the blackened outlines of shops and stores, long since locked and shuttered for the night.

She refused to react in fear, even when she detected the faint sound of footsteps behind her. Des had gone after the murderer, all she had to do was reach the water.

The laughter grew louder, rising to an almost grotesque crescendo. She hesitated, then ducked around a corner, concentrating on the muffled footsteps. They weren't that close. She was overreacting.

Rubbing her clammy palms on the legs of her breeches, she started off again. The fog spread out before her, a shifting cloud of white. But suddenly there was motion inside that cloud, something dark and indefinite, moving across her path. A split second later, Rowen felt the steel hard clamp of fingers on her left wrist. A rough jerk brought her around until her spine was pressed against a man's flat, hard chest.

He didn't utter a sound; there was no need. The dagger that appeared below her chin said it all. Panicked, she used her free hand to push on his forearm with all her strength. In the same frantic motion, she twisted herself back around, bringing her knee up solidly into his groin.

His face was hidden by a voluminous hood. She heard the hiss of pain that issued from inside it and caught a glimpse of white skin and a long black beard. It wasn't the skull mask, but she had no doubt this was Harold's murderer.

Rowen kicked him again, hard. This time his grip on her slackened. The knife clattered across the dock. Wrenching her arm free, she spun and ran, toward the distorted babble of voices and the water that lapped against the pier.

He was chasing her, she heard his footsteps thundering along on the planks behind her.

Thoughts rushed blindly through her head. He was wearing a mask with a beard, and a black robe with some other black garment underneath it. There'd been something white hanging out of his pocket. The skull mask . . . ?

She hadn't received a true impression of height, but the aura of menace had been unmistakable. This man was pure, twisted evil. And he was after her.

Determination and blind instinct carried her forward. He'd drawn to within twenty yards of her, and he was still gaining. She began weaving a path through the shops and adjoining docks, but never lost track of the water.

Her breath came in painful spasms, her mouth was dry with terror. She raced around a small antique store only to find herself facing an obstacle course of rope, wood and glass.

It was déjà vu, almost exactly like the scene she'd witnessed the night of the Los Angeles fire, except it wasn't Val Mitchell dodging ladders and knocking over paint cans—it was her.

She glanced back only once, relieved to discover that she'd gained ground. The man behind her tripped on a coil of rope, stumbled into a ladder, and was badly off-balance by the time he staggered around it.

He seemed shaken for a moment, but it was a short reprieve. Kicking aside an empty can, he started after her again.

Rowen ran on, plunging through the deepening fog. Footsteps mingled with the laughter ahead of her. The voices grew louder. She glimpsed movement, a sea of black shapes that finally resolved themselves into humans. "Thank

God,'' she breathed, and stumbled, panting, into a crush of costumed bodies.

The people danced rather than walked along, but Rowen didn't care. The ceaseless wave rolled ever-forward, picking up more and more celebrants as it went. Rowen stayed right in the center of it. Only then did she dare risk another look at the man behind her.

He stood near one of the shops, watching her through the eyes of his bearded head mask. Then very slowly, the fog closed in, until nothing remained of him but a sinister memory.

Rowen stuck with the group. Witches and vampires and even a couple of Lizzie Bordens surrounded her. But all she could think about was that mask, those thin, pallid features and that long black beard. It was the face of Jonah Blackstone, the face of a ghost. And it seemed that ''ghost'' wanted her dead.

DES LOST SIGHT of the skull mask almost instantly. That meant either the killer wasn't after him tonight, or he had something in mind that didn't include having his victim follow him.

It took him a full thirty minutes to locate Rowen. She was sitting at a café table with a large group of people, none of whom he recognized. When she saw him, she jumped up and ran to him, then surprised him totally by throwing her arms around his neck.

''You didn't catch him, did you?'' she said, her face buried in his shoulder.

She was trembling, a bad sign. Des's senses, already alert, grew edgy.

''What happened?'' he asked, fitting her securely against his body.

She raised her head. ''He came after me with a knife,'' she said with a barely controlled tremor. ''He was wearing a black robe and a Jonah Blackstone head mask, but I think he had the skull mask in his pocket. I managed to lose him in this crowd of people. And for your information, Desmond Jones, there isn't a single cop to be found on the waterfront.''

But there were, unfortunately, three familiar faces headed in their direction.

Richard, in a curly brown wig and deerstalker cap, raised a hand in greeting. "Didn't I tell you there was atmosphere down here?" He worked his way toward them. "I've just been to an impromptu convening."

Rowen recovered her composure sufficiently to turn in Des's arms, although he noticed she didn't step away. "What's a convening?" she asked.

"Like a séance, only more pagan."

The music around them swelled slightly. Couples had risen from the tables to dance in the fog. It was a haunting spectacle—sleek, gyrating bodies topped with monstrous faces performing pantomime play scenes. Des spied Franz the Inquisitor rolling purposefully through their numbers. He was being pushed by Poole in his Mr. Hyde costume.

The gardener cum butler appeared to be having difficulty walking tonight, not that Franz cared. He glowered at Des through pouchy, accusing eyes. "You should be the one wheeling me around, Reggie," he snapped. "I'm tired of wheeling myself, and Poole's too damned slow."

"So you haven't been together long then," Des assumed.

Poole shook his head. "Only for a few minutes. I've been looking for Almira. She seems to have disappeared."

"Another vanishing lady." Grinning, Richard set his pale Ripper mask down and began dancing with two sylvan ghosts in white bodysuits, hoods and face paint.

Des glanced down at Rowen. Her eyes were focused on a wooden bridge above the café. She hadn't even acknowledged Franz.

"Last I saw of Lady Death," Richard continued, "she was being told off by some brave street monitor." His grin widened. "It seems she was caught going into a men's washroom."

Des digested that information, then shifted his attention to Franz who was still glaring at him from behind his black inquisitor's beard. He probably would have offered some humorously irritating remark if Rowen's elbow hadn't suddenly rammed backward into his stomach.

"It *is* her," she whispered. Then she straightened and said to the three men in front of them, "Excuse us, will you?"

Des allowed her to drag him away from the café, past a group of black-robed witches and up a flight of wooden stairs to the bridge, before his curiosity prompted him to ask, "Where are we going?"

She pointed to a man hurrying along the bridge, then started to run. "Come on."

Whoever this mystery man was, he didn't like being followed. He darted down the stairs, managing to conceal himself in the fog and shadows before Rowen and Des could reach the bottom.

Hollow strains of woodwind music wafted through a night that smelled strongly of seaweed, salt and burning incense.

"Who was it?" Des asked as Rowen combed the darkness.

"I think," she said slowly, "it was Almira."

"What?"

"Well, don't you see? She came here dressed as Vampira. Now she's wearing a man's suit and hat." Rowen arched a meaningful eyebrow at him. "When did she change, Des? And why?"

THE PARTY, especially on the docks, seemed destined to go on for hours. But as far as Rowen was concerned, a macabre air now overshadowed the revelry. She felt it inside, like a swirl of darkness drifting in behind the light.

Someone had dressed up as Jonah Blackstone tonight. And while that wasn't as strict a taboo as the wearing of the skull mask, according to Richard, it seldom happened.

Franz and Poole were gone by the time she and Des returned to the café. Unfortunately, Lester was just arriving. In his longshoreman's outfit with a knit cap on his head and greasy streaks across his cheeks and forehead, he looked anything but friendly.

"Let's go, Rowen," Des suggested. "We can take the Land Rover back to the manor. There are plenty of other cars for the rest of them."

Rowen hesitated, torn. They really should search some more for Almira. On the other hand, the murderer was still out there, disguised as God-knew-what by now. They'd be safer at the manor. And if she wanted to, she could always catch the housekeeper when she returned.

"I haven't seen Cooper once tonight," Rowen remarked as they trailed a group of Puritans along the foggy pier toward Cemetery Road where the Land Rover was parked. "You'd think he'd have popped up sometime, wouldn't you?"

Des lit a cigarette, smiling faintly. "Maybe he did."

That ironic tone from anyone else would have brought a sharp retort to her lips. But Rowen knew that dark humor was simply Des's way of keeping a clear head. And she had to admit, it tended to calm her during those moments when fear threatened to rush in.

"I suppose it could have been Cooper who attacked me," she agreed uncertainly. "He wouldn't tell anyone what his costume was. Then again, it could have been one of the others, Darcy included. He's had plenty of time to get to town since we left the house."

They walked in silence for a time. Rowen noticed that one of the Puritans ahead of them had a cast on his foot. The resulting limp brought to mind thoughts of Jonah Blackstone. Aloud she mused, "Some people think Blackstone limped because of a wizard's spell he cast that failed and injured him. Others prefer the payment-to-the devil theory. Almost everyone agrees that he placed his earthly soul in the skull mask to ensure that his curse could be carried out. His malice was very specific, Des. So why did someone dressed as Jonah Blackstone try to kill me tonight?" She glimpsed a flash of metal out of the corner of her eye and sighed. "What are you doing?"

"Being a pirate," he said with a lazy smile. He handed her an uncapped silver flask. "It's just a little brandy. I think you can use it."

Rowen hesitated, then raised the flask to her lips and took a large swallow, just barely managing not to choke. "Thanks," she said, handing it back.

His smile deepened, emphasizing his cheekbones, but he made no comment. After finishing off the contents, he tucked the flask into his cape and squinted at the park just coming into view.

Two dozen or more fortune and storytelling tents had been set up on the broad expanse of lawn, and all of them were crowded with partyers. It was madness here, with blaring rock music and people singing as they danced on benches and behind trees.

The cemetery loomed in the distance, a more forbidding sight. Although Rowen couldn't see it through the mist, she knew there would be people keeping vigil at Blackstone's grave. So it seemed there were five main areas of Halloween communion. The park, the cemetery, the waterfront, the village green and the coven house. She wondered how the witches were doing.

"Maybe we should sneak into the séance," she said, glancing in the direction of the shadowy house.

Des put out his cigarette as they came to the park entrance. "Would Reggie do that?"

"No, but let's do it, anyway. At least we can peek through a window."

It didn't really surprise her that he relented. Curiosity was an insatiable hunger—and she'd be willing to bet it wasn't the only hunger Des possessed.

She couldn't let herself think about that, however, so she settled for dragging him to the coven house.

It was a daunting place at the best of times. At night, in the fog, the lines were even more austere, the area surrounding it doubly menacing. Careful not to rustle the bushes, they crept up to one of the narrow windows.

"Well?" Des asked when Rowen raised her head over the sill.

"They're sitting in six separate circles," she whispered back. "Chanting."

"In ancient Egyptian?" Des teased.

"Could be. They have candles burning, and there's a huge portrait of Jonah Blackstone on the wall. God, but he must have been a formidable man with that black beard and those silver eyes. I'm surprised William and Edmund would have crossed him."

"Any sign of his ghost?"

Rowen kicked him lightly, but she had to admit she was disappointed. She'd expected greater drama, or at least a more theatrical approach.

"Don't worry, it'll get more theatrical," Des said when she dropped down beside him in the bed of dirt beneath the sill. "By Halloween night, they'll be heavily into the ritual stuff."

She dusted off her breeches. "Do you want to go back..." she began, then broke off as one of Des's hands suddenly clamped itself across her mouth.

"Over there," he hissed in her ear. "That person's wearing a Blackstone mask, isn't he?"

He'd turned her head so she could see the mist-shrouded figure and the mask he wore. Rowen's heart began to race at the sight of it. Both the mask and the figure were cutting across the coven-house grounds.

It might have been an errant noisemaker that had him slowing his stride, or a sudden moan from inside the house. Whatever the case, he spotted them and froze. But only for a split second, then he was running, straight for the park and the myriad black tents.

Des was on his feet and gone before the man reached the street. Rowen was close on his heels. The masked figure bobbed and weaved, and finally plunged into the heart of the crowd. Rowen, hard-pressed to keep Des in sight, gambled and took a shortcut around the rear of the tents.

To her shock, the strategy worked all too well. She collided with the man full speed, slamming into his shoulder as he burst from the crowd.

With a startled snarl, he shoved her aside, but not before she wrapped her fingers around the sleeve of his robe.

As hard as he yanked on it, Rowen held fast, a stubborn, stupid thing to do, she knew, but there were witnesses everywhere, many of them turning now to watch the struggle.

"Over here!" In her peripheral vision she saw Des emerge from the crowd. Unfortunately, so did the man she was impeding—if in fact it was a man, she thought, recalling Almira and the black suit she'd been wearing on the docks. He twisted himself around, then wrenched his arms free of the encumbering sleeves and started running again, toward a high fence that bordered the woods.

Dropping the robe, she went after him. She might have abandoned all wisdom and followed him over the fence if he hadn't knocked down a pair of elderly women in his rush to get out of there. Rowen almost stepped on one of them but managed to jump over her at the last second.

"Are you all right?" she asked, going to her knees to help the smaller of the pair to a sitting position.

"Fine," the woman said shakily. "Who was that?"

Short of breath, Rowen shook her head. "I don't know."

A glance at the fence revealed that the man was long gone. And Des, who'd paused to help the second woman up, was heading back toward her.

"It's a bog out there," he told her once the women had recovered and were on their way. "By the time I got to the top of the fence, he was well into the trees. I found this, though." Crouching beside her, Des opened his hand.

Rowen fingered the torn piece of cloth in his palm. "Black velvet. From his jacket?"

Des nodded. "He caught his sleeve on a nail."

"It's good quality," she noted. "Like the one Richard was wearing the night Anna went missing."

He arched an eloquent eyebrow. "Or the bolt of velvet that Cooper stole?"

She nodded, her uneasiness mounting.

Tucking the swatch in his pocket, Des reached for her hand. "Let's get back to the manor and see who has or hasn't got a black velvet jacket in their room."

"THE ROBE HAS a Masque Factory label, Richard's velvet blazer is in his closet, so is yours, and Cooper's door is locked." Rowen leaned against the upstairs wall and sighed. "Not a very profitable search so far."

"We could break in," Des said, examining the lock.

"I'd rather not, if you don't mind. Cooper might not keep his bedroom bugs in jars. He might even be in there,

sitting in a corner like a demented bat waiting for some un-
suspecting animal to blunder into its cave.''

Des chuckled. "Well, we could always knock."

"We did knock. He didn't answer. Means nothing and
you know it." She took hold of his arm with both hands.
"Let's go through Almira's room instead. It's only midnight. She won't be back yet, and even if she is, we might get
a glimpse of the inside when she opens the door."

"And how do we tell which door is hers and which is
Poole's?"

"It doesn't matter. His room could stand a search, too.
He certainly has a motive for wanting Reggie and Harold
dead."

Des didn't resist as she maneuvered him down the stairs.
"What about his motive for wanting you dead?" he asked.

Rowen shrugged. "I admit he doesn't appear to have one.
But then nobody does really, aside from the fact that I'm
connected to you."

"It doesn't fit with Blackstone's curse, Rowen."

"I know." Pushing through the kitchen door, she took a
precautionary look around. "Almira? Are you here?"

When no one answered, she crossed to the light switch
and flipped it on. "It's not much better than a candle, is it?"
she said, shivering at all the lingering shadows. "Oh well. I
think the bedrooms are through here."

Her guess proved correct, although it wasn't actually
much of a guess. There were only four exits from the kitchen
and she already knew where three of them led.

Five bedrooms opened into a narrow, uncarpeted corridor. Three were unoccupied and the fourth, with the excep-
tion of a padlocked seaman's chest, held little of interest.

"Must be Poole's room," Des said, opening the closet.
"Butler's uniform, gardening overalls—ah, and a black
jacket."

"Velvet?"

"Wool."

Resting her elbows on the top of the dresser, Rowen sorted
through a wad of papers she'd discovered in the drawer.
"Bolton's Shipyard," she read aloud. "It's the employee

list, dated four years ago. This must be what Almira was talking about."

"Is Poole's name on it?"

"Well, there's a Poole here, but the initial is S, not T for Terrance."

Des shrugged. "Terrance might be his middle name. Desmond's mine."

"Really?" She shoved the papers back in the drawer, switching her attention to a Florentine box with no visible hinges. "What's your first name?"

"Not Desmond," was all he would say. "What are you doing?"

"It's a puzzle box," she said, turning it over. "Nineteenth century, Italian. A friend of mine gave me something similar on my twenty-first birthday. I never could get it open." She held the box up. "I wonder why Poole has something like this in his room. It's very valuable."

"So's the painting over the bed, Rowen, and the candelabra on the table. It probably all came with the room. There are antiques and portraits throughout the manor. Remember the Lalique bowl you found our first night here, and the Gwydon Byron in the study."

"And the fake painting you found in the great hall," she reminded him.

He made an uncertain motion, moving like a cat across the carpet. "All possibly combining to tell us something, but I'm not sure what. Do you want to try Almira's room?"

Yes and no, Rowen thought, glancing over covertly as he raked the loose curls from his forehead. He'd changed from the pirate costume to a pair of baggy black cords and a black shirt. The beard was gone, although it had suited him, and so was the eye patch. He was Des again, and as hard as she tried, she couldn't quite keep her mind off the bed in the corner, or the even bigger one in her own room.

"Bohemian," she reminded herself and straightened with a resolute motion that brought his knowing eyes to her face. He didn't press her, however. He simply waited for her to leave, then followed her wordlessly into the corridor.

Almira's bedroom door was unlocked. At first glance, her sleeping quarters looked Spartan, like a monk's cell, clean

and uncluttered. It wasn't until Rowen opened the close
that the first tendrils of unease began to curl through her.

"Men's clothes," she said, her eyes sweeping along th
rod. "Pants, jacket, shirts." She sniffed one of the shir
sleeves. "All freshly laundered. And only two dresses."

"Gilbert's things?" Des suggested from the oak bureau

"I guess so." She fingered the worn cuff, then let it drop
staring at it. "But he's been dead for a year now. Why is sh
keeping his clothes? More to the point, why do they sme
like fabric softener? And where are her things? There ar
only men's shoes on the floor."

"Almira wears men's shoes, you know that," Des sai
over his shoulder. He crouched to open the bottom drawe
"Interesting," he mused. "She also wears men's under
wear and socks by the look of it."

Rowen rubbed her arms, backing away from the closet
Her eyes climbed the gray papered walls. "So what then? I
this room some sort of shrine to her dead husband?"

Des gave his head a faint shake while Rowen sank ont
the bed. The discovery of Gilbert's clothes shouldn't dis
turb her. It was probably natural enough for a woman wh
loved her husband to keep his possessions after his death
But then she recalled seeing Almira on the docks dressed i
a man's suit, and she shivered.

The bedspread she sat on was patterned, red swirls on
black background, so Rowen didn't notice anything unu
sual at first. It wasn't until she set her hands down behin
her and leaned back that she felt the long strands of hai
beneath her fingers.

Startled, she sat up.

Des frowned. "What is it?"

For a long moment, Rowen simply stared. Then slowl
she reached out to pick the thing up. "It's a beard," sh
said, her stomach curling into a resistant knot. "A lon
black beard. Just like Jonah Blackstone's."

THE FOG FORMED an insidious shroud over Midnight Mano
and the Masque Factory. It spread filmy fingers throug
cemetery trees and headstones alike.

It was three a.m. and the street party was finally over. The murderer walked alone across the graves, head downbent, eyes trained on the leaf-strewn ground.

When a black mood descended, there was no fighting it. A letter might help, but it would have to be a mental one for now.

An imaginary paper and pen took shape in the murderer's mind. A seat on the damp mossy surface of Blackstone's grave, legs drawn up, eyes closed, and it was begun.

Dear Dr. Sayers,

Frustration and turmoil are my companions tonight. I thought it was all so clear; it usually is. But now the fog seems to have crept into my head. Death to Reggie, but not to Rowen. I never meant for her to die.

I want her with me, you see, not to stick a knife in her throat. Blackstone would have no reason to kill her. I have no reason to kill her. So why did what happened tonight happen?

Help me to understand, Doctor. Sometimes I feel strong, almost invincible. Then the smugness vanishes and the weariness crowds in. Your prescribed breathing exercises aren't working the way they used to. My mind's only clear about half the time now. I don't think anyone's seen through my disguise yet, but it only takes one small slip, doesn't it, one blunder and everything's gone.

Reggie would understand that. His life's been a tapestry of slips and blunders, all neatly covered up by Harold. Approve, disapprove, who knows how the old man felt about the only grandson he deemed worthwhile. One way or another, Reggie always came out on top.

Well, not this time, Doctor. I *do* have a plan, and this one *will* work—barring interference of course. I'll have to keep a sharp eye out for that.

I half wish Blackstone's ghost were here right now. I know what he'd say. 'Kill Reggie, but not Rowen.' I really must keep that straight in my mind. Maybe if I just go to bed and have a good long sleep, I'll be back to normal tomorrow.

Kill Reggie, I'll tell myself. Wreak Jonah Blackstone's revenge at the same time as I wreak my own.

Rest assured, dear Dr. Sayers,

A former patient

Chapter Fifteen

It was a nightmare, a distorted blend of past and present. Rowen awoke with a start to a cloud of fog outside her bedroom window. Frogs croaked in the woods, an owl hooted, the last of the autumn insects chirped in the darkness. But it was the hushed memory of terror that haunted her, like the wings of a giant bird flapping over her bed.

She sat perfectly still for a long time, willing her pounding heart to be calm. It took several minutes, but at last she could breathe again with something approaching normalcy.

Wrapping her arms around her upraised knees, she rested her forehead on top and tried to recall the dream. But it was cloudy, a blur of indistinct shadows.

Well, fine, she probably didn't want to remember, anyway.

Fully awake now, she allowed her mind to drift back over another very real memory. The man who'd attacked her tonight, the one who had chased her on the docks.

Raising her head, she rubbed her temple and concentrated on the image of the running man. But another image intruded, this one also of a running man, except that the second man hadn't been chasing her, he'd been escaping from a fiery building.

So why did she picture both men in the same thought?

The man running from the burning building had been nimble, she recalled, but something about the picture bothered her. Had he stopped? Yes, that was it. He'd halted suddenly as if he was surprised or startled. But why?

Rowen knit her forehead, wondering. The man chasin her tonight had stopped, too, or rather he'd paused, an wasn't that an odd coincidence?

A chill crawled along her spine. Was there a connectio between the two men? Did all of this go back to the fire i Los Angeles, to the man she'd seen running from the buri ing building? Was he the one who'd attacked her tonight No, that didn't make sense. Why would he wait so long t come after her?

With a sigh, she dropped her forehead onto her knee "Deductive reasoning," she mumbled into the quilt. "Bu how do you apply reason to a houseful of ghouls?"

Well, not quite a houseful, she had to admit. But if sh allowed herself to think about the one person who didn't f that description, she'd be in deep, deep trouble. So sh turned her mind to the others, instead.

She pictured a wheelchair with no occupant, then Frar with mud on his shoes. He wanted blood money, she knev and the prospect made her blood run cold.

And what of Almira dressed like a man, eluding them c the bridge tonight and telling Poole she knew about his s cret before that. "You're wrong, Almira," he'd replied. ' never worked in shipbuilding. There's no connection."

She pictured Cooper with his bug jar, Darcy wringing h hands over Anna's disappearance and Richard smiling, a ways so cheerful, with no apparent motive to kill anyone.

Lester was more of a background figure. A dark, broo ing silhouette, skulking about like a hungry wolf. On tl other hand, if Reggie died, Lester would inherit the Masqu Factory.

The whole thing felt malignant to Rowen. She shivere when she pictured Anna's face, bloodless, bloated for son reason. What did that mean? Was Anna dead?

A feeling of horror prevailed no matter how hard Rowe fought it. Horror and sickness and death. Ah, but Des cou take all of that away, couldn't he? She only had to think c him and the malevolence vanished.

Her sigh was gentle this time, more wistful. One thir Reggie had never understood was how to touch her. F didn't coax or tease, or smile, not the way Des did. It w

Des who had the exquisite cheekbones and the sensual mouth, Des whose eyes could rivet or laugh, Des who made her whole body ache from wanting him.

Of course, she might be fantasizing a bit about him. Des wanted to make love to her, she was pretty sure of that. But she doubted he was prepared to fall in love with her.

So what was she really frightened of? Rejection? That was silly—wasn't it? Being rejected by someone you didn't want couldn't hurt. She was safe with men like Reggie. She would never be safe with Des.

Her head came up at that dreadful thought. Safe? Good Lord, is that what she'd been doing all this time, locking her emotions away in a safe place?

Her eyes strayed to the door that connected her room with Des's. The shivering that had started up inside her began to subside as something much more demanding took its place, a hunger she longed to satisfy.

"Oh, Des," she sighed. "You aren't a safe place at all, but I want you."

Her gaze traveled to the fog beyond the window, then back to the connecting door. There was danger in there, she knew. But then, there was danger everywhere.

Shoving back the covers, she reached for her coral silk robe and slid from the bed. It was time to confront the biggest threat of all.

SHE CAME TO HIM in his sleep. He thought it was a dream at first, but his dreams weren't usually as arousing as the hands and mouth that currently touched his body. Des awoke with a jolt and a searing impression of heat in his lower limbs.

"You sleep very soundly," Rowen said, her lips moving against his cheekbone.

Her hair hung down around his face, her hands slid over his shoulders. It was dark, and he was on fire. She was straddling him, pressing herself against him with only the thin barrier of a sheet and blanket between them.

"Nothing to say?" she teased, kissing his eyelids. "I'll go away if you want me to."

Des shifted beneath her. If she went away, he'd have to follow her and make love to her wherever he happened to catch her. She knew it, too. She had to feel his arousal digging into her. But she couldn't possibly know how urgent was, how desperately he wanted her. He wasn't sure he' known how much until now.

The last traces of sleep vanished. His hands came up circle her waist. "No," he said, managing a smile. "I don want you to go."

She didn't move as he slid the robe from her shoulders The peach camisole she wore shimmered in the ghostly ligh of the fog. He could see the curve of her breasts, the darke nipples delineated against the flimsy material. Raising h head, he touched his mouth to one soft breast, dampenin the silken fabric over it.

Her back arched in response, her nails biting into h shoulders as he drew the hardened nipple into his mouth an ran his tongue roughly over the tip.

She wriggled against him, sending a hot stab of pai through his entire body. A hissed breath of reaction and h removed his mouth, sliding the camisole off and pulling he down on top of him. In one not particularly deft motion, h reversed their positions, laying her down on her back an running his eyes over her slender body.

He kissed her thoroughly, her mouth first, then he breasts, suckling her until he thought he'd go mad. Or wa it her hands on him that made him feel that way? H couldn't think in this state, couldn't really see her throug the curls that tumbled into his eyes. But he knew what sh was doing, and he was grateful for her care. He'd alway preferred to be safe with sex.

She brushed the hair from his face, kissing him slowl coaxingly. Then her fingers closed around him and he jerke in astonished response.

But he didn't want it like that, fast and one-sided. H forced himself to roll away, just enough that he could slid his hands to the peach silk panties that still covered her. H lowered his head deliberately as he removed them, pushin the barrier away and replacing it with his mouth.

She convulsed against him, her hips rising from the be her fingers curling into his hair.

"Des ... !

It was *his* name she whispered, *his* body she stroked. She'd come to him tonight, come to his bed and woken him up. She wouldn't have done that if she hadn't wanted him.

With his mouth and tongue he explored the sweet intimate part of her, savoring the heat his touch aroused. Her skin was soft, the taste and scent of her too delicious to resist. He felt the waves of pleasure that shuddered through her and then the final surge that had her crying his name again.

He swallowed the sound with his mouth, moving back over her. He almost lost control when her hands closed tightly around him but he managed to hold on.

Her touch, the sight and feel and sound of her wiped out all his doubts and lingering fears. Tonight might be all they'd have, but he didn't want to think about that. He had Rowen here and now. It was all he needed to know.

IT WAS LIKE FLYING or doing some other impossible thing. Rowen couldn't describe the feelings Des evoked in her. So she didn't try. She simply kissed him and teased him until he was as hungry for her as she was for him.

There was an exquisite pain when he entered her, a delicious burning between her legs. She wrapped herself around him, pulling him deeper, matching the rhythm of his body with her own. It felt so spontaneous and natural with him. It had never been like that before.

"Meant to be," she murmured, but then that probably wasn't true, only a romantic ideal.

Well, what if it was? She didn't care. He was hot and sleek, his skin satin smooth beneath her hands. They were together and it was right for this moment in time. Why should she deny something so wonderful?

The night sounds dissolved around her. She heard Des's uneven breathing and her own. She felt his heartbeat and saw the intense look of pleasure on his face. All of that in a split second, and then came that wonderful burst of light and heat inside her, and she couldn't see or hear or think about anything, except that she wanted to capture the moment and keep it forever, just take it and Des and herself to a place outside of time and never return.

It was a fairy-tale wish, but Rowen had never really seen the harm in fairy tales. With Des, wishing came very easily. So did wanting. And this wanting sustained, even when the flood of pure physical sensation began to recede.

Rowen clung to him, loving every part of him.

He collapsed exhausted on top of her and she cradled his head, kissing him, not wanting him to move, not wanting the confusion to return. That would happen soon enough.

There were other problems, too, something that stalked them, that seemed to grow more twisted and malevolent as Halloween night approached.

But it wasn't Halloween night yet. Death didn't live in the darkness of this room. And there were still many hours left until dawn....

A MISTY AUTUMN morning in Maine, with a canopy of colorful leaves still clinging to the trees and a blanket of those same leaves carpeting the ground, was a glorious thing to behold. At seven a.m. there wasn't a soul in sight. Des could walk and smoke a cigarette and be alone to think.

His first thought was of Rowen. He'd never spent such an astonishing four hours with anyone in his life. They'd made love three times and each time had been different, better in fact as they became more familiar with each other's bodies.

He hadn't wanted to leave her, but he'd needed to. There were too many obstacles for him not to hesitate, the biggest one being that he'd been alone for thirty-eight long years. He'd grown to like it that way. Now he wasn't sure. He also wasn't clear as to what Rowen wanted. They never had gotten around to talking about that.

Oh, they'd talked, all right, about themselves mostly and their lives to this point in time. Des told her about some of his shadier deals, and about his parents who lived in Suffolk. Rowen told him about her family in New Mexico and all the cities she'd lived in since graduating from college.

She hadn't been in love with Los Angeles, ergo, she hadn't stayed long. Even now when she thought about it, she only really remembered the fire and the inquest where she'd met Reggie.

"But there *was* something else, Des," she'd confided near dawn. "Something about that night that I'm not remembering..."

Des shivered in the early-morning mist. He wanted to go back to her, quite badly, but that would only confuse things more. He was headed for the cemetery. He might as well keep going and have a look at Jonah Blackstone's grave.

Blackstone's curse. Now there was a mystery. Was the murderer playing it out or not? Since Rowen had been attacked last night, Des tended to think not. But why then did the killer use a symbolic skull mask?

Damp leaves squelched underfoot as he crossed the mossy ground. Swirls of mist lent an unearthly feeling to the graveyard, floating about the crosses and headstones and the oak tree where Harold had been hanged.

There was a man standing in front of Blackstone's grave. Des had never seen him before. He looked like a beachcomber, with bleached-blond hair and a golden tan. Only the bandage on his head gave him away.

Taking a last drag from his cigarette, Des crushed it under his heel. "Peter Pettiston?" he inquired when the man glanced up.

"Yes." The confusion cleared instantly. "You must be Reggie Forbes." He stuck out his hand. "I've heard about you."

Not a promising start. Des smiled. "From Harold, I presume."

"And your cousin Richard. He ignored the 'family only' visitors' rule, and snuck in to see me in the hospital."

"Did he?" Des's smile didn't falter. "Social call?"

"More along the lines of a probe, I'd say. He wanted to know about Harold's will. I think he was hoping the old man had changed it."

"Really? Had he?"

"Damned if I know. I'm still looking for the thing. As you know, my father took over Harold's personal affairs a couple of years back. I inherited the job when he died. I hate to speak badly of the dead, but my old man, for all his flare, was about as organized as a junk collector. Nothing is where it should be, and having my office ransacked hasn't helped matters any. Between my father's disorganization and your grandfather's eccentricities, God knows where the thing is. All I've been able to find so far is a bill from a private investigation firm with a note attached that read, 'Re: D. and A. Forbes.'"

"Darcy and Anna?"

"Sorry, I don't know that, either. Anyway, I'm going to have a thorough search for the will today and see if I can't get things moving for you. Lester's been having kittens about the opening of the Masque Factory."

Des frowned. "The reading of Harold's will won't affect that, will it?"

"Not at all, but I can't convince Lester." The lawyer studied him thoughtfully. "I must say, Reggie, you're not what I expected."

Des's expression gave nothing away. "No?"

"I've heard about some of your business deals. Harold told my father you had a brilliant mind but the morals of..."

"A guttersnipe?" Des suggested.

Peter chuckled. "I suppose it all balances out in the end."

"Not really." Des glanced at the stone marker before him. "What do you make of all of this curse business?"

"You mean do I think Blackstone's back?" Peter shrugged. "I think a lot of things are possible."

"Including homicidal ghosts?"

Peter didn't answer directly. "They say in town the skull mask's been found. They also say you've had a few close calls yourself."

"The small town grapevine still flourishes, I see."

"Well, yes, although in this case your cousins have given it a helping hand."

Des raised impassive eyes to the man's face. "Which cousins?"

"Richard, and the one in black who likes bugs. He's been in Midnight a few times."

"Doing what?"

"I don't know. Buying things, I suppose. Cooper, that's his name. He's been to the tailor shop more than once. The owner's a friend of mine. He says this particular Forbes cousin is a little—unusual."

Des smiled. "That's an understatement, I'm afraid." He took a last look at Blackstone's grave marker. "Let me know when you find the will, hmm?"

"You'll be the first to know."

Would he, though, Des wondered, recalling the lawyer's ransacked office. Or had one of his "cousins" already beaten him to it?

"IT SEEMS we've misplaced another of our small group," Franz stated baldly at breakfast.

They were eating in the great hall today, in front of a roaring fire. Darcy looked pale and nervous, Richard appeared to be hung over, Poole was his usual subdued self, Almira refused to acknowledge Rowen, and Rowen was too tired to care about any of them. Only Franz's comment made an impression, and only because, for a horrible moment, she thought it might be Des who'd been "misplaced."

"Which one of us?" she asked when no one else bothered.

"Cooper," Franz revealed. "I knocked and knocked on his door but got no answer. So I went in."

Rowen propped her elbows on the table, her coffee mug in her hands. "Wasn't his door locked?"

"I used my room key. The locks up there are so old that almost anything long and flat will open them now."

Now *there* was an interesting piece of information. Keeping her expression blank, she inquired, "And what did you find inside? Obviously not Cooper."

Franz had Poole roll him up to the table. "Well, to begin with, his bed hadn't been slept in."

Richard laid his forehead on top of his folded arms. "He probably spent the night hunting for fireflies."

"In his costume?" Franz countered.

"What was his costume?" Rowen asked. "Do you know?"

Franz shrugged. "He wouldn't say, but I didn't see any sign of one in his room."

"Had a good search, did you?" Rowen said, mildly amused. Franz continued to eat, unperturbed, so she pressed. "What did you want with Cooper?"

He looked her straight in the eye. "I thought we might discuss old Harold's will."

"What?" Richard's muzzy head came up.

"Nothing," Darcy said gloomily. "Idle speculation. It's all a waste of time. Reggie'll inherit everything. Anna was right. We won't even get a token."

"We'd bloody well better get a token," Richard mumbled, dropping his head back down.

Franz buttered a piece of toast. "I know I will. Harold could be a very generous man when his conscience dictated. He had an elevator put in here especially for me, and that mechanical ramp thing in the basement, which I despise."

"All that to make up for Reggie's recklessness?" Rowen studied him contemplatively. "You must have been planning to visit Harold in Midnight quite often in that case."

Franz made a gruff sound in his throat but didn't really answer. Rowen decided to let the subject drop. Des had gone out walking; she didn't know when he'd be back and she wanted to search Cooper's room.

Aside from possibly being profitable, a search would keep her mind occupied with thoughts of something other than Des. She had no regrets about last night, none at all, but her feelings for him were another matter. What should she do about them? And where, if anyplace, might they lead?

Rowen had no doubt whatsoever that she loved him. But with that love came an emotional fear she couldn't begin to name—and a mounting sense of desperation that terrified her. What if Harold's murderer succeeded in killing him?

Well, that simply couldn't happen, she decided as she climbed the stairs. They'd have to expose the killer. Barring that, she would expose Des as an impostor.

But would the murderer believe her, or would he simply see it as a ruse to save Reggie's life?

Frightened but determined, Rowen took the key from her door and inserted it into Cooper's lock. As an afterthought she knocked, but there was no answer. She slipped inside, shut the door and looked quickly around.

It was a ghastly place, like the other rooms, yet the atmosphere seemed somehow more macabre, if that was possible. Of course that might have something to do with the bug jars on the desk.

She avoided them and went for the closet. The garment bag still hung inside. It had been torn open and something removed from a metal hanger. There was only one item left, a black velvet jacket, undoubtedly made from the bolt of material Cooper had stolen from the Masque Factory.

Since it hadn't been worn, this jacket wasn't ripped; however, a glance at the bill pinned to the bag revealed that there had been two jackets made, identical ones.

Which meant what? That Cooper had worn the missing jacket last night? That he was still wearing it?

"So where are you now, Cooper?" she wondered out loud, closing the door. "Why didn't you come back?"

With a sigh, she shoved the layers of dark hair from her face. All she had were questions, about Cooper and everyone else. Just once she'd like to find a useful answer.

The thought broke off sharply as a soft scrape of metal reached her ears. She looked up and saw the doorknob beginning to turn.

Her chest tightened. Hide, she thought, backing up. If it was Cooper, he wouldn't take kindly to an invasion of his privacy, and those bugs of his would probably love nothing better than to crawl on her.

The door opened a crack, and suddenly there was no time left to hide. Rowen had only one option. She took it swiftly. Grabbing a heavy brass candlestick from the dresser, she ducked behind the door. Then she waited, breath held, heart slamming against her ribs, for the person on the other side to enter.

She heard a tiny click as the key was withdrawn. A shadow fell across the carpet, and the door swung slowly inward...

Chapter Sixteen

Rowen thought her lungs were going to burst. But she didn't dare breathe. The shadow had nothing to distinguish it. She only knew it couldn't be Cooper because he wouldn't be so furtive in his entry.

Her damp palms gripped the candlestick tighter. Soundlessly, she raised it. The shadow lengthened. Then slowly a head came into view.

She was in the middle of a prayer when she spied the blond hair. "Richard!" she breathed in dizzying relief. Her body went limp, so limp she actually felt light-headed for a second. She lowered the candlestick, pressing a hand to her forehead. "For Chrissake, what are you doing in here?"

His grin was aggravatingly cheerful. "I was walking by," he explained, with an unconcerned glance at the heavy brass object she held. "I heard a noise and decided to investigate." He teased her with his blue eyes. "Your turn. Why the weapon? I can't believe you'd hit anyone at the manor, weird though some of them are."

She flashed him a mildly exasperated look. Her heart was still racing. "I was looking for a clue that might tell me where Cooper is," she said, leaving her post behind the door. "For all I know, you could've been Harold's murderer. I'd have hit him in a minute, whether he was staying at the manor or not." Recovered now, she gave the candlestick a cursory inspection. "So what happened to your hangover?"

"Poole whipped up a cure."

"Hair of the dog?"

"No, root of some nameless plant in the garden." He kicked the door closed with his heel and started for the desk. "Good Lord, what are those big black things?"

"Spiders," Rowen said, not looking. She took the candlestick to the window to examine the stamp on the base. "Italian," she murmured. "Something, something Salio, 1633. Hmm. Do you know antiques, Richard?"

"Not really." He was crouched down in front of the desk inspecting Cooper's insect menagerie. "These aren't spiders, they're beetles of some sort... I had a girlfriend that did, though."

"Did what?"

"Knew antiques. She was a real natural apparently. There's a name for her talent, I think."

"'A divvy," Rowen told him, her tone absent. "They get a sense of an object's authenticity just from seeing it."

Richard straightened. "Yes, well I get a sense of dread from being in this room. What say we get out before Cooper shows up."

Reluctantly, Rowen set the candlestick down. She didn't particularly want to linger, but the name Salio struck a familiar note in her memory, something to do with antiques she was sure.

Richard sailed through the door. "I wouldn't drag my feet if I were you, Rowen," he called back. "I caught a glimpse of the floor next to the desk. Not all of Cooper's bugs are in jars."

That got her moving, but it didn't quite disrupt her train of thought.

There were antiques on display throughout the manor. Of course there would be, the Forbes Corporation dealt in antiques. But she couldn't help recalling the partial letter she'd discovered.

What if Harold and Reggie had conspired with someone in an attempt to defraud their insurance company? Set a fire in a building where all the valuable antiques had either been replaced or removed. Except that the man with whom they'd conspired had found his wife inside the building when he'd arrived—his wife whom he suspected of having an affair with Reggie. He'd killed her in a fit of anger and jealousy, set the fire and fled.

"But that doesn't make sense," Rowen reminded herself. "Val Mitchell checked into the building. An arsonist wouldn't do that."

Richard's teasing voice in her ear interrupted her thoughts. "Do you always talk to yourself, pretty lady?"

She recovered her composure swiftly. "It's the only satisfying conversation you can have around here. Everyone's so secretive."

"Not me." He laughed. "Well, not much, anyway. I did meet an interesting witch last night. She said they made contact with Jonah Blackstone at their séance."

"How nice." Rowen paused outside her room. "And did Blackstone confide to them why he killed Harold?"

"I shouldn't think he'd have to. His curse is self-explanatory. My witch did say, though, that the feeling they got from him was one of great malevolence."

"Toward Reggie?"

"I imagine so, although she mentioned something about deceit as well, whatever that means." One blond eyebrow rose, as if in a challenge of some sort, but the expression vanished before Rowen could be sure.

With a cheerful, "I think I'll do some meditating," he was off, leaving her alone in the shadowy corridor to ponder yet another question.

Did Richard know about Des? Was that the reason for the momentary taunt in his eyes? Or was he the deceiver and deliberately trying to goad her?

Frustrated, Rowen shoved open her door. The situation was becoming impossible. One man dead, two people missing, skull masks, curses and now riddles into the bargain. She glanced at the telephone, then at her watch. Reggie should be awake by ten o'clock. Given the right questions, maybe he'd have an answer for her.

"Look, I haven't got time to go searching for a freaky Forbes," Des heard Lester growl from the back room as he entered the Masque Factory.

It was organized chaos in the converted mill. Halloween decorations were being hung in strategic places around the bottom floor. They didn't go in for garish; the atmosphere was more autumnal than anything, with corn-husk wreaths, clusters of pumpkins, corn and berries in the corners, trestles set up for food, a bandstand on the far wall and even a few fake cobwebs fluttering in the rafters. The displays of death masks and costumes remained, a space had been cleared for a dance floor, and a stack of freshly cut logs sat beside one of the old stone fireplaces.

"Very seasonal," Des remarked to a passing worker. "What's Lester ranting about?"

"A missing person, I think."

"A missing ghoul," Lester's surly voice interjected. "We need more death masks, Liz, and another trestle." He turned his attention to Des. "Is this call social or business?"

Des ignored the question. "What happened?"

"Cooper's gone," Lester answered gruffly. "I don't know where and I don't care. That other cousin of yours, Darcy, is looking for him. He'll be poking around in the barn by now. I gather he thinks that Cooper's disappearance is linked to his wife's. If you ask me, the little freak got whammed, and he's sleeping it off down on the docks. Hell, he could've crawled into one of the fishing boats for all anyone knows."

"He could have," Des agreed. Tugging his hat down over his eyes, he started for the staircase that would take him to the barn.

Darcy was indeed poking around the building, although it took Des quite some time to locate him. He was on his knees in a small room off the loft, examining the walls.

Des watched through the cracked door for at least twenty minutes. He was contemplating revealing himself when Darcy exclaimed softly, "He was right!" and jumped back from the section of wall he'd been probing. A second later, he pulled part of it away.

A hidden door. Clever, but not uncommon. Des had seen similar doors in old buildings before.

He waited until Darcy had crossed the threshold, then followed him. A set of plank stairs led down to another door, a trapdoor this time that Darcy only located because he tripped on the finger crevices.

A silent shadow on the staircase, Des waited until Darcy had worked the door up. More stairs awaited. Since they were already at ground level, Des knew this flight must descend into the tunnels.

He was half-right. From the top and with the aid of Darcy's flashlight, he perceived a six-by-six-foot space at the bottom. And one padlocked door.

Darcy sighed, then swore out loud, which was Des's cue to make his presence known. He came partway down the stairs, leaned against the stone wall and arched a deliberately mocking eyebrow at his "cousin."

"Looking for Anna?"

Startled, Darcy spun around. "What are you doing here?" he demanded angrily.

"Following you." Eyes locked on the man's wary features, Des came all the way down. "What's behind the door, Darcy?"

"I don't know."

"Yes, you do."

"And you don't, I suppose," Darcy challenged.

Des glanced at the padlock. "Do you have a key?"

"Of course not."

"Then we'll have to improvise, won't we? Give me your tiepin."

Darcy hesitated, but finally obeyed. "Where's your key, cousin?" he asked with a poor attempt at sarcasm.

"Point your flashlight at the lock." Kneeling on one knee, Des worked the silver pin into the lock and began to coax it. He noticed a series of scratch marks on the metal. Obviously someone else had done the same thing earlier. "I don't have one," he answered as an afterthought. "I didn't know this room was here."

Darcy looked unconvinced. He also appeared agitated. Des kept one eye on him and the other on his task. "I thought you and Harold shared everything."

"Did you?" Des glanced up, smiling from under the brim of his hat. "Well." The tumblers gave and he stood, motioning the other man forward. "Shall we see what's inside?"

Darcy's movements were edgy and alert. He clearly didn't trust his cousin, which was fine, because Des didn't trust him. He'd had very little trouble locating this room.

A good-size chamber spread out behind the door, twenty feet square at least, crammed with barrels and crates of every imaginable shape and size.

"A roomful of boxes," Des mused. "What treasures do they hold, I wonder?"

"Knock it off, Reggie," Darcy snapped with uncharacteristic rancor. "You know this place well enough."

"So do you, it seems."

"I only know what Cooper told me. And he's gone now, isn't he? I find that rather convenient. But just in case you're planning to make me the next missing person, let me warn you, I told at least three of the others where I was coming today."

"That was smart of you." With Darcy several feet away, Des took a moment to lift one of the barrel lids. "Lalique," he said, delving past straw and soft cloth. An ironic smile curved his lips when he recalled the bowl Rowen had discovered at the manor. "Of course," he murmured. "The fire."

"Yes, the fire." Darcy's defiant tone held just a trace of fear. "Los Angeles, three years ago. We all heard about it, Reggie. I wouldn't have given it a second thought, but Anna's not as trusting as me. She said the whole thing was a scam from the start."

"Did she?" Des surveyed his cousin from under his hat. "So who found this room first?"

"Cooper. He told me about it last night before he left the manor."

"So you saw him in costume, then. Was he wearing a skull mask?"

Darcy jerked visibly. "A what?"

"Nothing." Des forced a bland smile. "So you thought I knew about this, did you?"

"You and Harold. It's your style, Reggie. You'd defraud your own mother if it suited your purpose."

"You know me that well, hmm?"

"Snakes only shed their outer skin. Underneath it's all the same. Anna said you weren't as nasty as she'd expected, but she still didn't trust you. You don't know Anna the way I do. She's like a bulldog with a bone."

"Tenacious."

"Yes. She didn't trust you, and she's gone. Cooper found this room and now he's gone, too." Darcy's fist clenched but his features were rigid with strain. "What have you done with them?"

Des stared at him for a long moment. Finally, he gave his head a weary shake. "Nothing, Darcy. I haven't got them."

"Then who does? Blackstone's ghost?"

There was no answer to that, so Des didn't attempt one. He made an imperceptible gesture with his head, indicating the door.

Reluctantly, Darcy started toward it. He held the flashlight in one hand. The other one, Des noticed, rested lightly on a small bulge in his jacket pocket.

"Insurance fraud," Des told Rowen later that evening.

He was back at the manor. The bulge in Darcy's pocket had turned out to be a second flashlight, not the gun he'd momentarily suspected. The revelation had been almost anticlimactic.

Would Darcy take his discovery and all his dark suspicions to the Midnight police? Des had known the answer from the start. Of course not. Darcy believed that Anna was being held hostage in order to ensure his silence.

"I don't care what you do to Cooper," Darcy had muttered through clenched teeth. "Just please don't hurt Anna."

Des could've denied it all again, but what would be the point? Darcy wouldn't believe him, and this way the police, a lackluster bunch at best, were kept well out of it.

Bringing his mind back to the present, he watched as Rowen walked past him. She was pacing the upstairs drawing room, telephone in hand, receiver pressed to her ear while she waited for the line to clear. "So what you're saying," she said, clarifying his earlier remark, "is that the partial carbon copy of the letter we found in Harold's study is very likely connected to the crates you found hidden in that room Darcy led you to under the barn today."

He grinned. "Yes."

"But then who was the letter written to? Val Mitchell or someone else?"

"There's no way to know, Rowen." Des leaned back, enjoying himself as she paced the floor in a clingy tan knit dress. "I went through Harold's study when I got back, but I couldn't find the first part of the letter."

"Well, I still think it must have been written to Val Mitchell," she maintained. "If I'm right about that letter, Harold said he couldn't condone murder, and it *was* Mitchell who ran from the burning building."

"That doesn't mean there wasn't somebody else involved. Reggie for one, and possibly another person or people."

"One of his cousins?" Rowen frowned. "No, that wouldn't work. He wouldn't have sent you here if there was a chance that one of them might recognize you."

Des shrugged. "I said 'might.' Reggie wasn't necessarily involved. He and Harold led separate lives. They probably worked more than a few separate deals."

"Which I could ask Reggie about if this stupid line would come back for more than ten seconds at a time." She rattled the phone. "There must be a storm down the coast."

"Like the one here."

"Don't remind me."

He smiled faintly. "There's no thunder, Rowen."

"Not yet. Ah!" She halted, her eyes widening. "It's ringing."

Perched on the windowsill, Des waited patiently for the connection to be made. Although neither of them had mentioned last night, the ease of Rowen's movements told him she wasn't uncomfortable with their lovemaking. It didn't change things between them, but at least when the opportunity presented itself, they'd be able to talk like adult human beings. Maybe.

"Reggie?" She practically had to shout his name into the receiver. "I have to ask you something." A pause, then, "No, I can't speak up, not unless you want everybody in the manor to hear me." Her forehead wrinkled as a blast of wind and rain hit the outer walls. "What rabbit's foot?"

Des held out his hand. "Let me talk to him."

She raised her voice. "Reggie, Des wants to talk to you."

Reggie was blustering over the static-heavy line when Des came on. "What the hell's the problem now?" he demanded. "Did you screw up?"

No, but you bloody well did, Des thought darkly. Aloud, he asked, "What do you know about an insurance scam, Reggie, and a room under the old barn filled with antiques and paintings?"

"Room under the what?"

"Barn." Des enunciated the word with theatrical precision. "Remember the fire at your antique store three years ago? Well, unless I'm mistaken, what should have been destroyed is currently residing in a room under the barn."

The static cleared fractionally. "Keep your voice down," Reggie snapped, "and explain to me from the beginning what the hell you're talking about."

Des went over it all, while Rowen watched from the sofa. "Darcy and Cooper know about the room," he finished five minutes later.

"But Cooper's disappeared, you say. Well that's something, anyway. He can't go blabbing to the police if he's not around."

"You're missing the point, Reggie."

"No, I'm not. You want a confession from me that Harold and I did this insurance fraud thing together. Unfortunately—" his tone soured "—we didn't. And let me tell you, I'm none too happy about it. All I know is that some guy who worked for us . . ."

"Val Mitchell."

"Whatever. His wife was killed in the fire, and he was seen fleeing from the scene. Rowen can tell you about that. For myself, I'm more interested in this underground room."

"Naturally."

"And what Darcy's going to do now that he's found it," Reggie finished tightly. "Does he know what you suspect?"

"He suspects the same thing," Des said. "But he won't call the police. He seems to think that I or rather you are holding Anna as a hostage against that eventuality."

"That's a break."

"I thought you'd see it that way," Des murmured, his tone dry.

"Look, cousin," Reggie snapped. "I told you I had no part in any scheme to cheat our insurance company. Anna's being gone is a bonus. Same thing for Cooper. Don't expect me to mourn the loss. I know Anna by repute and Cooper by misfortune. They can stay missing forever for all I care."

Rowen left the sofa and walked over to Des. Her eyes were on the storm as she said quietly, "Ask him about Grace Mitchell. Just say her name and see how he reacts."

"Tell me about Grace Mitchell, Reggie," Des complied.

"What about her? She's dead." Reggie's words were a flat statement of fact, with no reaction beyond mounting impatience. "Look, as far as anyone knows, she was in the building the night her husband burned it. The hows and whys are still up in the air. Grace Mitchell's dead, Val Mitchell's vanished and that's how it's been for three years now."

"Unless he's here."

Reggie's laugh had an incredulous edge. "In Midnight?"

"Why not?"

"Because—well, for one thing I'd recognize him, wouldn't I?"

"Except that you're not here and I wouldn't know him if I fell over him."

"You're being obtuse."

"I know," Des agreed, smiling. He'd always enjoyed irritating Reggie.

"Well, cut it out," Reggie growled, properly annoyed. "I'm not in the mood. Mitchell can't know you're me, ergo, he couldn't risk letting 'me' see him."

"He could if he was wearing a disguise."

"Fine, have it your way, but I still say your best bet f[o]
murder is one or more of my greedy cousins. Do whateve[r]
it takes, Des, to catch the bastard. Just make sure you d[o]
catch him. And keep the knowledge of that room under th[e]
barn quiet at all costs. Offer Darcy money if you have to.'

"Not my money."

Reggie snarled something unflattering, then added a surl[y]
"Let me talk to Rowen."

Tired of games, Des handed the receiver over and sli[d]
from the windowsill. Lighting a cigarette, he started pu[r-]
posefully for the door.

"Where are you going?" Rowen asked, her tone tole[r]
ant.

"To my room," he said over his shoulder. On the thres[h]
old he turned to look back at her, a mocking smile grazin[g]
his lips. "Tell Reggie I've gone to break a mirror."

"Don't be so disagreeable, Reggie," Rowen sighed sever[al]
minutes later. She heard a click and frowned. "Reggie? A[re]
you there?"

The drawing room went dark less than ten seconds aft[er]
the phone line went dead. Releasing a tired breath, sh[e]
dropped the receiver into the cradle. It didn't matter. Sh[e]
could hardly hear him above the storm and the static, an[d]
he wasn't admitting anything, anyway.

Well, maybe he isn't guilty, she allowed, waiting for h[er]
eyes to adjust.

She sank onto the window ledge Des had recently va[
cated and pressed her fingers to her temples.

Harold could have arranged it so that Val Mitchell woul[d]
deliberately check into the building that night. Harold ha[d]
money and power. He might have promised Val a new li[fe]
and a new identity in exchange for Val's taking the blame f[or]
the fire. That way Harold would never be a suspect. H[e]
could collect the insurance money, stash the antiques an[d]
sell them off on one of at least a hundred black markets.

To a degree that would explain the letter she'd found i[n]
Harold's study, particularly if Val had accidentally disco[v-]
ered his wife in the building that night. He could have a[

sumed she was waiting for Reggie and either knocked her out or killed her. Her death would in turn have given Harold the perfect opportunity to renege on his deal with Mitchell. To which Mitchell might have later responded by using Blackstone's curse to kill Harold.

"But why then, if Reggie's innocent, is Mitchell also after me?" Rowen wondered out loud. "Unless Reggie *is* guilty. Or unless Mitchell wants revenge on Reggie for having an affair with his wife." She paused. That last idea made some sense. Take her away from Reggie the way he thought Reggie had taken Grace away from him.

Still, it was an inconclusive theory at best, full of ifs, maybes and question marks. Rowen massaged her aching temples, then turned to regard the storm behind her.

The gloomy air in the manor seemed to have settled right into her bones. She wasn't accustomed to such negative feelings. Part of it might stem from Des and the fact that she wanted quite badly not to fall for him. However, the point was moot now. She did love him, and feelings that deep couldn't be wished away.

So what was frightening her? Was it irrational fear or simply confusion?

She let the question slide, closing her eyes for a minute and allowing the darkness and the storm to flow through her.

Rain lashed the windowpane and a howling sea wind blew upward from the rocks below. When she finally looked, she saw the cliffs, stark and deadly and strangely haunting, illuminated in the candlelight glow from the manor. But the haunted aspect was just fancy, surely. Blackstone's ghost didn't wander the town or the estate.

She stood, hesitating as she glimpsed a movement near the edge of the woods. It looked like a line of people emerging from the trees, black-robed and solemn, purposeful in their advance.

The Midnight witches? Rowen squinted into the murk. Why would they go into the woods on a night like this?

Shivering deeply, she watched the line trudge toward Cemetery Road. What a macabre sight, she thought, leaning closer to the window. They were probably planning to chant over Blackstone's grave as a preamble to their second séance.

Tapping her palms restlessly against her elbows, Rowen started for the hall.

Already Almira and Poole had lighted scores of candles. Unsure as to her ultimate destination, she let herself wander. She might have wandered right up to Des's door if, from her vantage point above and aided by the fact that there were no railings to impede her view, she hadn't happened to notice the shadowy figure that was creeping laboriously across the great hall below.

"Poole," she whispered in soft puzzlement.

He made his way awkwardly to the archway, prompting Rowen to make her way cautiously down the stairs.

She lost sight of him briefly, but located him again at the bottom. He was heading for Harold's study. She saw a light filtering through the crack at the bottom of the door.

Her curiosity overriding her common sense, Rowen inched forward. Poole was staring at the bottom of the door, pressing his ear to the heavy panels.

Then suddenly, his head jerked back. The door flew open to blackness, the light inside having been extinguished. From the shadows, an intruder dressed entirely in black erupted. He burst across the threshold, knocked Poole aside and bolted for the front door. Or rather he would have if Poole's fingers hadn't twined themselves around his jacket.

More déjà vu, Rowen reflected grimly, recalling the previous night when *she'd* grabbed the murderer's robe.

Giving no thought to the consequences, she rushed forward. The intruder was still struggling with Poole, so she made a grab for his black head mask.

Although she fully intended to kick him, the action proved unnecessary. Her removal of the mask paralyzed the man. That and the fact that Almira had materialized in the hall with a weighty bronze statue in her hand.

Light from the candles streaked across the man's angry features. "Bitch," he swore through his teeth.

But all Rowen could do was stare in amazement as she whispered his name. "Lester!"

Chapter Seventeen

"Let me go," Lester growled at Poole. He snatched the ski mask rudely from Rowen's fingers. "Give me that."

"What were you doing in there?" Almira demanded. "What's that paper in your hand?"

He glared at her, his lip curling. Something told Rowen this wasn't over. Uneasily she stepped back and shouted up the stairs, "Reggie!"

Footsteps sounded on the upper landing. From the shadows, Richard's voice called back, "What's going on down there?"

"Give it to me," Almira ordered Lester.

His response was a crude curse that told her exactly what she could do with her suggestion. His eyes darted to the stairs. "You!" he snarled at a rumpled-looking Des. "I'll talk to you. The others can..."

"Yes, we got the message the first time," Rowen said with forced calm. She laid a cautioning hand on Des's arm as he came up beside her. "Something feels wrong."

His eyes moved to Lester's dour features. "It'll be fine," he said, squeezing her fingers. Then he arched a questioning eyebrow. "The study?"

"Whatever."

The click of the door was like a death knell as far as Rowen was concerned. She should have insisted on going with them. She was very good in a scrap, not a fair fighter at all.

"I saw him sneak in while I was setting the table for supper," Poole explained, righting himself with difficulty.

"I wonder what was on that paper he was clutching?" Richard mused. He buttoned his blazer, glancing back at Darcy who was halfway down the stairs. "Don't worry, cousin. If Lester's responsible for Anna's disappearance, Reggie'll get it out of him."

Darcy said nothing. For a long moment, no one moved. It was Almira who broke the stormy silence, setting the statue down and pushing her black hair under a net she'd pinned at the nape of her neck.

Her hair looked wrong, Rowen noticed suddenly. It lay flat on her head except for a few wild strands, as if she'd been wearing a hat that she'd pulled off in haste.

Rowen's eyes strayed downward, over the housekeeper's starched black dress to her flat oxford shoes that were several sizes too large for her.

Rain beat hard against the stone walls. Richard was murmuring something to Darcy. Poole was still pondering Lester's presence in the house. Almira didn't move a muscle. When Rowen glanced up, she saw a quick look of horror cross the woman's sharp features.

"I'd better check on dinner," she said hastily, and dissolved into the shadows. But not before Rowen glimpsed something creeping down her leg below the line of her hem.

It was the cuff from a pair of pants. Almira was wearing long pants under her dress. And quite obviously she wished to keep that fact a secret.

DES SELDOM GOT blinding headaches, but he had one now, an incessant pounding in his temples that made it virtually impossible to concentrate.

"I didn't kill him," Lester insisted. He waved a sheet of paper under Des's nose. "This is a manifest, a list of items reported destroyed in that Los Angeles fire three years ago. I've seen things around the manor, Reggie. Antiques. And I talked to old Harold."

"About the fire?" Des tried to focus on the list, couldn't do it and gave up. He couldn't imagine where Lester had found it. "I find it hard to believe he'd have confided in you."

"So did I at first. He was a crusty old codger. He'd have scammed the president and not thought twice about it. But he wouldn't have scammed the Pope or even the local minister. He was God-fearing. I learned that about him. Harold would never have killed for gain."

"Whereas I would." Rousing himself from the desk, Des crossed to the window. "Are you Val Mitchell?" he asked without inflection.

"Who?"

"Don't play games, Lester. You know about the fire, and you just told me that Harold wouldn't kill for gain. That means you know about Grace Mitchell's death in the fire. Are you her husband, Val?"

This time Lester faced him squarely. "No."

A faint smile grazed Des's lips. "Am I supposed to believe that?"

"Believe what you damned well like, Reggie, I'm not her husband. But I do know those antiques are around here somewhere. Harold may not have been a murderer, but he had plenty of gall." Lester balled the paper in his fist. "Some of these pieces are on display in the manor. All I have to do is take this to the police and you'll be in jail so fast it'll make your head spin."

"Unless?"

"Unless what?"

Des summoned a pleasant smile. "Well, aren't you going to offer me a deal? I give you the Masque Factory, you give me the list and a chance to stash my antiques elsewhere?"

Lester's lips thinned. "I'm not a criminal."

"Oh, I'd be willing to bet that's exactly what you are," Des returned easily. "But it doesn't matter. I'll think about it. I'll let you know what I decide after Halloween night."

The other man's stance grew challenging, all attempts at pretense vanishing. "Tomorrow's Halloween, Reggie," he said in a rough voice. "What if you don't live past midnight?"

"Then it won't make much difference to me what you do with that list, will it? You'll be the only one who loses, Lester."

"There's always Rowen."

Des's insides hardened. His eyes came around to Lester's face, filled with a deadly intent that even the darkness couldn't conceal. "Touch Rowen, Lester," he said softly, "and I'll kill you."

IT WAS A WILD NIGHT, turbulent and portentous.

The man didn't like it. Tomorrow was Halloween. Reggie had to die by midnight tomorrow, possibly at the Masque Factory party, but that might take some doing.

As he watched the wind snap limbs from trees that had stood for hundreds of years, the man reviewed the situation. Anna was gone and Cooper was missing. That made for less human clutter to trip him up. But what about the fire? How much did anyone really know about that?

Panic fluttered in his stomach. He tamped it down. It would be all right as long as he didn't lose his nerve.

Play the game, he thought, wiping a sweating palm on his pant leg. A lot can happen in twenty-four hours. Blackstone's curse can still triumph.

And that would leave only one problem. Rowen.

IT WAS A bizarre night, Rowen reflected. The police arrived as Des and Lester emerged from the study. They were looking for Cooper, a little matter of his having charged his purchase at the Midnight Tailor Shop with a credit card well over its limit.

"We haven't seen him since yesterday," Franz informed them. The power was still out, so he had the police carry him downstairs in his wheelchair. "Richard tells me, however, that we did have a prowler in the study."

"No, we didn't," Des corrected, coming into the drawing room and heading for the bar. Rowen intercepted him and steered him toward a chair by the window.

Poole looked up from setting out fresh candles, but it was Darcy who protested, "Well, of course we did. Lester..."

"Was here at my request," Des lied. He tugged Rowen onto the arm of the chair beside him.

"You should have told us you were expecting him," Almira said coldly.

Her hair hung past her shoulders now, a long ghoulish frame for her pale features. No pant legs dipped below her hem, and her composure was firmly back in place.

The officers didn't care about Lester. They marched up to Cooper's room and confiscated the remaining velvet jacket.

"So he did have two identical jackets made," Rowen clarified. "Both black velvet?"

The more garrulous officer nodded. "I assume he's wearing the one that's missing."

"That's difficult to say," Poole replied, quietly polite. "Since as we told you, none of us have seen him since yesterday."

It was a vicious circle. The police left and Almira summoned everyone to dinner.

As the storm grew increasingly violent, Rowen noticed that the guests grew increasingly somber. They talked about Halloween and trick or treat, but not about Blackstone's ghost.

Des wasn't in the best of moods. He recapped his conversation with Lester for her, yet when he finished, she sensed he'd left something out.

"Do you think he's the murderer?" she pressed as they walked through the shadowy maze of halls that formed the rear of the manor.

"I wish I knew, Rowen."

It was an abstracted response. She could feel the tension in his body. Lester must have said something, either to anger or to unsettle him. Whatever it was, though, he obviously didn't intend to tell her.

They followed the line of jack-o'-lanterns to the doors they'd discovered their first night there. "Feels like a million years ago," Rowen sighed. She motioned at the door with the ramp behind it. "Harold had that cable system put in especially for Franz, did I tell you that? He must have felt very badly about the accident."

"Harold had a conscience."

"I guess so." She slid him a speculative look. "Do you want to talk or something?"

The question earned her a grudging smile. "Talk?"

"About last night."

The shadows that fell across his face softened the sharper planes. Where had she ever gotten the impression that he wasn't handsome? She couldn't remember. Maybe it had something to do with Reggie and the feelings she'd never had for him.

Des looked down at her, his eyes traveling the length of her suddenly hot body. "No, I don't really want to talk. Not now."

A tremor far stronger than desire ran through her, but all she said was, "Good."

His smile deepened. "I doubt that, Rowen." His hands came up to cup her face, his thumbs gently stroking her cheeks. "It isn't good for either of us."

"I know."

"We should stop now."

She nodded, her eyes not leaving his.

A small sigh escaped him. "Bloody fool," he said more or less to himself. And he covered her hungry mouth with his.

IT WAS MIDNIGHT, the witching hour, the dawn of Halloween. As it had been two hundred years ago, so it would be again. Reggie would die tonight.

Hands trembling with anticipation, a new letter was composed.

Dear Dr. Sayers,

I've come so far, survived so much. All I need to do now is to hang on, breathe deeply when I feel my control slipping and see this thing through to its agonizing end.

You know all about agony, don't you, Doctor? You know, I know, even old Harold knows. And soon Reggie will know, too.

Yesterday, I prepared a trap within the manor. Don't worry, I'm sure no one will discover it. I don't like to kill people, Doctor. I explained that to you the last time we were together, at least I tried to—although I got the feeling you weren't really listening, or that you didn't entirely believe me.

But I'm straying from the point.

Harold and Reggie took something precious from me. I can't replace that, I can only have my revenge, and of course set the story straight as well. That's an absolute must.

I don't know if Rowen will understand, or if her attitude toward Reggie is merely a clever ploy. Maybe it doesn't matter.

Yes, I know, breathe with deliberation, think with deliberation, move with deliberation. All fine words, but you don't know the hell I've suffered because of them. Only Blackstone could understand that.

Ah yes, Jonah Blackstone, whose soul inhabits the skull mask that I possess. Tonight I'll deliver another Forbes to hell, on his behalf and mine. A sweet treat for a tricky ghost.

Happy Halloween, Blackstone...

> Please rest assured, dearest Dr. Sayers,
> A former patient

NIGHT AND DAY melded, the stormy darkness at last giving way to a sludgy gray dawn.

Rowen spent most of the night wrapped in Des's arms, his sleek, hard body warming hers. Talking had resolved nothing, so they'd abandoned that idea and made love instead—in the bed, in front of the fire, on the carpet by candlelight with the storm still raging outside.

No thunder had intruded. No lightning shot through the skies. But it was a strange night even so, disquieting in its silent revelations.

Des could live without her, Rowen knew that, just as she knew she could live without him. They were survivors, two people who wanted quite desperately to be together but who would undoubtedly be better off apart.

And yet she had to wonder how dangerous it would be to give her heart to this man, to trust him and take the risk, to deal with any problems that cropped up as they went along.

It could go two ways. Life on the move—though probably not in the fashion of Monte Carlo or St. Tropez—or settle down in one place for years, someplace where she could draw her pictures, make friends, learn to cook, and maybe even have babies. She wasn't sure about that yet. On the other hand, if they were Des's eccentric little babies...

The fantasy persisted throughout the night, an endless stream of possibilities. But close behind them lurked the horror. Someone wanted Des dead, and her as well it seemed. It was Halloween, the peak time of Blackstone's curse, the turning point, as Rowen saw it.

It felt like Halloween, too, rainy, with the last leaves clinging to the trees and Poole up at dawn, raking the fallen ones despite a steady drizzle.

There was still no sign of Anna. The police came by twice to check for Cooper. On their second visit, they accepted Richard's offer of coffee and hot rolls he'd baked himself.

"Almira's been in her room most of the day," he explained to Rowen later. "I don't know why."

"Her husband died on Halloween," Poole said from the kitchen doorway. He clumped awkwardly over to where Des stood leaning against the table and drinking coffee. "I wondered if I might have tonight off, Mr. Reggie. From serving at the party, I mean. I'll be glad to take Mr. Becker to the factory in his wheelchair, but I would really like to rest after that."

Des nodded, staring at him. "Tell me, Poole," he said slowly. "Did you ever work for us?"

Poole shifted his weight. "I work for you now."

"He means before now," Rowen said, strolling over.

Poole's face paled slightly. "I..."

"They know, Poole."

Almira appeared at the door that led to the bedrooms. She looked tired and disheveled. There were shiny blotches on her jaw and chin. Her hair was flat and pulled back, and her makeup seemed to have been applied in a rush. Rowen did a better job at stoplights in her rearview mirror.

The housekeeper regarded Des. "It's the shipbuilding firm, isn't it? You checked and learned the truth."

"I never worked for any shipbuilding firm," Poole said with conviction.

"What else have you turned up?" Almira's eyes hardened. "You've been spying on all of us, haven't you? What skeletons are hidden in whose closets? Who has reason to want both you and Harold dead? You think I do, because Harold killed my Gilbert with overwork, and because I'll inherit the manor if you die. And Poole worked for a company you dissolved."

"I didn't," Poole growled.

"Your cousins want money, Franz Becker just plain hates you and Lester wants the Masque Factory." Her lips were white with suppressed rage. "Yes, Reggie, we have our motives, all of us, including Jonah Blackstone. Look outside sometime today and you might catch a glimpse of the Midnight witches. Gilbert noticed them this morning. The covens are massing in the woods around the factory. They're going to bring Blackstone over. And when they do, you, Reggie Forbes, are going to die."

"SHE'S MAD, Des, completely mad."

Rowen's words echoed in Des's head well into the evening. She was right, of course, although her conclusion had nothing to do with Almira's dire predictions that Blackstone was going to kill him. It was the other statement Almira had made that had given her away.

"Gilbert noticed them this morning," she'd said in reference to the witches.

But her husband, Gilbert, was dead. Still, there was that closet full of men's clothing in her bedroom, wasn't there? Des hated to think what those things in combination might portend. It could be a harmless delusion. It could also be a split personality.

The day passed with agonizing slowness. The fear inside him had become a living thing. He wasn't afraid for himself, however. His concern was entirely for Rowen's life.

If he'd thought it would work, he would have put her on the afternoon train for Portland, but there was about as much chance of that succeeding as there was of Reggie becoming a philanthropist.

Which left only deductive reasoning, and neither of them had done very well in that department. Now it was Halloween night.

He and Rowen had been to the factory earlier in the evening. The decorating was complete, the interior looking almost early American.

"It's like Sleepy Hollow, the party at Van Tassel's farmhouse," Rowen remarked in delight. "With a few death masks, witches and Puritans thrown in, of course."

She was going to be a witch tonight, Des recalled with an inward smile, a sexy one in a black flowing shroud. For his own costume he'd chosen bedouin robes rather than his former pirate persona.

"Great, then you can lend me that flash cape of yours," Richard said as they all went upstairs to change.

Des agreed, but managed to forget about the cape during the next hour. His thoughts turned to Rowen instead, and what the two of them could have together if they'd simply let themselves take it.

But life was never easy. His eccentricities would be hell for her to handle. Add to that Rowen's very definite opinion on life, and you came up with trouble every time.

The rain began in earnest at seven o'clock, full driving sheets of water sweeping over the manor. By eight it was a deluge, with thunder and lightning creeping inexorably down the coast from the north.

"I knew it would do this," Rowen said from the mirror in her bathroom.

She was wearing her black shroud with its high waist, huge bell sleeves and low neckline. Des had trouble dragging his eyes away.

"I think almost everyone's left," she went on, fastening the sides of her hair back with silver barrettes.

"Richard, too?" Des didn't stir from the bed where he was sprawled in his brown cords and white flannel shirt.

"I don't know. But if you're going to lend him your cape, you'd better do it now."

The thunder, still some distance away, edged closer. Des heard it above the lash of wind and rain as he walked down the hall. The lights were flickering, too. He saw the electric sconces in Franz's room flare, then dim, then flare again.

Then he saw something else, two things actually, cause enough for him to make a wary detour.

The lights continued to flutter as rain pelted the manor. There was no sign of life from within the room, only the door moved, blown inward by an errant draft.

Franz should have taken greater care, Des reflected on the threshold. The evidence before him was incriminating and irrefutable.

The wheelchair sat at the foot of Franz's bed. Next to it, resting against the wall, stood his two wooden canes. But there was no sign of Franz Becker anywhere.

Chapter Eighteen

A low peal of thunder rumbled through the night sky, burying itself deep in Rowen's bones. She had to ignore it, she told herself resolutely, finish getting into her costume and prepare to do battle with Blackstone's curse. This was no time to confront an old childhood fear.

She was halfway across the room when the electric candles faltered. A power failure on Halloween in the middle of a thunderstorm—her nerves were certainly being tested tonight.

She made it all the way to the closet and her witch's cape before she detected the displaced shuffle. Nothing definite, just a sound that didn't belong, the soft brush of a heel on the carpet.

Her head came up, eyes alert as she searched the walls for shadows. The sound was behind her, she was sure of that, an eerie little scrape, closer this time than before.

Her heart gave a panicky lurch. She started to spin around, but the moment had passed. Whoever had made the sound was right there, so close that she could feel the heat of his breath on her neck.

Black-gloved hands ensnared her wrists. "Don't," a gravelly voice whispered in her ear.

She fought him anyway, struggling against his iron grip, kicking his shins. Even as she fought, she felt the power in his muscles. But no one was indomitable.

Flinging her head back, Rowen attempted to hit him in the face. He jerked sideways and she missed. What she gained was a glimpse of a rubber skull mask and the certain terrifying knowledge that the person behind her was Harold's murderer.

Jerkily, he transferred her wrists to one powerful hand. "I said don't," he warned again in that indefinable growl. "I need you with me."

Rowen felt the cold steel of a knife blade being pressed to her ribs. "Who are you?" she managed to choke out.

He shoved her forward, not answering.

"No." She squirmed against him. "No!"

The knife dug into her skin. She had no doubt he'd use it. Her only chance was to drag her feet and pray that someone would see them in the hall.

The lights quivered but held at a dim level. He poised the knife over her racing heart. The thunder crept closer.

It was worse than the cave, worse than anything Rowen had ever been through.

She continued to fight him as he thrust her down the stairs. Where was Des? If she screamed, would he hear her? Or would the murderer kill her first?

She knew he would, he'd already tried several times. She swallowed the scream.

"Where are you taking me?" she whispered above the noise of the storm.

Again he didn't answer. He propelled her forward despite her struggles. In a remote corner of her mind, Rowen wondered why he didn't simply stab her and be done with it. She had to be bruising him with all her kicking and flailing; their progress was at best slow and awkward.

Like an albatross around his neck, she thought, refusing to release the sob that climbed into her throat.

On the second to last step, she succeeded in freeing one wrist. Her fingers curled instantly around the knife handle, pushing it away.

She wasn't really sure what happened after that. She knew he screamed and that the knife clattered to the floor. Then his arm clamped tightly around her waist and he hoisted her up, hauling her resistant body toward the rear of the house.

Her struggles impeded him, but not sufficiently to stop him. She saw the burning jack-o'-lanterns in her peripheral vision. Distorted shadows seemed to hang everywhere. She

heard thunder and rain and his labored breathing in her ear
She screamed again, and again. Finally, as they ap
proached the junction where she and Des had come thei
first night here, she felt the murderer fumbling in his pocket

The handkerchief he removed smelled strangely familia
Like a miniature ghost, it rose to cover her mouth and nose

She couldn't avoid it, and she couldn't hold her breatl
forever. The noxious fumes slithered into her lungs.

Her head began to spin. Huge black shapes crowded int
her mind. She pictured a man. What was he doing? Sh
couldn't tell. A large piece of wood rose up in front of her
wood and glass and paint, a ladder leaning against the wall
She saw movement, swift, uncertain, someone darting, the
hesitating, but was it real or something from a distan
memory?

Rowen heard a door slam somewhere close by, then fel
herself being carried through the darkness. The murderer se
her down with sweeping gentleness, her hazy mind noted.

"Shh." His mouth moved against her ear. His finger
stroked her hair.

She couldn't see his face, but it was a man, she was sur
of that. "You killed Harold," she heard herself murmur a
the blackness settled in around her.

His mouth moved again. And she knew with a muzz
sense of horror that the word he whispered back wa
"Yes."

THE SCREAM on the staircase sliced sharply through Des'
thoughts. Rowen!

He was out of Franz's empty bedroom before the screar
stopped. It had come from the bottom of the stairs.

Des raced along the corridor, aware that the lights wer
flickering badly. If they went out, he might never find her

The sound of a scuffle gave him direction when h
reached the entry hall. "Let me go!" Rowen shouted. He
words confirmed his worst fear. The murderer had her.

But why did Harold's killer want Rowen dead? There wa
no provision for her death in Blackstone's curse.

The whys weren't important, he reminded himself, focusing his mind on the struggle ahead. What mattered was that the bastard had her.

He ran past the jack-o'-lanterns, the clamor of the storm momentarily blotting out all other sound. Still, they had to be heading for the junction at the back of the manor. Were they heading for the ramp as well? Possibly. There was an outside door at the bottom that would take them straight...

"To the cliffs," he finished through gritted teeth.

He wasn't thinking clearly, and he knew it. That's what love did, shoved logic and intellect out the window. He heard a door slam and reacted instinctively, bursting from the corridor and heading straight for it. He did pause for a precious second to check the other doors, but they were all locked. The killer must have taken her down the ramp.

Des almost ripped that door from its hinges when he yanked it open.

Lights first, his brain cautioned, but for once he didn't listen. He stepped across the threshold, prepared for the ramp, ready to wrap his fingers around the murderer's throat.

He was envisioning the moment when he entered, not looking, not anticipating anything except finding Rowen. It took only a split second for him to understand. He had time to squeeze his eyes closed after the realization hit him. He didn't quite have time to stop his forward momentum.

There was only black air beyond the door, moist, surprisingly warm air. The ramp was gone, the railing had been removed, even the cables had vanished.

Des felt himself tumbling downward, just as he had when he'd been shoved from the cliff. Except that this time there was no water to break his fall, only the darkness and an unforgiving stone floor.

ROWEN HAD NO idea what was happening, but she knew something must be. The chloroform hadn't completely knocked her out. It had come close, but she'd clung to consciousness, enough to realize that the murderer had left her side, whispering an agitated, "No! That's not right! You shouldn't be there."

What was he talking about?

She felt him step over her, felt his pant leg graze her cheek. It was damp and smelled of must and mud.

Rowen's eyes fluttered open. Her mind was thick and fuzzy. Shadows enveloped her. Where was she?

Pale light filtered through a window to her right. She lay on her back, staring up at it. Whoever he was, he'd left the room at a dead run.

She twisted her head slightly, wincing at the pain that washed through her skull. It must be an effect of the chloroform. He hadn't hit her, she remembered that.

Another sliver of light trickled through the door, which he'd thoughtfully left ajar.

She sat up, groggily, a hand pressed to her forehead. He'd admitted that he'd killed Harold. But who was he?

Thunder shook the floor beneath her. Rowen's muscles clenched in response. She didn't want to move.

"You have to!" she whispered out loud.

Her chest felt tight; her breath came in uneven spurts. But she couldn't, she wouldn't live in the past. The murderer might have gone after Des.

Every square inch of her body ached as she climbed to her feet. She was cold and shaking, her palms clammy, her mind numb with fear, but it was fear for Des's life, greater than her fear of thunder, that released her from her momentary paralysis.

She stumbled to the door, hanging on to the edge as she peered cautiously around the frame. The corridor was empty, the lights had, for the moment, steadied.

Des, she thought desperately, pushing the hair from her face. She had to get back upstairs and find him.

She wasn't sure why she noticed the other cracked door or what compelled her to tiptoe toward it. Maybe she heard a tiny sound and didn't realize it. As she drew nearer, she knew she heard something, a moan, a thump, she couldn't tell.

Her fingers wrapped around the brass knob. Uttering a prayer that the door wouldn't creak, she eased it open all the way.

The ramp was gone, she noticed instantly. Her eyes slid downward, fixing in horror and disbelief on one of the shadows.

There was a body, a man lying on the floor. And next to him, coiled and alert, sat a very long, very deadly copperhead snake.

THE FALL left Des dazed and disoriented—and vaguely surprised that he wasn't dead or even unconscious. He'd landed on something lumpy. Not a cushion, but not the floor, either.

He rolled away, bruised, heaving himself to his knees. A tiny beam of light shone through the door. It must have swung shut behind him. He could make out a black blob beside him but nothing else.

It didn't matter. Standing, he steadied himself and groped his way to the outer door. He wasn't particularly surprised when it didn't open. This whole situation felt off to him, a plan of some sort that either hadn't succeeded or wasn't quite finished.

Holding the tangled curls from his eyes, he studied the black outline. Finally, he went over to it and crouched down.

His eyes had adjusted somewhat, enough that he could make out a human shape. There was something in its hand, a flashlight, he suspected from its shape. He only needed to touch the rigid fingers wrapped around it to know that this person had been dead for some time, a day at least.

Stoically, he worked the flashlight free. His mind was still on Rowen. Even when he rolled the body over, he couldn't summon more than a passing glimmer of remorse for his dead "cousin."

Cooper's eyes stared blankly up at him. Des closed them and sat back, rubbing his chin with the side of his hand.

Had Cooper fallen accidentally, or had the murderer pushed him? He was wearing a black velvet jacket, but whether it was ripped or not, Des couldn't say. It was a moot point. Cooper couldn't be the murderer. That person had taken Rowen. Which meant he had to get out of here now.

He stood, switching on the flashlight. Only a faint glow emerged and it faded quickly to nothing. But not quickly enough that he missed the movement on the other side of Cooper's arm.

So that's why it was warm down here. Reptiles didn't function well in the cold. And ramps didn't move themselves.

Des gave the flashlight a shake, winning a full second's worth of beam. It was a copperhead, he realized, his eyes fixed on its spotted coils, poisonous and in motion. It slithered over Cooper's inert body, and directly toward him.

"DES!" Rowen could scarcely choke out his name. "Oh my God."

"Rowen?" To her shock, she heard his voice on the far side of the room, from the shadows near the outer door.

Her head snapped up. "You're alive!" she exclaimed. "Where are you? Who's that on the floor? No, wait, the snake." Relief turned to exultation, then swiftly to fear. "Where did it go?"

She tried the light switch but it didn't work. Her frantic eyes searched the corridor. "Wait a second. There was a curtain..."

She ran for the room where the murderer had deposited her and tore the heavy muslin drape from its rod.

"Here," she said, when she got back. "I'll throw this on the snake, and... I can't see it. Des, are you all right?"

"Fine. And it's at the top of Cooper's head."

"Cooper!" She spared a look at the shadowed body. "Is he—dead?"

"Very. He probably stumbled in here by accident. Throw the curtain, Rowen."

Hands trembling, she sighted the patch of darkness just above Cooper's body. Cooper's dead body. God, she felt heartless. She didn't even flinch when she thought the words.

She could reproach herself tomorrow. The snake was moving, crawling away from Cooper toward Des. Forcing a calm motion, Rowen flung the curtain down.

It settled over Cooper's head. She couldn't see the snake. Had she covered enough of it?

"Des?" she whispered softly.

He didn't answer. There was a flurry of sudden motion, a hissed breath and then a loud clap of thunder that drowned both sounds out.

Rowen waited on her hands and knees, shuddering. She couldn't see anything except Cooper. She couldn't think of anything except Des. And Jonah Blackstone's damnable curse.

IN THE NOISE and confusion of the storm, the man stole through the manor. The trap was sprung. Had it succeeded?

He crept along the shadowy corridors to the juncture—and wanted to stomp his feet in fury at what he saw.

How could he possibly be alive! Rowen had found a rope and tied it off. Damn, now he was climbing out!

The man's face burned with rage. Of all the inept, stupid . . .

He stopped himself midtirade. This was no time to let his temper reign. He had to do something. Think. A better trap awaited if he could only lure them into it.

His eyes located a folded piece of paper on the floor near one of the jack-o'-lanterns. He saw the white handkerchief farther on. Ignoring the handkerchief, he picked up the paper. A smile touched his lips. Yes, this might do the trick.

He glanced out the window. There was someone moving about, skulking around the crypt, visible despite the heavy rain.

He fingered the paper, then let it flutter back to the floor. His gaze roamed the corridor. In one of the shadowy niches sat a Grecian urn, a fake, he suspected, like the other Greek pieces that had been "destroyed" in the fire three years ago. Genuine or fake, however, it would do very nicely.

Rather, he hoped it would. This maneuver might require more luck than skill, but he was due for a little luck, surely.

"Fortune is a fickle thing, Reggie," he whispered. "But the pendulum swings both ways."

Carefully, he picked up the urn. One final look out the window to reassure himself and he released his grip. The urn shattered on the stone floor.

Turning, he ran for the nearest door and the sanctuary of the storm.

"WHAT WAS THAT?" Rowen's arms froze about Des's neck. She twisted her head around. "It came from the hall!"

Des wasted no time. "Come on," he said, taking her hand.

She considered mentioning that they might be running into the blade of a knife, but decided against it. The copperhead in the cellar was bagged; Des, thank God, hadn't been bitten. But the danger wasn't tied up with a snake. It emanated from a human source and that source was still out there.

If a confrontation, ill-advised though it might be, would put an end to this nightmare, then bring it on. Rowen was sick of skull masks and curses and death. She cast a longing look at the ceiling. If only the thunder would go away.

No human shadows lurked in the hall. There was only a handkerchief—no doubt the chloroformed one used to knock her out—a smashed vase and a piece of paper, all lying scattered about on the floor. She picked the paper up while Des checked the rest of the corridor.

"'Dear Dr. Sayers,'" she read out loud. "Des." She motioned him back. "Look at this."

He came to stand behind her, his curls brushing her cheek as he squinted at the uneven black scrawl.

"'I've come so far, survived so much,'" he read. "Ah here's something." Frowning, he indicated another line. "'Yesterday, I prepared a trap within the manor.'"

"The snake and the missing ramp," Rowen presumed. "And look, farther down it says, 'Harold and Reggie took something precious from me.'"

"I wonder what that could be?"

"I wonder." She shivered at the final paragraph. "Oh, I don't like this. 'Tonight I'll deliver another Forbes to hell, on his behalf and mine. A sweet treat for a tricky ghost.'"

"Blackstone's curse. Well, we knew he was using it."

"Not to kill me, he wasn't."

"No." Rowen saw his eyes reflected in the rain-slick window as Des rested his cheek against her hair. "It's not quite right, is it?"

She opened her mouth to agree, but stiffened her spine instead. "The skull mask!" she exclaimed, staring through the diamond pane.

"Where?"

She ran to the window. "Near the old pool. You can see the white face. It looks like he's struggling to keep his balance."

"It looks like he's heading for the Masque Factory," Des said. "I'll try to catch him."

"We," Rowen corrected as they started for the kitchen, which was the nearest exit.

She expected an argument. What she got was a grudging, "Come on then. But stay close to me."

That was easier said than done, Rowen quickly discovered. They collected raincoats on their way out, but that only kept them from getting soaked through. The grounds had been transformed into a giant mud puddle. No wonder the murderer was floundering.

Dogged persistence coupled with her fervent desire to end this nightmare drove Rowen on. Rain streamed over her face, and several times she had to push sopping strands of hair from her eyes. She could no longer see the murderer. "Has he gone into the factory?" she shouted.

"I think so," Des shouted back above the lashing wind.

A clap of thunder rocked the ground. Rowen glanced up, ice-cold inside and out. She only had so much mental energy. With that energy currently divided between masked murderers and childhood memories, she felt small and shaken, scarcely up to the challenge of facing either one.

Thank God for Des. His grip on her never slackened. He dragged her relentlessly forward and finally through the door of the Masque Factory.

The old mill was a pastiche of color and music and wonderful warm smells. Costumed bodies drifted through the shadowy parts, but there was nothing sinister about the gathering. Well, not compared to what had been happen-

ing lately. This was Halloween the way it was meant to be
spooky and cobwebbed and deliciously dark.

"Here, put this on." Des handed her a huge black cloak
with a hood. She had no idea where he'd found it. Tugging
off her raincoat, he dumped it by the door and smiled at her
"We can't chase killers in wet clothes."

"In other words, we want to blend in," Rowen trans
lated. "With luck, we'll spot him before he spots us."

"Exactly."

Des settled for a black cape stripped from one of the dis
plays and a floppy black hat, which hid a full half of hi
face. He was so tall though, noticeable even disguised. Tha
was the problem with his brand of physical presence
Skulking was a virtual impossibility.

Heads turned as they forged a path through the party. O
course, they were the only two people not wearing masks, a
oddity in itself, and a disquieting one at that.

It seemed to Rowen that seventy or more pairs of eyes
bored into her, everything from Phantoms to vampires to
Frankenstein's bride. There was no way to identify anyone
and no way to know if the murderer had changed masks.

The music became Bach's *Toccata*. The lights dimmed a
the crowd began to dance, if you could call the macabre gy
rations dancing.

A tremor rippled through Rowen's body. It had to be he
imagination that all of these people had suddenly turned
into ghouls.

"I feel like I've walked in on *Night of the Living Dead*,"
she murmured to Des.

"Or a séance?" he suggested with a shrewd arch of hi
brows. Nudging her arm, he nodded toward the rear wall
"Does that collection of people remind you of anything?"

They were standing in a line, black-clad and individually
masked. The costumes, however, were identical, long robes
belted with red rope. Motionless, they watched the pro
ceedings, a line of witches hovering in the shadows.

In their own way, they were entirely mesmerizing. Rowen
stared back, then jumped a little when something slunk into
view behind them.

"Des, that man in the black hood was wearing a skull mask."

Des peered at the doorway. "I don't see him."

"He went into the back room, the one where all the death masks are." She stopped speaking when he dragged her roughly sideways into a large shadow. "What are you doing?"

"Over there." Des's mouth was close to her ear. "He must have doubled back."

Rowen frowned. "Is he trying to hide?"

"Or to be inconspicuous. He's probably looking for us."

"In that case, he should have led us to the ruin. He can't kill us in front of all these witnesses. Can he?" she added, swallowing hard.

Des responded by pulling her tighter against him. "He's seen us," he hissed. "He's going for the back room again."

Rowen didn't like any part of this. The murderer's actions were too erratic. What exactly did he intend to do to them? Why hadn't he killed them both at the manor?

Undulating bodies impeded them, but at last they reached the mask room. The Midnight witches stared openly at Rowen and Des, following their progress with shielded eyes. But Rowen didn't see how they could be involved in this madness. Their sole aim was to bring Jonah Blackstone over from the other side.

Darkness enveloped the smaller room. The porcelain faces shone ghostly white in the glow from the party. Eerie strains of music created a perfect backdrop for the thunder outside. Rowen tugged her cape closer as Des held out a warning hand.

"There." He fixed his eyes on the corner. "A door."

"Conveniently left ajar."

"He wants us to follow him."

Rowen struggled with the lump of fear in her throat. "I don't suppose you brought your gun."

He sent her a rueful look. "I hadn't planned on leaving the manor quite so soon."

"So what should we do?"

"Absolutely nothing," a guttural voice behind her whispered. Rowen started badly, not recognizing it. A blade jabbed her in the spine. "No, don't move, Reggie," the man cautioned when Des's muscles twitched. Who was it? Rowen wondered desperately. The murderer's voice came into her ear. "Your elusiveness tonight has made me angry, but now the cat becomes the mouse. Turn and walk very slowly ahead of me. I don't want to hurt Rowen, but I will if I have to."

Rowen's mind worked frantically. What did he mean, 'The cat becomes the mouse'?

He gave her a shove. "Go," he ordered, his raspy words muffled by the skull mask. "Reggie first. Walk under the ladder. Walk right under the rungs and through the door."

There was no mistaking the mockery in his voice or the unnerving tinge of hysteria that underscored it. He was mad, as Rowen had somehow known all along. And he was going to kill them both, no matter what he said to the contrary.

She saw the tension radiating from Des's body. But he turned and walked under the ladder as he'd been instructed.

The murderer gave a papery-soft laugh. "So, you do love her, after all. Then my punishment for you may be a fitting one indeed. Now go down the stairs to the basement. We're entering Jonah Blackstone's world tonight, Reggie. Rest assured, it's a world you'll come to know extremely well."

Chapter Nineteen

The tunnels spread out endlessly before him, echoing with sounds Des couldn't begin to identify. He was aware of the murderer behind him, holding a large knife to Rowen's spine.

"Walk slowly," the man instructed. "Don't do anything stupid."

The voice sounded male to Des. That let Almira out. American accents, however, could be faked, so he couldn't dismiss Franz.

"Why don't you let us see you?" Rowen asked with a slight quaver.

"When we get there," he promised.

They wound an arduous path through the underground maze, past patches of dried mold and minor cave-ins, then up a set of stone stairs until they emerged into the ruin.

"A roundabout route. Most of the tunnels are blocked," was all the man would say. "We'll reenter over there." He gestured toward the room that Des and Rowen had discovered their first full day at the manor.

"Why did you clean out this particular room?" Des asked as they proceeded.

"Harold did that." The murderer sounded odd but alert. "He used to come here at night to search for the tunnel entrances."

"You mean he was looking for the skull mask?" Rowen said.

The man's voice dropped to a bitter, low, barely audible whisper above the wind and rain. "No," he said, reaching out to pull a charred timber from the wall. "He was look-ing for a place to store his antiques. This room was out of the way. He would have used it if he hadn't discovered a better one under the barn."

A portion of the wall slid away. Des started down the stairs. "So you know about the antiques Harold stashed there."

"Yes, Reggie, I know all about it."

That meant he could be Darcy, Des mused. He heard the storm in the distance and the closer sound of their foot-steps in the dried ruts—unmeasured, slow, heavy steps. No limp that he could detect, but on this ground it would be difficult to tell.

The tunnel broadened. Des continued to listen. A num-ber of archways appeared to their left and right, some with doors, some without.

"The safe room caved in while I was excavating it," the man finally said in his indistinct undertone. "But this is Blackstone's workshop. Stop here and turn right. Walk through the door, Reggie, into the darkness. It's waiting for you there."

The soft, mad sound of laughter filled the damp air.

"See the candles flickering before it? I light them every night. I thought you might never see it, but now you're here, and I know this was how it was meant to be, why you didn't die when I pushed you over the cliff, or when I made the lights fall in the factory, or when I tried to trap you with that snake in the basement. You ran away from me, Reggie, you slipped through my fingers tonight, you made me chase you. But you didn't win. You only did what Blackstone intended from the very beginning."

Des stared at the object in front of him. It sat on a ped-estal on an old wooden table surrounded by fat candles, taunting him with its empty black eye sockets. This was no rubber reproduction, it was the real thing, scarred and sooty, the embodiment of Jonah Blackstone's curse. The original skull mask.

Dragging Rowen with him, the murderer reached for an old-fashioned torch on the wall and touched the tip to the candle. When it flared, he held the burning wood over a scattering of dried straw and began to laugh.

"Say goodbye, Reggie. You die the way you left me to die." His voice rose above the crackle of flames. "Burn, you adulterous bastard murderer. Go and join old Harold in the fires of hell!"

"No, don't!" Rowen screamed, grabbing his wrist. He was holding the knife in the same hand as the torch. He could shove her away but he couldn't stab her. "Please," she begged, but he wasn't listening.

Burn, he'd cried. As you left me to burn. Adulterous, bastard, murderer...

Rowen's head spun. Adulterous! Reggie's rumored affair with Grace Mitchell?

Thrusting Rowen behind him, the man flung the torch at Des's head. Des ducked and it missed, landing on the floor near the back wall. Although slightly dazed, Rowen saw the flames catch on the bits of wood lying there. Then she saw Des lunge.

Scrambling unsteadily to her feet, she ran to them. Surely one man couldn't overpower both of them.

The murderer spun, almost falling in the process. His feet seemed to be tangled underneath him. Des pounced on the stumble, seizing the man's arms and wrestling them into a painful position behind his back.

Even trapped, the killer refused to submit. He twisted and swore and kicked Des very hard before Rowen's fingers were able to latch on to the rubber skull mask and rip it from his startled face.

She shouldn't have been shocked. Maybe she wasn't.

Wisps of smoke from the flames crept insidiously across the rear of the room, stinging her eyes and blurring her vision. She pictured the tunnels. Walk slowly, he'd instructed Des. Of course, he would need to go slowly, she realized now. If she was right, this man's injuries, though perhaps not as extensive as he'd led them to believe, were undeniably real.

Rowen let the mask slip from her fingers. For a shocked moment, the man simply stared at her, a pathetic creature, his sandy hair a flattened cap on his head, his eyes shining with something more desperate than hatred.

"Val Mitchell?" The question came out as a whisper, a choked thread of sound from Rowen's throat.

His head jerked. "Yes—Val. Val Mitchell. Grace was my wife. Mine..." His voice trailed off, but his eyes continued to glow. They were the eyes of a madman. And they were set in the face of the man they'd known as Terrance Poole.

ROWEN STARED, disbelieving. "Why?" she whispered, because it was easier to ask than to try to piece it all together. "Why did you do it?"

She shouldn't have spoken. Her words had the effect of rousing him from his temporary state of submission.

Releasing a violent roar, he kicked Des hard in the knee, then he worked one arm free and took a swing at his head. To do that, he had to twist himself around. But Des wasn't about to release him. Rowen heard an agonizing crack of bone and Poole's subsequent shriek of pain. Then she saw something flash in his free hand.

"Des!" she screamed. "He's got another knife!"

There was no way for Des to avoid the blade. But he was quick enough that it slashed mostly through his shirt, leaving only a thin line of red across his chest.

"You killed Grace and left me for dead," Poole, or rather Mitchell, accused, scurrying backward until he stood in the doorway.

"No, I didn't," Des replied calmly. His advance on the man was smooth, almost imperceptible.

He bared his teeth. The knife came up in a defensive gesture. "You did! You murdered your lover because that's what you are, Reggie, a murdering snake. You knew I was in the building, you saw me, I know you did." His face contorted. His broken arm hung limp at his side. Smoke swirled in a sinuous spiral about his head. "I dragged myself out of there. I was burned and bleeding and half-unconscious. But even while I was crawling away, I promised myself that one day I'd make you pay. You and Harold. You did it together. I figured that out later. You wanted to get the insurance money by destroying a bunch of phony antiques. But why did you have to kill my wife?"

Des glanced meaningfully at Rowen. She responded, forcing her shaky legs to carry her away from the wall.

In her peripheral vision, she noticed the table smoldering at the far end of the old workshop. The skull mask seemed to taunt her, but she knew that had to be an illusion, a trick of the flickering candles. Then, at the base of the skull, she spied a small brown object, something curved and furry, too small to be a mouse. Besides, it wasn't moving.

It didn't matter. Marshaling her defenses, she faced Val Mitchell. "Why did you try to kill me?" she demanded.

Her question captured his attention, although it seemed that he was beyond answering rationally. Red-rimmed eyes blinked at her. "I don't like to kill," he whispered. "I keep telling people that. Why don't they listen? I only kill when I have to. I tried to explain that to Dr. Sayers, but she said I shouldn't want to kill at all."

Rowen fought to keep her voice steady and at the same time not choke on the smoke that was growing thicker by the minute. "Is Dr. Sayers your psychiatrist?"

"She was." Poole's voice faltered. "I left her a few years ago, when I came here. I needed to make a plan. I found out that Harold was coming to live in Midnight. I wanted to be near him." His voice became distant. "Wasn't I lucky that the grounds keeper here just happened to disappear? I liked Almira's husband. He hired me when Mr. Simms—that was the old grounds keeper's name—went away."

"Went away?" Rowen repeated carefully. She saw Des drawing nearer. Five more steps and he'd have the man within his grasp. "That *was* lucky, wasn't it?" she said, willing a composure she was far from feeling.

His expression darkened. "No," he said in a dangerous tone. "It wasn't luck. But I needed to be here and he was in my way. I don't think Dr. Sayers approved, but it didn't matter. Old Harold was going to retire here. It was all perfect." His voice rose. "Even Blackstone's curse fit my plans. I knew I could use it to..."

He cut his confession off sharply, his head snapping around. "No!" he hissed. "Not this time, Reggie."

Raising the knife, he threw himself at Des. But the blade missed its target completely. Des knocked the weapon away and grabbed the man's shirt, slamming him hard against the wall.

Rowen heard a sharp crack, then saw Poole's head loll to one side. His eyes rolled back in his skull, his body crumpling as his legs gave way beneath him. Unconscious, he dropped with a dull thud to the floor.

The sound released Rowen from her terrified trance. She ran to Des. He was bleeding, the knife had sliced deeper into his chest than she'd thought. The front of his shirt was stained bright red.

"It's not as bad as it looks," he assured her, but he didn't protest when she used the tail of his shirt to wipe away some of the blood.

She spared a look at the fire, which was more smoke than flames at this point. "We have to get out of here. We can send someone back for Poole."

"Mitchell," Des murmured. He steadied himself with an arm around her shoulders. His puzzled eyes surveyed the fallen man. "He said he crawled out of the building."

Rowen's fingers tightened on Des's shirt, but she kept doggedly at her task.

The memory returned even so, the picture of a man running toward the parking lot. Running. But there'd been something before that, hadn't there, a detail she'd never been able to pin down. He'd woven a path through the construction equipment, hesitated, stumbled and run on.

She envisioned the site with its coils of rope and paint cans, its sheets of plywood and glass, its scaffolding and ladders. She'd run through a similar site on the Midnight docks the night of the Halloween street party. Her pursuer had hesitated that night, too. And there was that other thing she'd seen on the table only a few minutes ago.

Her knuckles white on Des's shirt, Rowen stole a look at the table. Even with all the smoke, the skull mask was visible. So were the candles and the brown, furry object she'd noticed earlier.

Not a mouse, her brain informed her.

"Des," she whispered, her skin cold and clammy despite the rising heat. "If Poole, or Mitchell, did crawl from that building three years ago, then who was it that I saw running toward the parking lot?"

Des made an abstracted sound, and suddenly Rowen didn't want to acknowledge anything more. She certainly didn't want to leave Des and dash over to the table. But she did.

Her fingers closed on the thing. She'd always thought they were horrible. How could a rabbit's foot be lucky? How could running under a ladder be unlucky?

She didn't realize that Des had come up behind her until she felt his shoulder brush her arm. It wasn't a casual gesture.

"He always carries a rabbit's foot," he muttered through his teeth. "The bastard!"

Smoke coiled through the tiny room. The skull mask seemed to Rowen to be laughing now. At them?

Des grabbed her hand, rabbit's foot and all. "We have to get out of here," he said, hauling her backward.

Rowen's mind swam. A vivid image of the man running from the fire shot through her head. She closed her eyes, groaning. "That's it, Des," she whispered. "My elusive detail. He didn't almost collide with the ladder that night, he almost ran under it. That's why he hesitated. It was never Mitchell at all. It was..."

A sharp click from the doorway warned her that they were no longer alone. He was behind them, as he'd been behind so much of what had happened in Midnight.

Raising her head, Rowen turned slowly and glared at him. "You!" she whispered, shocked in spite of herself to actually see his face. "It was you I saw."

He smiled at both of them. "It was me," he agreed. Then he raised the gun in his hand until it pointed at Des's chest. "Time to die—Reggie Forbes."

ROWEN'S REACTION was instinctive. Protect. She flung herself in front of Des before the man could pull the trigger.

"No, you can't," she gasped in panic. "You won't get away with it."

"Oh, but I will," he said softly.

For a numbed moment, Rowen could do nothing except stare in shock. How could she have been so blind? Her fist clenched around the rabbit's foot. Poole must have accidentally found it. There was no chance that the two men were working together.

Her eyes closed briefly, terror and revulsion sweeping through her. He would have killed two people the night of the fire. He intended to kill two more tonight.

She couldn't really see his features in that endless second of time. She didn't need to. He was a pale imitation of his cousin...and everything Mitchell had said earlier now made perfect sense.

This man was the true source of the evil, Harold's partner in crime, his beloved grandson, the real Reggie Forbes.

Des set Rowen aside, his eyes not wavering from Reggie's face. "He'll kill you, Rowen. Won't you cousin? That must have been your plan all along. Why, I can't imagine, but the fact that someone else wanted you 'dead' was apparently perfect for your purpose." Des gave a humorless laugh, regarding Reggie through the tangle of his curls. "I should have known you'd pull a stunt like this. You knew all about Mitchell and his plan for revenge from the start, didn't you?"

"Not at all." The gun dropped a notch. The danger level didn't.

Rowen glanced at the flames behind them. Was the fire spreading more rapidly now?

Reggie continued, "I only knew that someone had murdered Harold. I had no idea who'd done it, or why. But I figured that whoever it was would probably come after me next. And if he didn't, well, then I'd just have to do the job myself and let the blame fall where it may. I'd have been dead, you see. Reggie Forbes would have been buried in the Midnight Cemetery next to his grandfather, and anyone who didn't attribute the death to Blackstone's curse would undoubtedly lay it at the feet of whoever murdered Harold."

Dense layers of smoke drifted in front of Rowen's eyes. She waved them away. "I don't understand," she said. "You intended to kill yourself?"

"Technically speaking, yes. Only it would have been Des who died in my place. Not that anyone would have known that." He arched an ingenuous eyebrow. "Except for you, Rowen dear. Fortunately, your presence in my life was about to be ended, anyway. You see, I really couldn't have let you live much longer. I think you know why."

"Because it was you I saw running from the fire in Los Angeles."

"Exactly. Luckily for me, you thought the man you saw was Val Mitchell. Everybody thought that, which was what I intended when I took his keys and drove off in his car. I even went into his house and packed up a few of his things—to support my story, you understand. But I knew you'd seen me better than your friends had. I also knew that if you ever mentioned the bit about my almost tripping in my rush to go around that construction ladder rather than under it, I'd be found out, or at least suspected. I'm a self-confessed believer in superstition. Val Mitchell isn't."

Des regarded him through narrowed eyes. "Yes, could we get back to the part about why you wanted yourself dead?"

"Don't push me, cousin," Reggie warned. Then he smiled and continued. "As I was saying, I couldn't have suspicion falling on me for starting the fire, could I? So I came to the inquest, just to see how much you knew. Strangely enough—and this is to your credit, Rowen—I found I was attracted to you. You never mentioned anything about the person you saw trying to avoid running under a ladder, so I thought to myself, I won't kill her. Not yet. I'll . . ."

"Have some fun first?" she interrupted angrily.

His smile was placid. "You could say that." He moved the gun. "Back up, Des," he warned. "I haven't gone through all of this to let you jump me in a smoky tunnel. I *am* going to die tonight. Well, you're gong to die in my place, actually, but the end result will be the same. You two will be dead. Mitchell here—" he nudged the unconscious man beside him with the toe of his polished boot "—will take the blame, and I will simply disappear."

"Why?" Des persisted.

Reggie rubbed his thumb and fingers together. "Money," he said succinctly. "Harold disinherited me on the sly. Only he wasn't sly enough. I found out that he'd changed his will. As you can imagine, I wasn't terribly happy. So I began embezzling heavily from the corporation. In case you're not aware of the law, that's a crime, and I'm guilty up to my ears. At some point, Peter Pettiston is going to find Harold's will, and the police are going to allow it to be read. Once that happens, I'll be a wanted man. But only wanted if I'm still alive, so to speak. My solution to that problem? I am going to 'die' tonight."

Des studied his cousin's face. "Why did Harold disinherit you, Reggie?"

"Because of Grace Mitchell. She learned about Harold's and my plan to defraud the insurance company. She was blackmailing us. I decided to do something about it."

"You killed her," Rowen said flatly.

Reggie shrugged. "I prefer permanent solutions, present company temporarily excluded. Harold disagreed. He wasn't into murder. Of course until Poole confessed he was Val Mitchell, I had no idea that he had gotten out of the building that night. I assumed that both Val and Grace died in the fire. You see, Mitchell didn't realize what his wife was up to. He believed that Grace and I were having an affair. He stormed into the building that night, ready to accuse us like the jealous idiot he was. Only the scene he stormed in on was scarcely one of intimate passion. He found me with my hands wrapped around Grace's throat. He attacked me, so I knocked him out. I'd set off a fault in the wiring system earlier. The place was already starting to burn. I decided to let the fire finish him off." He waved at the gray smoke that circled his head. "And speaking of fires, this one seems to be getting a bit thick."

Yes, it was, Rowen thought, dizziness crowding her terror, but not as quickly as it should. She had a bizarre sense of something keeping it at bay, like a giant hand cupped around a flame to stop it from spreading.

Black eye sockets bored into her spine. Reggie was raising the gun. He was too far away for either she or Des to knock it from his hand. Unless...

Rowen backed up, her fingers groping for the table. She singed them on a candle but managed to locate the skull. As Reggie started to squeeze the trigger, she heaved the heavy skull mask at his arm.

The gun fell, hitting the floor and discharging. Outraged, Reggie dived to retrieve it, but Des was right there.

Rowen saw Mitchell stir as she ran toward the men. Des was already struggling with Reggie. The gun must have been kicked away; she couldn't find it. She also couldn't see the skull mask anywhere.

She went to jump over Mitchell, then started badly when Mitchell's fingers closed around her ankle.

"Let me go." She tried to shake him off.

But he merely pointed at the back wall, his mouth dropping open in shock.

Whatever caused the reaction, Rowen couldn't see it. She received a hazy impression of something black stirring in the corner. The floor seemed to vibrate, then she felt herself being thrown backward as an explosion took out the entire rear section of the room.

Flames, previously contained, shot upward in a violent plume. Bits of stone and timber showered them. Hot sparks flew in all directions.

Rowen's cloak began to smolder. She tossed it off, coughing in the billowing smoke. She could no longer see Des or Reggie.

Through the chaos, a voice she didn't recognize said harshly, "Run, Rowen."

Maybe it was the voice of panic. The roar from the fire was infinitely worse than any thunder she'd ever heard.

"Des!" she screamed, distantly aware that Mitchell was using her leg to haul himself to his feet. "Let me go!" She kicked at him. "Des!"

"Get out of here!" A body rushed past, grabbing her as it shot into the smoke-filled tunnel. "Take Mitchell and get the hell out." Des shouted, panting. "I'm going after Reggie. Go on, Rowen."

"No, you . . ." But he was already gone, swallowed up by the smoke. " . . . can't," she finished in a choked whisper.

Another explosion rocked the tunnels. Earth and stone cascaded down the walls.

"Please, help me," Mitchell begged from the doorway.

He was on his knees, a more pitiful sight than her brother had been huddled in that cave.

Squaring her shoulders, Rowen took one last look down the tunnel after Des, then with a resolute, "He'll be all right," she went for Mitchell, helping him awkwardly to his feet and setting his good arm over her shoulders.

She had no idea which way was out, and Mitchell was only semiconscious, whimpering in her ear about Dr. Sayers, apologizing for all the monstrous things he'd done. "I killed Harold. I didn't mean for Cooper to die. Reggie was supposed to fall into the cellar."

It felt as if he weighed five hundred pounds. Rowen could scarcely cope. The smoke was everywhere, and deafening explosions sounded throughout the passageways.

Would Des get out, she wondered, but didn't dare dwell on that. A fork loomed before them. Should they take the left or right passage?

"Go right," a voice in her head instructed. Now she was sure it wasn't her voice or the voice of instinct, but she obeyed it anyway, without hesitation.

Five minutes later, a set of stairs came into view. "Thank God," she breathed, stumbling forward. "Wake up," she grunted when his knees almost buckled.

He roused himself and staggered upward to a door Rowen had never seen before. Please let it open, she prayed.

It didn't. She rattled the knob, whispering a disbelieving, "No!"

Mitchell sagged against it. She shoved him aside and yanked with both hands. The wood frame gave a pop and the door swung open. Rowen dragged Mitchell through—then stopped dead in surprise on the other side.

They'd emerged under the staircase in the Masque Factory. But it wasn't the same festive factory she'd left. Smoke poured from the back room and from the loft of the adjacent barn. Tongues of orange flame licked the walls, running along the beams overhead.

How could the fire have spread so quickly and over such a vast distance?

She shook herself. The shrieking partyers were evacuating en masse. The last to go were the Midnight witches. The entire group of them trudged across the burning room. One witch glanced at Rowen but didn't stop. She saw it in his eyes, however. He believed that Jonah Blackstone had done this.

They were all mad, Rowen decided grimly. She wrestled Mitchell across the floor and out into the pouring rain.

Thunder crashed above the trees, barely drowning out the roar of the fire. Too exhausted now to be afraid, Rowen unwrapped Mitchell's arm from her neck.

She spotted Richard in the excited crowd and called to him. "Watch him for me. He killed Harold."

"What?"

She started off. The police, she thought, exhaustion pressing in. She had to find someone in authority. It was the only thing left that she could do. Explain the situation. And pray that Des could find a way out of the flames.

HE TACKLED Reggie inside the new Masque Factory.

Des had chased his cousin all over hell in the tunnels, running in circles, he suspected. They'd broken out under the burning staircase in the old mill. It seemed the only available exit.

"Let me go," Reggie squawked, panting for breath.

Des took pleasure in ramming his fist into Reggie's mouth. "No." He grabbed his cousin's lapels. "You tried to kill Rowen and me so you could take off and start a new life under another name. You killed Grace Mitchell. Did you kill Anna, too?"

Reggie squirmed beneath him. "Yes," he finally burst out when Des threatened to hit him again. "She must have spotted me from her window while I was watching the house. I didn't realize I'd been seen until I heard her come up beside me. She knew the truth. I had to kill her, didn't I?"

Des leaned forward. "How?" he demanded through clenched teeth.

"I shoved her over the cliff."

"The way you shoved me?"

"It was Mitchell who shoved you, you idiot. Mitchell or Poole, or whatever the hell name he's using. He was just an anonymous dupe as far as I was concerned. Now let me up or we'll both die."

Heat from the fire seared Des's skin but he refused to move. "You caved in the tunnel on Rowen and me, didn't you?"

"Yes. Only that idiot, Mitchell, butted in. You heard him in the tunnel. He wanted me dead, not her."

"So it was you who attacked Rowen on the docks."

"Yes!"

"And shot at us."

"For Chrissake, yes!" Reggie shrieked. "I've been living in the cellar at the coven house. I didn't know who the murderer was until tonight, and even then I would never have recognized him if he hadn't admitted who he was. The man's obviously had extensive plastic surgery. I saw someone wearing a skull mask grab Rowen. I knew that whoever he was, he had a plan to kill you, or rather me, but I also knew his plan had failed when I saw you climb out of the cellar. Mitchell must have spotted me on the estate, that's why he left Rowen. He didn't understand what was happening. He thought I should be trapped in the basement. He chased me but I doubled back to the manor. I saw him skulking around outside so I broke the vase, ran out and got him to chase me to the factory while you chased him. Once he spotted you, all I had to do was follow you into the tunnels. Now will you please let me up before we're both burned alive."

Des had no chance to respond. A portion of the wall unexpectedly blew, knocking him sideways. Reggie scrambled out from under him and made for the door.

Dazed, Des climbed to his feet.

"There's no way out!" he heard Reggie shout above the clamor. His cousin rushed toward the staircase, pausing just long enough to kick a piece of burning wood at Des. "You stupid son of a bitch! We're trapped!"

There was nowhere to go but up, Des realized. Choking, unable to breathe, he followed his cousin up the stairs.

The entry to the barn was a wall of flames. They had to go higher, and higher still, until at last they arrived on the top floor.

It was Des who noticed the trapdoor and climbed up onto the window ledge to thrust it open. Reggie clawed at his leg, but Des kicked the flailing hand away and hoisted himself through.

The roof breathed underneath him, like the chest of a sleeping giant. Red lights flashed on Cemetery Road and on the ground below. He held the hair off his forehead, his mind working swiftly as he caught his breath. Where was the ladder truck?

A snarl from behind distracted him. Reggie was charging across the roof, a murderous glint in his eyes. He lunged, wrapping his fingers around Des's throat and squeezing tightly.

Des lost track of things after that. He knew he succeeded in removing Reggie's fingers from his throat and even managed to trip him up. But the roof seemed suddenly alive, an angry monster heaving beneath them. Portions of it actually blew open, allowing the flames to break through.

The rain did nothing to douse the fire. "I'm burning!" Reggie cried. He grabbed Des from behind and held fast to his waist. "My legs, I can't feel them."

"You're not bloody burning," Des retorted, but he re-ented and hauled his cousin upright. "Walk," he ordered.

"I can't." Reggie's face contorted with fury. "I'm not going to die alone, Des."

He didn't have to die at all, Des thought, coughing from the smoke while he pried Reggie's clinging fingers from his flopping shirt.

Another explosion rent the roof, splitting it apart very close to them. Reggie staggered backward, off-balance, clutching at Des as he went. All he caught was Des's foot, but he gave it a mighty yank. Des broke free, tripping in the process and hitting his head.

Great clouds of black smoke engulfed him. He'd fallen dangerously close to the edge. Lights from the fire trucks flashed below, barely visible to him. He saw the smoke billow up around Reggie's cringing form.

"Nooo!" his cousin screamed. He seemed to grapple with something, then in desperation he flung himself at Des. "Help me!"

But for some reason, Des couldn't seem to get his legs under him. He must have hit his head quite hard, he reflected blearily.

Reggie's fingers groped for his pant leg, then slowly began to recede, as if the smoke were sucking him backward. A huge explosion sent plumes of flames into the air, scattering fiery bits of wood over the roof. For a fuzzy moment, Des thought he saw a pair of giant arms and above them the smoking outline of a bearded face.

He closed his eyes, fighting a wave of dizziness, and crawled to his feet.

"Des, help me!" Reggie shouted.

Des almost reached him. But just as his fingers were about to close on Reggie's wrist, the smoke thickened. His cousin's hand was ripped away. With a final panicky shriek Reggie pitched through the hole in the roof behind him.

On his knees, and thoroughly exhausted, Des dropped his head forward. The smoke filled his lungs and his mind. He was dimly aware of activity in the background, of someone calling his name.

Rowen...

The dizziness increased. The blackness rushed in. It had to be his imagination, but just before he passed out, Des thought he heard a soft satisfied chuckle, as the flames in the Masque Factory slowly began to die down.

Epilogue

"So there were actually two maniacs running around loose," Richard summed up three days later. "A man named Val Mitchell, known to us as Terrance Poole, and Reggie himself. Mitchell wanted revenge—he wore the skull mask and used the legend to cover his murder attempts—while Reggie simply wanted to cover his crooked tracks by killing 'himself' so to speak, and also by murdering Rowen in case it ever occurred to her that the man she'd seen running from the fire in Los Angeles had deliberately avoided going under a ladder. Is that right?"

Des nodded and lit a cigarette. Midnight Manor was being temporarily closed pending an investigation by the FBI and God knew what other interested agencies.

"And there's still no sign of Anna's body?" Richard asked, picking up his bags.

"None," Des said, "but she's down there somewhere on the rocks."

The two men walked out the front door. "What about you?" Richard said. "Are you in trouble with the authorities for your impersonation?"

Des grinned. "I'm always in trouble with the authorities for something, but in this case, probably not."

Chains clanked behind them as the manor was securely locked. "Weird Halloween," Richard observed with a shake of his head. "Anna and Cooper dead—by the way, Cooper's death was an accident, wasn't it?"

Des's eyes roamed the misty estate. "According to Rowen, Cooper just stumbled in where he shouldn't have."

"Into one of Poole's traps."

"Mitchell's."

"Same difference. So now Mitchell's under police guard in a Boston psychiatric ward, Reggie's dead, Darcy's in mourning, Lester's totally pissed off about the factory burning, Franz has admitted that he's been able to walk for several years—he was simply playing on Harold's guilt to get what he could from the old man—and there's a legal freeze on the Forbes's personal and corporate assets. Does that cover everything?"

Des let his gaze stray to the newly burned Masque Factory. "Pretty much. Almira's been dressing up in her husband's clothes, sticking a beard on her face and talking to his ghost, but the doctor says it's a harmless enough delusion. She doesn't want to let Gilbert go. And Mitchell, aka Poole, never did work for any shipbuilding firm in Boston. That was just an unfortunate coincidence that Almira happened to stumble upon."

Richard frowned. "Should I know what you're talking about?"

Finishing his cigarette, Des dropped it on the wet ground. "Not really. Have you seen Rowen?"

"She's with Darcy on the cliff. He wanted to say goodbye to Anna. Are you flying back to London?"

"I'm not sure." Des started for the cliffs. "Hold the cab for us, will you?"

Richard held up an acknowledging hand, then turned to one of the policemen milling about the estate. "So what do you make of all this? Was it Blackstone's curse, do you think...?"

Des preferred not to think, not right then. He could see Rowen through the mist, heading toward him in a long black raincoat she'd borrowed from Almira.

"Goodbyes finished?" he asked when she drew near.

"More or less. He's awfully upset." She glanced over her shoulder. "He must have really loved her."

Des summoned a smile. "Well."

She narrowed her eyes. "That's it? That's all you have to say to me? No impassioned, 'I know how he feels, Rowen'?"

"I know how he feels, Rowen," Des complied with forced solemnity. With gentle fingers, he brushed the hair from her cheek. "I didn't think I'd ever see you again when I was up on that roof."

He felt the shiver that ran through her. "You almost didn't," she said softly. Sliding her arms around his neck, she stared up at him. "The whole roof caved in after we got you down. Another few seconds and you'd have been as dead as Reggie." She laid her forehead against his chest. "God, what a horrible way to die. Impaled on a spike. I know he caved that tunnel in, and left us to suffocate..."

"And shot at us," Des added.

"Yes, I know. It's still an awful way to die. The police found a black velvet jacket in the basement of the coven house, did you know that?"

Des kissed her forehead. "Ripped?"

She nodded. "I gave them the scrap of material we found. They also discovered a stack of letters in that locked sea chest in Poole's—Mitchell's—room, letters written to a Dr. Sayers. They were all addressed to a Los Angeles cemetery."

"So he killed her."

"I gather he felt he had to. He's crazy, Des. Although he did get us out of the tunnel, didn't he? I wonder if he thought Reggie was Blackstone's ghost. You'd almost think the possibility crossed his mind from the tone of his letters." She paused, wriggling against him. "What are you doing?"

"Kissing you."

"So you do love me?"

He suppressed his amusement. "Very much."

"So, what's your first name then?"

He grinned a little. "Elijah."

"Elijah Desmond Jones. Sounds prophetic."

"Doesn't it, though?"

She laughed. "Well, I guess I love you, too, Elijah Desmond Jones. But you are a Bohemian, and I still don't want to live like my mother does."

"Then we'll just have to work on a compromise, won't we? What about Casablanca?"

"What about London?"

"Or Boston."

Her eyes clouded slightly. "How did he do that, Des?
Reggie, I mean. He was never in Boston and yet I phoned
him there."

"You phoned a number there. He simply had the call
forwarded to him in Midnight."

Rowen's finger traced the line of his cheekbone. "You
know Reggie died on Halloween, don't you?"

"Blackstone's curse come true?"

"Well, it did. And you admitted yourself that you weren't
altogether sure what you saw up on the roof."

"True." Des kissed her, his lips curving against her
mouth. "But Blackstone didn't kill Harold, Rowen, that
was Poole's doing."

"Yes, it was," she agreed. A trace of irony shimmered in
her eyes. "You know what that means, don't you, at least
in terms of Harold's death."

"What?"

Pressing her mouth to his ear, she whispered a soft, "It
means, Des, that for once, the butler did it."

THE AREA AROUND the gutted Masque Factory smelled of
charred wet wood. A layer of heavy mist had settled in. The
man standing in the middle of the rubble couldn't see the
witches in the woods. He only knew that since he was here,
they must be there.

A smile grazed his lips beneath his long black beard. He
moved purposefully through the scorched remnants of the
mill and barn. It was all gone, including the antiques stored
below. A just ending, all things considered. Another fate-
ful Halloween come and gone.

The object he sought lay beneath a pile of black ashes. It
was sootier now than before, but intact as always. He picked
it up and brushed it off. Maybe it would be needed again
someday. Where the Forbes family was concerned, one
could never be sure. For now, though, he would take it and
leave Midnight.

Soundlessly, the man made his way back through the
rubble. Tucking the skull mask under one arm, he limped
through the mist toward Cemetery Road.

It was done.

Chapter One

. . . . And here's more of the best in romantic suspense!

Turn the page for a bonus look at what's in store for you next month, in Harlequin Intrigue #253 WHAT CHILD IS THIS?—a special Christmas edition in Rebecca York's 43 Light Street series.

In the hallowed halls of this charming building, danger has been averted and romance has blossomed. Now Christmas comes to 43 Light Street—and in its stocking is all the action, suspense and romance that your heart can hold.

Chapter One

Guilty until proven innocent.

Erin Morgan squinted into the fog that turned the buildings on either side of Light Street into a canyon of dimly realized apparitions.

"Guilty until proven innocent," she repeated aloud.

It wasn't supposed to work that way. Yet that was how Erin had felt since the Graveyard Murders had rocked Baltimore. Ever since the killer had tricked her into framing her friend Sabrina Barkley.

Sabrina had forgiven her. But she hadn't forgiven herself, and she was never going to let something like that happen again.

She glanced at the purse beside her on the passenger seat and felt her stomach knot. It was stuffed with five thousand dollars in contributions for Santa's Toy and Clothing Fund. Most were checks, but she was carrying more than eight hundred dollars in cash. And she wasn't going to keep it in her possession a moment longer than necessary.

Erin pressed her foot down on the accelerator and then eased up again as a dense patch of white swallowed up the car. She couldn't even see the Christmas decorations she knew were festooned from many of the downtown office windows.

"'Tis the season to be jolly..." She sang a few lines of the carol to cheer herself up, but her voice trailed off in the gloom.

Forty-three Light Street glided into view through the mist like a huge underwater rock formation.

Erin drove around to the back of the building where she could get in and out as quickly as possible. Pulling the collar of her coat closed against the icy wind, she hurried toward the back door—the key ready in her hand.

It felt good to get out of the cold. But there was nothing welcoming about the dank, dimly lit back entrance—so different from the fading grandeur of the marble foyer. Here there were no pretensions of gentility, only institutional-gray walls and a bare concrete floor.

Clutching her purse more tightly, she strained her ears and peered into the darkness. She heard nothing but the familiar sound of the steam pipes rattling. And she saw nothing moving in the shadows. Still, the fine hairs on the back of her neck stirred as she bolted into the service elevator and pressed the button.

Upstairs the paint was brighter, and the tile floors were polished. But at this time of night, only a few dim lights held back the shadows, and the clicking of her high heels echoed back at her like water dripping in an underground cavern.

Feeling strangely exposed in the darkness, Erin kept her eyes focused on the glass panel of her office door. She was almost running by the time she reached it.

Her hand closed around the knob. It was solid and reassuring against her moist palm, and she felt some of the knots in her stomach untie themselves. With a sigh of relief, she kicked the door closed behind her, shutting out the unseen phantoms of the hall.

Reaching over one of the mismatched couches donated by a local rental company, she flipped the light switch. Nothing happened. Darn. The bulb must be out.

In the darkness, she took a few steps toward the file room and stopped.

Something else was wrong. Maybe it was the smell. Not the clean pine scent of the little Christmas tree she'd set up by the window, but the dank odor of sweat.

She was backing quietly toward the door when fingers as hard and lean as a handcuff shot out and closed around her wrist.

A scream of terror rose in her throat. The sound was choked off by a rubber glove against her lips.

Someone was in her office. In the dark.

Her mind registered no more than that. But her body was already struggling—trying to twist away.

"No. Please." Even as she pleaded, she knew she was wasting her breath.

He was strong. And ruthless.

Her free hand came up to pummel his shoulder and neck. He grunted and shook her so hard that her vision blurred.

She tried to work her teeth against the rubbery palm that covered her mouth.

His grip adroitly shifted to her throat. He began to squeeze, and she felt the breath turn to stone in her lungs.

He bent her backward over his arm, and she stared up into a face covered by a ski mask, the features a strange parody of something human.

The dark circles around the eyes, the red circle around the mouth, the two dots of color on his cheeks—all wavered in her vision like coins in the bottom of a fountain.

The pressure increased. Her lungs were going to explode.
No. Please. Let me go home. I have a little boy. He needs me.

The words were choked off like her life breath.

Like the rapidly fading light. She was dying. And the scenes of her life flashed before her eyes. Climbing into bed with her parents on Sunday morning. First grade. High school graduation. Her marriage to Bruce. Kenny's birth. Her husband's death. Betraying Sabrina. Finishing college. Her new job with Silver Miracle Charities. The holiday fund-raiser tonight.

The events of her life trickled through her mind like the last grains of sand rolling down the sloping sides of an hourglass. Then there was only blackness.

Don't miss this next 43 Light Street tale—#253 WHApT CHILD IS THIS?—*coming December 1993—only from Rebecca York and Harlequin Intrigue!*

Relive the romance...
Harlequin and Silhouette
are proud to present

by Request ™

A program of collections of three complete novels by the most-requested authors with the most-requested themes. Be sure to look for one volume each month with three complete novels by top-name authors.

In September: **BAD BOYS**
Dixie Browning
Ann Major
Ginna Gray
No heart is safe when these hot-blooded hunks are in town!

In October: **DREAMSCAPE**
Jayne Ann Krentz
Anne Stuart
Bobby Hutchinson
Something's happening! But is it love or magic?

In December: **SOLUTION: MARRIAGE**
Debbie Macomber
Annette Broadrick
Heather Graham Pozzessere
Marriages in name only have a way of leading to love....

Available at your favorite retail outlet.

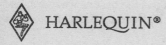

HARLEQUIN®   *Silhouette*

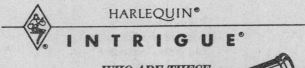